I0655702

Forever Home

Sequel to The Bee Charmer

Ali Spooner

Affinity
Rainbow Publications

2022

Also by

Ali Spooner

Single Books
The Ghost of East Texas
The Trophy Wives Club
The Bee Charmer
Ruined
Back in the Saddle
Open Your Heart
South of Heaven
Shotgun Rider
The Settlement
Love's Playlist
Cowgirl Up
Twisted Lives
The Epitaph
Terminal Event
Bailey's Run

Series
The Island Series
Neptune's Ring
Venus Rising

The Hunter Series
The Devil's Tree
Bound

Sasha Thibodaux Series
Sugarland
Bayou Justice
Line of Sight

Strong Southern Women Series
Diamond Dreams
Gator Girlz
True North
Footprints

Cast Iron Farm Series
The Mountain Whispers
The Star Child
Soul on Fire

Co-authored with Annette Mori
Heart Strings Attached
Free to Love

**Co-Authored with
K.L. Gallagher**
Hat Trick

Forever Home

Sequel to The Bee Charmer

Ali Spooner

Affinity
Rainbow Publications

2022

Forever Home
© 2022 by Ali Spooner

Affinity E-Book Press NZ LTD.
Canterbury, New Zealand

1st Edition

ISBN: 978-1-99-004962-0 (paperback)
ISBN: 978-1-99-004959-0 (EPUB)
ISBN:978-1-99-004960-6 (PDF)
ISBN: 978-1-99-004961-3 (KINDLE)

Editor: Angela Koenig
Proof Editor: Alexis Smith
Cover Design: Irish Dragon Designs
Production Design: Affinity Publication Services

ACKNOWLEDGMENTS

I would like to thank my fans for following my stories, providing great feedback, and encouragement. Writing wouldn't be so much fun without you. Thanks to Affinity, Irish Dragon for the cover art and the team of editors, readers, and publishers who continue to help me grow as a writer.

DEDICATION

In memory of my wife Rhonda, who was my loving friend and partner for twenty-six years. I love and miss you every day. Thank you for all the great memories we shared and sticking by me when life was hard. Love you...MOST!

TABLE OF CONTENTS

PROLOGUE

In the Pacific Northwest, fur trapper Nat St. Croix has lost her love of spending months alone trapping along the Canadian border. The death of her father, Nathan, helped her decide to find a more permanent home. When Nat meets a young widow, Marissa Mason, they begin a life together in a cabin that Nat had built for them on the shore. When James, Marissa's legally declared deceased husband, returns to claim her, Marissa's new life and freedom become jeopardized. A sharp-witted and clever mayor discovers that James' desertion of duties, and his defrauding the government by not returning to service after a minor injury, could land him in jail. When faced with the option of imprisonment, James begrudgingly accepts the opportunity to leave town forever. Nat would have preferred to carve him up and feed him to the predators in the bay but was satisfied when James tucked his tail between his legs and left town.

Nat couldn't be sure James would be smart enough to move on with his new life, but she was sure his claim on Marissa was null and void. She promised him that if he ever crossed their paths again, he would feel the edge of her sharpest knife.

Nat struck an agreement with Jacob at the general store and Randall at the hotel for them to purchase the seafood, jerky, and other items Nat could deliver to keep a steady income. Nat would still have plenty of opportunities to hunt and run a small trapline while Marissa and Maggie, their Native American companion, ran the homestead.

CHAPTER ONE

Spring had arrived and with it a plethora of chores as the women began their busiest season. Nat would begin harvesting her traps for beaver pelts and keep their smokehouses filled with meat while her lover Marissa, and their friend Maggie, tended the garden and made fresh goods to take to town to barter. With the threat of Marissa's husband extinguished, life at the shore slowly returned to normal.

Winter was still months away, but as time allowed, Nat would cut trees to add to the woodpiles. With the addition of the indoor cookstove, wood was even more critical to their way of life, and someone was always splitting short logs to feed the fire. The addition of the cookstove had been a housewarming gift from Smithy and Tom. Not only did it speed up cooking their meals, but it made it easier for Marissa and Maggie to make jelly from the berries they harvested.

The ocean water was still too cold for the tidal pools to fill with the seafood they harvested and took to town to supply the growing need of the hotel. The town's population was also rapidly increasing, adding to the demand for fresh seafood. Nat hunted to fill the smokehouses with meat for the jerky that had become so popular in town, while the others tended the newly planted garden.

Nat had filled the last of her jars with golden honey and was taking them back to the cabin as a flock of geese flew overhead on their way to the lake. She smiled, thinking that the migrating animals were returning north, which meant the bison would soon be heading her way.

Maggie was sitting on the back porch when she arrived. She was shelling a fresh batch of clams that she would fry for their supper. Nat sat the crate of honey down and wiped a bead of sweat from her forehead.

"How do you feel about sleeping on the ground for a few days?"

Maggie looked up from her task. "I think I could tolerate that. What do you have in mind?"

"I thought we could take Quincy and the wagon south for a few days. I'd like to clear a path for Rusty and the larger wagon before we go down to begin hunting. We can use the trees we cut for firewood on our hunting trips, and maybe even build a small shelter to keep us out of the weather."

"That sounds like a good idea. When would you want to leave?"

"Soon. Our chores here have slowed, and the garden doesn't need much tending yet, so it would be a good time to go."

Marissa had walked out to the porch as they were planning. "Where are you going?"

"I'd like to go ahead and blaze a trail to prepare for our hunting trips," Nat said. "The smokehouse is full, and the traps set, so I thought it would be good timing. Maggie has agreed to go with me this trip."

"I can keep things going here," Marissa said. She hated sleeping on the cold ground, even with Nat pressed close against her. "You don't mind me staying behind, do you?"

"Not at all. I know sleeping under the stars is not a pleasant thing for you, but the work we do now will make the hunting trips much easier."

"I will pack some jerky and fresh ham biscuits if you plan to leave tomorrow."

Nat looked at Maggie, and she nodded her head. "That sounds good. I'll get some gear packed into the wagon, and we can head out at first light."

Marissa spotted the crate full of honey. "I'll make another batch of biscuits that you can take with you with some honey. I know you could use the energy it gives you."

"I'll cook up a few jars of chowder that we can take if you'll dig another bucket," Maggie said. "I'm sure you can hunt something for fresh meat."

"That I can," Nat said as she bent down to pick up an empty bucket and the clam rake.

"Would you like some company?" Marissa asked.

"I'd love some," Nat said as she reached for her hand. "We'll be back soon."

"Take your time," Maggie said with a chuckle.

†

Nat held Marissa's hand as they walked down to the shore. The small footprints from Maggie's previous trip had all but washed away. Nat released her hand to start to rake for the clams.

"I can get these if you want to take a break to enjoy the morning," she said.

"That's a sweet thing to say, but I enjoy working with you. You rake, and I'll pick the clams."

"Get us some juicy ones," Nat teased.

It didn't take them long to fill the bucket. Nat looked over at the pools, evident with the tide out. "I wonder if there's anything in the pools yet."

"Go ahead and look," Marissa said. "I know you are eager to begin harvesting again."

Nat removed her boots and socks and waded into the shallow water. "It's still plenty cold," she said as she walked quickly to the first pool and then to the next. There were a few small fish, but no sign of the shrimp or lobsters yet. Her mouth watered at the thought of lobsters. The succulent meat had quickly become her favorite, and she would once more eat her fill when it was available. She turned back toward the shore and waded back to Marissa. "Still too early. There's a few small fish, but nothing else."

"I'll check while you are gone. I know you are eager for the lobsters to return."

"I'm more than ready for some of that sweet meat."

"I'll walk down to the other pools, too, and check them."

"Just be sure to take Maggie's pistol with you if you venture that far."

"I will," she answered.

"Do you want me to leave Gyp with you?"

"No, she would be miserable the whole time you're gone. I'll be just fine."

"I wouldn't leave you if I thought any different," Nat said with a smile. "With Maggie's help, the work will go a lot faster."

"Just don't be gone too long. You know I'll miss y'all."

"We'll miss you too," Nat said as she picked up the bucket and handed the rake to Marissa. Nat took her hand, and they walked up the hill.

†

Nat left the bucket of clams with Marissa and walked to the barn to pack her supplies. She loaded hay and feed for the horses along with her cookware, axes, and hatchets in the wagon. She also put a small box filled with nails and a pair of hammers to use to build a shelter. Tom and Smithy would be surprised when they joined them for a hunt if they had already prepared a camp. As an afterthought, she added a small jar of molasses to add to Quincy's feed.

When she walked back into the cabin, Marissa and Maggie were busy in the kitchen. Maggie was cooking the chowder to take with them while Marissa was preparing fresh biscuits for their trip. "Is there anything I can do to help?"

"I think we've got things covered. We'll start on supper soon, so you can relax on the porch until we're ready," Marissa said.

"I think that's our clue to get out of the kitchen," she said to Gyp and Luna. "Let's go."

Nat took the whalebone she was carving and walked to the front porch. She sat in her chair as the dogs dozed in the sun. Maggie had suggested they make Tom a new knife for all of his help last fall. Nat continued carving the whalebone they would use for a handle. When she had started cutting the dense bone, she had no clue what would emerge under her knife, until the shape of a whale came to life. How fitting, she thought. The design also made a comfortable handle for a large hand. She continued to carve until she was called inside for supper and then wrapped the piece in a soft cloth. Nat would take it with her on the trip and finish it at night while they sat around the fire. She wanted to give it to Tom when he arrived in a few weeks to deliver supplies, and hopefully return to town with a supply of goods to trade.

†

Maggie cleaned up from supper while Marissa finished packing the supplies for their trip. "I've got jelly and honey for your biscuits, a small bag of flour if you need to cook more, and a large bag of jerky. I'll bag up the biscuits for you in the morning."

"Thanks for getting us ready," Nat said. "I've got the rest of the supplies in the wagon." Nat took a new box of shells for her rifle and tucked them in the crate.

"If you don't need me for anything, I think I'll go enjoy my bed for one last night," Maggie teased.

"We won't be far behind you," Nat said. "Rest well."

"You, too."

Nat laid firewood in the fireplace and the cookstove, then turned to Marissa. "Are we ready?"

"I think we are," Marissa smiled and followed her to the bedroom.

Marissa had taken Nat's favorite pair of buckskins and a heavy work shirt out for the trip. "I know you'll probably shed this during the day, but it's still cool at night," she explained when Nat smiled at her.

"Thanks for thinking of everything," Nat said as she slipped out of her clothes. "These are due for a washing," she added as she dropped them in the corner.

"You noticed, too, huh?" Marissa teased. "I'll wash them while you're gone."

Marissa blew out the lantern, then joined her in the comfortable bed, and snuggled in close. "I'm going to miss this," she said.

"We'll be back in no time," Nat said as she wrapped her arm around her lover.

"You better hurry home to me," Marissa teased.

"Always," Nat said, and kissed her softly.

†

Rufus woke them at the break of dawn the following morning with his loud crowing. Nat smiled as Marissa opened her eyes. "I think I've finally gotten used to him."

"He definitely won't be ignored," Marissa said. "He gets louder if he doesn't see movement in the cabin."

"You noticed that, too."

"Oh yes, it didn't take long to figure that out."

Maggie was already in the kitchen, making coffee and warming the ham for their biscuits. "Good morning," she said when they walked into the room. "Coffee and biscuits will be ready soon."

"I'll go get Hardy and Quincy ready while we wait," Nat said.

Maggie waited until Nat left the cabin and then handed Marissa her pistol. "Keep this close in case you run up on a snake or other critter while we're gone."

Marissa nodded and tucked it away in her apron pocket. "You two stay safe and hurry back home."

"We will," Maggie smiled, and brought their coffee cups to the table.

†

They ate breakfast and drank the pot of coffee. Maggie picked up the bag of fresh biscuits. "I'll wait for you outside."

Nat nodded and took Marissa in her arms. "We'll be back soon. Is there anything else you need before we go?"

"Just a kiss to hold me until you return."

They kissed deeply, and Marissa's eyes shone with tears.

"Are you going to be all right while we're gone? I can go alone."

"No, I think Maggie is looking forward to an adventure with you. I'll be fine, I'm just missing you."

"See you soon then," Nat said, and they walked out the back of the cabin.

10

†

Nat mounted Hardy, and Maggie chose to walk beside Quincy for a while. They started, and when they passed the barn, Nat turned to wave to Marissa.

On her last trip south, Nat had marked a path, and when they spotted the first marking, about a mile from the cabin, Nat dismounted and tied Hardy to the back of the wagon. "The path is light here, but the trees will be much closer the farther we travel," she said as she took an ax from the wagon.

"You start on the larger trees, and I'll take the saplings," Maggie said, taking a hatchet Nat offered.

Nat nodded and walked to the first tree to begin chopping. The fresh scent of the evergreens filled her nostrils. When she was nearly through the trunk, she turned to see where Maggie was. "This one's coming down."

Maggie smiled as Nat pushed the tree in the direction she wanted it to fall. The small tree fell in the perfect spot to mark the entrance to their trail. "We can pile your saplings there and come back for them later if we want."

"I'll handle moving them if you want to work ahead and take down the bigger trees."

Nat moved down to the next tree and cut it as close to the ground as she could. It was too large for her to move, so she worked on the next tree until Maggie caught up with her, and with her assistance, they moved the tree from the trail.

Nat was quick to remove the heavy work shirt as the sun had risen and was breaking through the canopy of trees. The exertion had left a coat of sweat on her skin, and she smiled as she picked up the ax. They were making good time, and by midday, they had cleared several miles of trail. Maggie moved the animals down the path and called to Nat.

"Let's take a quick meal break and rest for a few minutes."

Nat buried the ax in the next tree that she planned to cut and walked back to the wagon. Maggie had pulled out several of the ham biscuits and drizzled honey over them. She handed one to Nat and picked up one of her own.

"We seem to be making good progress."

"Yes, it's going much faster than I thought. Thanks for your help."

"No problem. You're doing the harder work."

"Maybe, but you're doing a lot more walking."

"That's never hurt me, and it'll help me sleep tonight."

Nat smiled at the tenacity of her friend. She took another bite of the biscuit and drank from her canteen. "We should be coming up on a stream soon, and then the trees will thin out for a while. We should make it through the saplings quickly there, but then we head into a stretch of dense forest."

"Is there any way to go around it?"

"No, it's solid back to the ocean, and for miles to the east. I figure if we can make it halfway through that today, we'll be in good shape."

"Do we need to put some of the saplings on the wagon to build a shelter tonight?"

"That's not a bad idea, and it shouldn't be a burden on Quincy. I'll dig a fire ring and cut some firewood for tonight if you'll start working on a shelter?"

"No problem," Maggie said. "I'm ready when you are."

Forever Home

Nat took another long drink, emptying her canteen, and then walked back to the tree she was chopping. Maggie had already downed the saplings in the area, so she pulled Quincy and Hardy ahead of them.

"Call for me if you need help moving a tree," she said and walked ahead of Nat.

Nat got back into rhythm, and looking around, she could see the trail was coming to life. She cut the trees and rolled them out of the path and moved to the next. She had lost sight of Maggie and the animals and was in her element as she downed tree after tree.

Maggie waited until Nat dropped the tree she was cutting so as not to break Nat's concentration.

"You need some cold water," she said as she handed her a full canteen.

"I see you found the creek."

"I did, and it's a beautiful spot," she said as she handed Nat a strip of jerky. "I'm a good way ahead of you. Would you mind if I start on some of the larger trees, and work back toward you? There's only a dozen or so between us."

"Just drop them, and we'll move them together," Nat said, and took another long drink before handing her the canteen. "Don't overwork yourself. We still have plenty of cutting to do."

"Yes, boss." Maggie laughed and walked deeper into the woods.

Hardy and Quincy were grazing on new grass when Nat finally reached the creek. Maggie had dropped four trees and was working on another when Nat arrived. She waited until the tree fell and then helped Maggie move them to the side.

13

"You need a rest break," Maggie said. "Go cool off at the creek."

Nat walked to the edge of the creek and knelt to scoop the water in her hands for a deep drink, and then she dunked her head into the cold water. When she lifted her head, the liquid streamed down her face and back.

"That's refreshing," she said as Maggie walked up.

"I won't look if you want to take a dip."

"I don't think it's that refreshing," Nat grimaced. "It's still a bit chilly for that."

Maggie sat beside her in the grass, and they rested while watching the animal's graze. Gyp and Luna had been scouting all morning and curled up together napping. "I have an idea," Maggie said. "Why don't we scout ahead, and find a spot to camp tonight, and then cut our way back to camp? I thought if we dropped the cut trees, we could move them on our way back to the cabin."

"It would get us to the end faster, but make for heavier work on the way back. Let's try it through the heavier section and see how it goes." She stood and offered Maggie her hand. "Let me get my ax, and I'll be ready."

Maggie gathered the animals while Nat collected her ax. They refilled their canteens and walked for another mile, deeper into the forest. When they reached a small clearing next to the stream, Nat called them to a halt.

"This spot looks good. If you want to settle the animals and begin the shelter, I'll start cutting."

Nat had counted the trees as they walked. Fifty remained in the path. She took another ax from the wagon and started back up the trail. The freshly sharpened blade cut through the wood smoothly, and she was glad she had remembered to pack the file to keep them sharp.

Maggie unhitched Quincy from the wagon and unsaddled Hardy to let them graze while she started to set up camp. She dug holes and buried thick saplings to make a three-sided lean-to that would give them adequate cover. Maggie used twine that Nat had packed to bind the saplings to the braces as the shelter began to take form. She could hear the steady stroke of Nat's ax followed by the crash as tree after tree fell to the earth. Maggie knew Nat would be exhausted by the time they decided to call it a day, so Maggie dug a fire pit and laid a fire from dry wood from the clearing. She was surveying the campsite when she heard movement off to her right, and she looked up to see a big rabbit emerge from the forest into the clearing. Maggie crept to the wagon and picked up Nat's rifle. The rabbit lifted its head when she pulled back the hammer, and Maggie held her breath, praying he didn't bolt back into the woods. He sat up to look around, and Maggie fired the rifle, making a clean shot.

"We will have roasted rabbit for supper," she told the dogs as she stored the weapon back in the wagon and went after the rabbit.

Nat was walking to her next tree when she heard the shot, and her panic brought her racing back to the clearing. Maggie was skinning the rabbit as Nat came skidding to a halt out of breath.

"I thought you were in danger," she said between gasps.

"I'm sorry, but this fellow was just begging to be our dinner," Maggie replied.

Nat looked around the campsite. "This looks good," she said, after taking a long drink from the canteen. She spotted a tree that had fallen during the winter. "Why don't I cut that up for some firewood while you get him dressed, and fashion a spit to cook him, then I'll get back to cutting."

"That sounds good to me, and then I'll start cutting close so I can keep an eye on dinner," Maggie answered.

"I'm about halfway down one side," Nat said. "There may be enough daylight left to make it back here."

"If not, we'll finish before we move on in the morning."

Nat took another drink and chopped the downed tree into firewood before returning down the trail. When she reached the spot where she had stopped, Nat picked up her ax and resumed cutting. When Nat made it to the end, she could hear Maggie chopping at the campsite. The smell of the smoke from the fire filled the cooling air. *Even the hard ground is going to feel good tonight,* Nat thought as she turned and started cutting her way back to camp. An hour later, she could see Maggie in the distance cutting a tree, and Nat knew the end was in sight. Nat reckoned a dozen trees were left, and they would finish for the day. The smell of the rabbit roasting had her mouth watering, and she picked up her pace, eager to be done.

Maggie was chopping on the last tree as Nat walked into the camp. The rabbit had roasted to a golden brown, and it smelled wonderful. She walked to the creek to fill her canteen and heard the crash of the last tree. She filled the container, took a long drink, and after refilling, walked to meet Maggie to offer her a drink.

"We made it before the sun went down," Maggie said with a grin.

"Yeah, we did. That was a good idea. I'm going to cut a few of the last trees to stack for the fire while you finish supper."

"I can do that if you need to rest," Maggie offered.

"No, I'm fine," Nat answered and walked to the first tree.

"Let me check the rabbit, and I'll stack while you cut."

Nat picked out a smaller tree and cut it into small sections after removing the branches. Maggie used some of the small branches filled with needles to lay a bed beneath the shelter to provide some comfort and insulation from the cold ground. Maggie checked the rabbit and then made a pile of branches to dry for their return trip. They would make excellent wood to start the fire upon their return. Then she carried the smaller logs and started a stack next to the shelter.

Nat finished the tree and moved to the next, a bigger tree she would split if her energy held out. Maggie struggled but carried the larger sections next to a stump Nat would use for a chopping block. Her arms were quivering with exhaustion as Nat cut the last log.

Maggie saw how tired she was. "You go sit by the fire, and I'll get this split, and then we should be ready to eat."

"I'm too tired to argue with you." Nat handed Maggie the ax. She walked to the wagon, took out the file and the two axes, and sat on the ground. It took the rest of her energy to sharpen the blades for the next day while Maggie finished splitting the wood. Nat stretched out in the bed of the wagon when she finished. She looked up to see the first of the stars twinkling in the sky. Her eyes grew heavy, and she could no longer hold them open.

When the rabbit finished cooking, Maggie cut sections from the carcass and dropped them on their plates to cool. She drizzled honey over the dark meat to add some flavor and give them both energy for the next day of cutting. Maggie loaded several biscuits, and more honey on the plates then carried them to the wagon.

"Time to eat," she said to wake Nat.

"Damn, I didn't mean to drift off," Nat said as she sat up.

"You worked hard today," Maggie said. "You can get started on this while I get some fresh water for us."

Nat accepted the plate gratefully and took a bite of the roasted rabbit. Maggie returned from the creek and sat beside her on the wagon, placing the canteens between them.

"Either I'm starving, or this is the best rabbit I've ever eaten," Nat said.

"Maybe both," Maggie said with a chuckle. "I used some of your honey on it."

"I thought so. It tastes great," Nat said.

"There's plenty of meat left, so eat up, and I'll give the dogs the rest."

Nat cleaned her plate, eating another portion of the rabbit before Maggie split the rabbit down the middle, and gave half to each of the dogs.

Nat reached for her work shirt and then walked to refill the canteens. She and Maggie sat on the wagon, enjoying the nightfall and the wide-open sky until they decided to crawl into their bedrolls for sleep. Maggie tossed extra wood on the fire and climbed into her bedroll as Luna and Gyp took up their spots. She turned to say goodnight to Nat, but she was already fast asleep. Maggie smiled, pulled the cover over her shoulder, and quickly slipped off to rest.

CHAPTER TWO

When the sun broke across the horizon the next morning, Nat had already cut another stack of firewood while Maggie cooked them breakfast. As she added the last armful to the pile, Maggie filled their plates with scrambled eggs and ham.

"That sure smells good," she said as she took a cup of coffee from Maggie.

Maggie drizzled honey across the ham, positioned several biscuits on her plate, and handed it to Nat. "Eat up, I feel you're going to need a lot of energy today."

"You're right about that if we're going to make it to the main campsite tonight. Once we clear this section, the going will be much easier."

"Do I need to cut saplings to take with us?"

"No, there will be plenty where we'll be making camp tonight. I'd like to make it there by early afternoon if we can."

"We will make it," Maggie assured her.

"The big trees start thinning out just ahead, and it's primarily small trees after that."

"We may make it by lunchtime then if we get as much done as we did yesterday. Do you want me to go ahead and set up camp?"

"That worked out pretty well for us yesterday," Nat said. "When we finish breakfast, we can scout ahead, and you can set up camp while I start cutting my way back here."

†

Maggie picked up camp while Nat got Quincy hitched to the wagon and tied Hardy to the back rail. They walked side by side as they wove their way down the trail, and it took less than an hour to reach the spot Nat wanted to use as the main camp.

"We were closer than I thought," she said, as they reached the clearing. "Just over that hill is where the bison will be grazing soon."

"Let's go take a look," Maggie said.

Nat nodded, even though she was confident the herd would not have migrated this far north yet. She released a breath slowly when they crested the hill to find an empty meadow. "This spot was filled with animals the last time I was here."

"It will be again," Maggie said. "It's a perfect spot for grazing." Maggie pointed to the new grass growth filling the meadow.

20

Nat nodded and turned to walk back to the clearing. "I'll drop some saplings for you before I go," she said, and picked up her ax.

"Just drop them, and I'll do the rest."

Maggie got the animals settled while Nat began to cut the saplings they would use for shelter. She quickly dropped two dozen and then took a short water break before taking her axes to start cutting her way back to the first shelter.

Maggie filled her canteen with fresh water. "I'll start cutting close when I finish setting up camp. Do you want some jerky to take with you?"

"I'll take a few strips with a couple of ham biscuits, and that way I can eat a quick meal on the go."

Maggie filled a flour sack with food and handed it to Nat. "I'll see you soon," she said and then watched Nat walk from the clearing.

†

Nat tied her flour sack on a limb and hung her canteen next to it as she began to cut. She cut the taller trees, pulling them off to the side as she made her way back through the dense forest. With those done, the smaller trees seemed simple, and she fell into a comfortable rhythm as the sun broke through the clouds.

Maggie went to work making a much larger shelter that would accommodate all four of them when they returned to hunt. She used the longer saplings for the back and roof and cut more for the sides. Pleased with the shelter, Maggie moved on to digging a wider fire pit and found rocks by the stream to ring the hole. When she was done with the fire pit, she took out an empty feed sack and walked to the meadow with the dogs on her heels. Gyp and Luna raced ahead of her and then stopped to sniff the ground. Maggie chuckled at them as they pawed at the fragrant piles. The grass was dotted with piles of bison dung that had survived the winter and she filled the bag with the droppings to use to start the fires they would need to build. The dried manure provided an excellent source as a fire starter and would get the fire burning much faster with the green cut wood. She carried her bounty back to the campsite, and tossed several of the bricks in the fire pit with some of the branches she had trimmed from the saplings. Later, she would scour the area for dead wood to use to keep their fire burning for supper.

The sound of Nat's ax had grown closer, and Maggie picked up her hatchet to begin cutting the saplings on the trail. Maggie cut several, dragging them to the campsite to chop for firewood. She was returning from the camp when Maggie heard Nat's ax fall silent.

"I hope you're taking a rest my friend," she said aloud.

†

Nat was pleased with the progress she was making. The soreness in her arms and shoulders disappeared once she started chopping the larger trees. She reached into the bag and took out a biscuit as she surveyed the trail they had blazed. It would serve them nicely in the coming months as they hunted the bison, making travel much more comfortable, and more direct from the cabin. With an early start, she thought they might be able to make the trip from the cabin to the first campsite in two days of travel. She took a long drink from the canteen as her mind raced ahead of her.

She and Tom could ride ahead at a faster pace, and get the main camp ready while Maggie and Smithy followed with the wagons. Rusty would do most of the heavy work, but Maggie and Quincy would be useful in carrying the slain bison back to camp to be processed. Just thinking about the hunt energized her, and she picked up a freshly sharpened ax to resume cutting.

†

Maggie finished off the saplings around the campsite, and took a short meal break before trading her hatchet for Nat's rifle. She would join Nat on the trail and keep her eyes open for something to shoot for dinner. Gyp and Luna trotted along beside her as they walked toward the sounds of Nat's ax. When she came into view, Maggie called the dogs close to her as Nat pushed a tree to the ground.

When Nat turned back to pick up her ax, she saw she had an audience. "Hey there," she said. Gyp came rushing up to her, and she knelt down to greet her canine friend.

"We thought we'd come check on you and see what we can do to help. The campsite is ready and I've cut the saplings that were close."

"We're making good progress then," Nat said. "You want to see what you and the dogs can scare up for supper?"

"I was thinking maybe you'd enjoy a break, and I'd keep cutting."

"What did you have in mind?"

"That rabbit was pretty tasty last night," Maggie said. "I'll clean and cook whatever you can kill."

"You sure you don't want to hunt?"

"You've been cutting all morning. Take a break, and I'll cut while you hunt."

"We'll take a walk down by the stream, and see what we can rustle up then," Nat said.

Maggie handed her the rifle and picked up the ax. "Happy hunting."

Nat shouldered the rifle and called the dogs to her as she walked into the woods toward the stream. She heard Maggie beginning to chop as she searched the area for signs of wildlife. Gyp and Luna ran ahead of her, noses to the ground, searching for scent as they headed north away from the sound of the chopping.

†

Nat followed the stream back to the campsite from the previous night without seeing anything to shoot. The stream was filled with fish, and when she located a pool with several large fish, she decided that would be their supper. Maggie could fry them and heat the chowder they had brought from the cabin. She took out her knife and cut several branches that she made into spears, and then sat on a rock to remove her boots and socks.

Gyp and Luna watched her curiously as she rolled her pants to her knees and picked up her spears. She stepped into the chilly water and slowly waded toward the pool. Once Nat made it through the initial shock of the water, she found it to be refreshing. She looked over to the bank to see Gyp sitting next to her boots, wanting nothing to do with the cold water. "Too cold for you, tough girl?" Nat asked her. Gyp answered by wagging her tail, but she made no move to enter the water. Luna was trotting down the streambed oblivious to anything beyond her nose. Nat shook her head and continued to the pool.

She took aim at a fish and released the spear, missing on her first attempt. "Guess who's out of practice," she spoke aloud as she took aim and tried again. The fish were lethargic in the cold water, so they did not travel far in the pool. Her second attempt was successful and with her confidence bolstered, she speared three additional fish before wading back to the shore where she gutted and cleaned the fish.

Nat sat on the boulder to allow her feet to dry before placing her socks and boots back on. Impaling all four fish on one spear, she picked up the rifle and started back to the trail. When she returned to the camp, she found that Maggie had dropped several trees and was busy chopping another.

Gyp and Luna ran ahead of her, and when Maggie saw them, she stopped cutting and turned to find Nat.

Nat held up the fish. "No rabbit, but we did find these. I thought they'd go well with some of your chowder."

"They'll do just fine," Maggie said, wiping sweat from her brow.

"Take them back to camp and put them in a bucket of water until you're ready to cook, and I'll take over here."

"Do you need anything from camp?"

"Bring the file back with you so that I can sharpen these blades. I'm sure they could use a new edge."

"Do you want me to help you move these few before I go?"

"I've got these," Nat said. Maggie nodded, took the fish, and started walking back to the campsite.

Nat moved the downed trees to the side of the trail and picked up the ax to continue chopping. They were getting close, and she thought maybe by early afternoon they would finish.

When Maggie returned with the file, Nat sharpened both axes and took a long drink from her canteen. "We'll finish here shortly," she said when Maggie took up an ax and walked to the next tree.

With both women cutting, they made short work of the smaller trees. When they had the trail cleared back to the campsite, Nat surveyed the work Maggie had done earlier. "You've made a great campsite."

"It'll be plenty big enough for all of us," Maggie said with a grin.

Nat noticed the bulging feed sack next to a small stack of firewood. "What's that?"

"Bison chips," she answered. "They make great fire starters."

"I reckon they would. I've never thought of that."

"They'll get a fire burning hot, much quicker when you've got green wood."

"That's very good to know. Let me take a short break, and I'll get started cutting some firewood."

"Take your time. I thought I'd see what deadwood I could find for tonight," Maggie said.

Nat took a long drink from her canteen and climbed onto the back of the wagon to sharpen the ax blades while Maggie carried armloads of dried branches and stacked them near the fire pit. "What do you say we put Quincy to work?" she asked when Maggie delivered a load.

"What do you want to do?"

"We've got plenty of downed trees. I thought you could hitch Quincy to the wagon, and I'll cut some of them into firewood, and he can haul them back for us."

"I think he'd love some work," Maggie said as she turned to look at the animals grazing on the sweet grass. "I'll get him ready if you want to start chopping."

She picked up the two axes and a hatchet to trim the smaller branches. "I'll see you on the trail."

Nat walked to the head of the trail where a pile of saplings was stacked. They would make perfect rounds for the fire pit, and she would use several more significant trees to cut sections to split. She pulled the first tree from the pile and began chopping it into sections, tossing them into a small stack for Maggie to load into the wagon. The sharp blade sliced through the softwood making her job easy. She had three saplings cut when Maggie and Quincy arrived.

"You must have gotten a second wind," Maggie teased.

"A freshly sharpened blade makes all the difference."

Maggie started loading the rounds onto the wagon, and when it was full, she took up Quincy's lead. "Do you need help?"

"No, keep cutting. We can get a good pile started today, and when we return for the hunt, it will be nicely seasoned."

Nat finished the pile and moved onto the more substantial trees. The ax chewed into the trunks as she sectioned them. Maggie could handle the smaller pieces but would need her assistance to get the thicker parts into the wagon.

When Maggie returned, she picked up the hatchet and started trimming branches from the trees, making it easier for Nat to cut sections. With the final load on the wagon, they returned to camp, and Nat started splitting the larger pieces while Maggie lit the campfire to begin cooking supper.

Nat split wood until darkness began to fall and then picked up their canteens to refill from the stream. Luna and Gyp rushed ahead of her. They startled a rabbit that had come to the water for a drink and took off in pursuit of the terrified animal. Several minutes later, she heard the squeal of the animal as the dogs caught their prey. She walked back into camp, shaking her head.

"Did the dogs catch their supper?" Maggie asked.

"I do believe they will be dining on fresh rabbit tonight."

"That's good. Fish gives Luna gas."

Nat chuckled at Maggie and stored their canteens on the back of the wagon. That had become a comfortable spot for them to share their meals. She reached into the flour sack for a strip of jerky as she took up a seat and sharpened the blades while Maggie fried the fish.

"Do you want some fry bread to go with the meal?"

"That would be good," Nat answered, slowly chewing on the strip of jerky.

"What are your plans for tomorrow?"

"I thought we'd start working our way back to the other camp, moving the trees, and cutting some firewood as we go."

"We've got a good stack here. I'm sure Tom will insist on cutting more once he arrives."

"I won't fight him for that job," Nat said. "I'd like to add to the small pile we left at the first campsite before we head for home."

"That shouldn't be a problem with the trees you've already cut. It's just a matter of chopping them into sections, and I can help with that."

"It will be a busy day, but I'm sure we can get it done."

"If you'll put your gloves back on, you can go ahead and pour bowls of the chowder to cool while I finish the fry bread."

Nat replaced the axes on the wagon and slipped the gloves on her hands. The jar was warm, and she quickly poured the thick chowder in their bowls before the heat burned through her gloves. She carried their dishes to the wagon to wait for Maggie.

Maggie had just carried their plates to the wagon when they heard the dogs return from hunting. Gyp and Luna sat in front of the cart in hopes of getting a hand out from Maggie. Their presence did not go unnoticed, and Maggie broke off pieces of fry bread to toss to them.

Nat started eating the fish while the chowder cooled. "These are very tasty," she said as she peeled a strip of the flakey fish and popped it in her mouth. "They have a different flavor and texture from the fish we get from the ocean."

"I bet they would smoke well, too," Maggie said.

"You're probably right about that. Maybe we can bring a small barrel with us and see if we can take some alive back to the cabin when we come for the hunt."

"I'll collect some reeds from the lake and dry them to weave into fish traps when we get home," Maggie said. "Maybe I can convince Marissa to help me."

"I'm sure she would," Nat said as she bit into a piece of fry bread.

"I found some blackberry bushes down near the meadow. Maybe when we return, they will be ripe and we can pick some fresh berries. They would go nicely cooked into some flapjacks."

"That sounds really good. I wouldn't mind some flapjacks for breakfast in the morning."

"You can load the supplies while I cook," Maggie said.

"Deal," Nat said as she picked up her bowl to sip on the chowder.

†

Nat sipped on coffee while Maggie washed the dishes from supper. "That was a great meal," Nat said when Maggie joined her on the back of the wagon.

"It was good, wasn't it?"

"Your cooking is always welcomed."

They sipped coffee as they watched the full moon climb into the night sky. "It's wonderful out here," Nat said.

"Do you miss your old way of life?"

"Not at all. I still get to trap and hunt, but I've gotten used to having a roof over my head, and a soft bed."

"Good. I enjoy living with you and Marissa."

"We make a good team. Between the three of us, I don't think there's anything we can't do."

"It's very nice to have money in my pocket, too, without having to rely on selling breeches and baked goods."

"Is there anything you need?"

"I have more than I ever could have dreamed," Maggie said, her eyes shiny with tears.

†

Nat broke down the campsite and packed the wagon while Maggie cooked breakfast. The hearty flapjacks would give them the energy to work through the morning, and they could eat the rest of the ham biscuits later in the day.

They were about to leave the campsite when they were surprised to hear a rider approaching. Nat cautiously eased toward the rifle on the wagon and broke into a smile when she recognized the rider.

"Tom. What are you doing here?"

"Smithy gave me a couple of days off, so I thought I'd check on y'all to see what help you need. Marissa told me what you were up to, so I started here yesterday after lunch."

"Well, it's good to see you," she said as he dismounted and hugged them both.

"You two have been busy. I stayed at your shelter last night and was impressed, but this one is even better."

"It will make a good campsite for hunting," Maggie smiled. "Have you eaten?"

"Yes, ma'am, Marissa packed me some biscuits."

Nat smiled at the mention of her lover. "How was she doing?"

"A bit lonesome, but I think she's cut a couple of hundred antler buttons for Maggie to bore."

"That will keep me stocked for a while," Maggie said.

"Are you ready for some work?"

"I noticed you dropped a lot of trees along the trail."

"We decided to cut and then move them from the trail on our way back. We want to get them moved, and some wood chopped for the other campsite today."

"Is this the spot where we will be hunting?" Tom asked.

31

"Yes, there's a huge meadow on the other side of the hill," Nat replied. "Do you wanna look?"

Tom nodded his head and the three topped the hill again. "This is really beautiful," Tom said as his eyes gazed across the green meadow.

"You ready to move some trees?" Nat asked, anxious to get started.

"I can certainly help with that. Let me give Buck a quick water break, and I'll catch up with y'all."

Nat mounted Hardy, Maggie climbed onto the wagon, and they pulled away from the campsite. They had done an excellent job of preparing the trail and would have no problem bringing Rusty and the larger wagon to the campsite.

Tom and Buck caught up with them quickly. "Do you want to ride ahead and get started moving the downed trees?" he asked.

Nat looked at Maggie, who nodded and said, "Go ahead, Quincy and I will be there as quickly as possible."

"Keep an eye open for something for supper," Nat said. "See you shortly."

Nat and Tom took off at a smooth canter and made good time back to where Nat had dropped the trees on the trail. They tied the horses off and began moving the trees to the side of the pathway.

"I can't believe how much you two have gotten done," he said, as they moved a large tree together.

"It was hard work, but the result was well worth it."

"I bet your body hurt after cutting all these trees."

"It reminded me it'd been a long time since I've worked this hard."

"I'll chop the firewood when we get the rest of these moved," he offered.

"We can both chop and it'll go faster. I'll gladly let you do the splitting though when we get it back to the campsite."

They heard the crack of a rifle shot, and Nat said, "It sounds like Maggie found supper. Ride back and see if she needs some help."

Tom nodded and trotted back to Buck.

†

Maggie had spied a small buck, his antlers no more than spikes, and she pulled Quincy to a halt and reached for the rifle. The dogs had trotted after Nat, so she didn't have to worry about the dogs catching the scent and chasing after the deer. She aimed and fired a single shot, watching as the buck staggered and fell to the ground. Maggie pulled the brake on the wagon and climbed down.

She carried the rifle with her if she needed to finish him off, but her shot was clean, and the deer was dead when she reached him. She propped the rifle against a tree and removed her knife to slit his throat to bleed him. Maggie smiled when she heard a horse approach and welcomed the sight of Tom as he approached.

"He's not big, but he will make more than supper," she said as Tom tied Buck to the wagon and started to walk toward her. "Grab that length of rope, and we'll hang him to gut him, and then we can carry him to the wagon."

"I can follow you to the campsite, and hoist him in a tree so you can skin him, and finish the processing if you'd like. Then I'll go back to help Nat."

"That sounds good. I'll get us a nice roast on the fire to cook for supper. Maybe some fresh biscuits too."

Tom's grin widened. "My mouth is watering already."

After they lifted the deer onto the wagon, they resumed the trip down the trail. Nat was steadily working and stopped for a break when they pulled up. "He will make a fine supper," she said when she spotted the buck in the wagon.

"I'm going to help Maggie get him strung for processing, and then I'll be back to help."

"How does a nice roast sound to you? Maybe I can find some wild onions, and I'll make some fresh biscuits."

"I'm ready," Nat teased. "My flapjacks are already wearing off."

"Darn, I missed flapjacks."

"If you had arrived just a bit earlier, you could have shared some with us, but Gyp and Luna finished them off," Maggie told him. "If Nat can handle those two days in a row, I'll cook more in the morning."

"I can always eat flapjacks," Nat assured them, making Tom smile.

"That's settled then. Let's go," she told him.

Nat watched them go and then hung her canteen over her saddle horn before returning to the task of moving the trees.

†

Tom hung the buck in a tree near the campsite, then laid and lit a fire, while Maggie started skinning.

"Is there anything else I can help with?"

"No, I can take it from here. Go help Nat finish, and I'll see you both soon."

Tom rushed back to where Nat was working and fell into rhythm with her. Not long afterward, they smelled the smoke of the fire pit, and the campsite came into view.

"Take Hardy on to camp, bring back the file for the axes, and Quincy with the wagon if Maggie doesn't need him."

Nat took a seat on one of the downed logs to rest for a few minutes while waiting for Tom's return. The sun was tucked behind the clouds, keeping the temperature moderate, making it a perfect day to perform manual labor. A slight breeze filled her nose with the fresh smell of aspens and fragrant pine as she enjoyed a short rest break. Tom's arrival had been unexpected, but with his help, they were way ahead of where she had hoped to be, and she knew that by late afternoon, they would have a healthy stack of firewood, and a hot meal on the way.

Tom returned with Quincy in tow and handed Nat a sharpened ax. They had left a dozen trees on the trail, and they went to work, cutting them into sections. When they had them all cut, they began loading the sections onto the wagon and led Quincy back to the campsite. They made two piles of rounds for Tom to split, and smaller sections that they would burn as whole logs. It took them six trips to haul the wood back to the campsite.

"Let me get Quincy settled, and I'll be back to help with the split wood," she told him.

"No rush, there's plenty for two," he teased.

Maggie had hung the last quartered section in a tree away from the campsite when Nat returned from the stream with Quincy.

"Good job," she said, "no need to attract a hungry bear to our camp."

"That's what I was thinking. I haven't seen any tracks, but I know they're out there. Do you need help?"

"You can mix some molasses into some feed for Quincy, and I'll help Tom split the firewood."

"I'll come and stack after I finish with Quincy. The roast is cooking fine, so I'm all set to help."

"I'll never turn down your help," Nat said as she handed her Quincy's lead.

She walked over to the pile, positioned a large section on a bare trunk, and picked up her ax. Tom had just finished a stroke and bent down to place the section back on the stump to split again.

"If we split all this, we should be set for some time."

"If we need more, we can easily access the trees you dropped to blaze the trail, and they will have already begun to season," he said with a grin.

"That was the plan."

"I figured it was." He smiled and split another section.

With Maggie's help stacking the split wood, she and Tom concentrated on splitting the sections, and by late afternoon the woodcutting was done.

They all sat on a log Tom had moved near the fire pit and took a water break.

"What's the next move?" he asked.

"Supper and a relaxing night," Nat said. "Tomorrow, we will head for home. When do you need to be back in town?"

"Not for three days yet. What can we do at the cabin?"

"I need to check my traps and finish the first set of pelts to send back to Smithy. Maybe there will be some seafood to harvest too."

"When do you plan to come back and hunt bison?"

Nat could see the excitement in his eyes. "Now that we have a trail blazed, I can ride out to check if the herd has arrived. I thought I'd come back in two weeks to check."

"I could bring a load of supplies from town and ride out with you," he said.

"That sounds like a good plan," Nat said. She turned at the sound of growling to find the dogs playing tug of war with a section of ribs they had chewed clean of meat.

"Supper sure is smelling good. How much longer until we eat?" he asked.

"Not for a while yet," Maggie said. "I'll put the biscuits on to bake, but it will be full dark before the roast is ready."

"Do you need some jerky to hold you over?" Maggie asked.

"No, ma'am, I can wait. I was hoping maybe Nat and I could take a ride. I'd like to see one of those goats she talks about if we're close to the bluffs."

"Saddle the horses," Nat said as she stood and stretched. "You don't mind us leaving you for a bit, do you?"

"No, not at all. Bring one of them back if you can. I've never cooked goat before."

"You know Smithy would go loony over a ram's head," Tom said. "No one in town has anything like it, so I'm sure he would keep it as a prized possession."

Nat smiled, thinking of how Smithy's eyes had grown wide with excitement when she told them about the goat. "You're right about that," she admitted.

Tom left them to saddle the horses, and Nat pulled her work shirt back on. "Hopefully, we'll make it back before dark. I don't think the rocky ridge is that far away."

"I'll keep the dogs here to keep me company," Maggie replied, as she stood and stretched.

"I'm leaving my rifle with you, too, in case a bear catches the scent of that buck."

†

Tom brought the horses and Nat mounted Hardy.

"We'll be back," she said, and they rode from camp. Gyp and Luna rushed over to follow, and Nat stopped and looked at Gyp. "Stay and protect Maggie," she said, and the dogs turned back.

Tom and Nat picked their way through the forest toward the scent of salt in the air. "How are things going in town for you?"

"Really well. I've learned a lot from Smithy, and he seems to be pleased with my work."

"You would know if he wasn't."

"I don't think I ever want to see him angry with me."

"In all my years, I've never seen him lose his temper with his staff, although he demands hard work."

"He gets that from me. I don't have any trouble sleeping at night."

Nat smiled, and they pulled up when they reached the bluffs. "They are the same color as the rock, so you have to be looking carefully to see them."

They scanned the bluffs with their eyes until Nat felt hers begin to water. She was about to suggest they start back to camp, when Tom said, "There," and pointed toward a ridge.

Nat strained her eyes, searching for movements, and finally saw what Tom had seen. "See if you can get a shot on him."

Tom nodded and dismounted, pulling his rifle from its sheath. He handed Buck's reins to Nat and crept forward several paces. She watched him as he stalked forward, keeping his eyes on the goat. It would be a tough shot, but possible, she thought when Tom dropped to a knee and took aim. Nat found herself holding her breath as his finger twitched on the trigger and slowly pulled it back. The crack of the rifle filled the forest with an echo as she watched the goat stumble and fall from the ridge, sliding hallway down the bluff.

"Great shot," she said. "Now comes the fun part. You'll have to climb up that ridge to claim your kill."

The base of the ridge was at least a hundred yards from the top. The goat had tumbled about halfway down the bluff. Tom would need to climb several hundred feet to reach the goat, shoulder him, and then climb back down.

"Be careful, that looks like it can be a treacherous climb," she warned.

"I'll be careful," he said and handed her the rifle.

Nat watched as he picked his way to the base of the ridge and selected his path upward. Movement off to his right caught her attention, and she glanced over to see the mountain lion a hundred yards away from Tom. The cat was sitting on an outcropping, watching Tom closely. Nat decided to wait instead of yelling to warn him of the cat's presence. She observed closely for any sign of aggression from the cat. Nat knew he was determined to claim the goat however, Nat would not allow him to be injured either. She decided to wait and watch, to give Tom his chance to retrieve the goat. The cat also seemed content to sit and watch.

Tom slipped a few times on his climb, but eventually reached the fallen goat, hefted him over his shoulder and began his decent. The cat's tail twitched as it watched him labor to climb down with the goat, but it only appeared curious and made no move toward her young friend. Nat breathed a sigh of relief when Tom cleared the ridge and started the climb back to her.

His grin was wide across his face when he returned and dropped the goat in front of her. "Man, he's heavy," he said, slightly winded.

Nat handed him a canteen for a drink of water. "I'm glad you made it back in one piece."

Tom looked at her with a curious look on his face. "Me too."

"You had company," she said. "Take a look at where you were climbing and then a hundred yards off to the right."

Tom turned quickly and scanned the ridge until he found the mountain lion. "I had no clue it was there."

"It was just curious to see what you were doing. I would have made a warning shot if it had moved toward you at all."

"I'm glad you were here to watch my back," he said as he took a final look at the cat. "There's no way I was coming back without that goat after that climb."

"I kind of figured that," Nat said with a chuckle. "Mount up, and I'll hand him up to you." She handed him back the rifle.

Tom climbed into his saddle and waited for Nat to hand the goat up to him. He stretched the carcass over his lap and took up his reins.

"Let's get back to camp before it gets dark, and you can dress him then. I don't think we need to tempt the cat with the scent of more fresh blood," she said as she mounted Hardy.

They rode back to camp, and Nat helped him process the ram while they waited for supper to finish.

Tom removed the head, and they marveled at the structure of the horns as the goat bled out. "That's a very nice head," Maggie said.

"Are you going to sell it to Smithy?" Nat asked.

Tom looked at her with disbelief.

"He's your kill to do with as you want," she said. "You did all the hard work."

"I don't think I could ask Smithy to pay for it," he said.

Nat nodded. "Smithy is a collector and a shrewd businessman and would gladly pay you for the head. It's your decision to make, though. If you want to give him a gift, I can't think of anything better."

CHAPTER THREE

After a hearty meal of flapjacks and venison chops, they packed the gear in the wagon and rode for home. Nat surveyed the trail as they rode and was proud of the work they had accomplished. She looked over at Maggie, riding on the wagon. "We did a good job."

Maggie returned her smile. "Yes, we did."

"I wish I could've been here earlier," Tom said.

"You showed up in time to be a big help," Nat told him.

"I just wish I could've done more."

"Don't worry. I plan to work you hard before you go back to town."

A grin broke out over his face as they rode. Tom enjoyed hard work as much as she did, and it was good to see the results come more quickly with his youth and strength helping her out. They would unload the wagon, and if there were daylight left, they would check her traps, while Maggie checked the pools for seafood. She hoped at least a few lobsters had arrived while they were gone.

†

When the air filled with the smell of salt, the dogs raced ahead. Even they knew home was near. By the time the rest of the group reached the clearing, Marissa waited for them at the barn with Gyp and Luna dancing circles around her.

"You go catch up with Marissa, and we'll care for the animals," Maggie said when Nat's eyes filled with excitement.

"Thanks," she said, then dismounted Hardy and handed Tom the reins.

She hugged Marissa, and they walked back to the cabin arm in arm. "I'm so glad you made it home," she said. "I missed you."

"I missed you too." Just inside the cabin, Nat spun Marissa into her arms and kissed her deeply.

"Did you have a good trip?"

"Yes, we blazed our trail and set up two campsites. We even brought some meat home with us," Nat answered.

"What did you bring?"

"Maggie brought down a young buck, and Tom got our first mountain goat."

"That had to be exciting."

"It was, and I think we are all eager to see how the meat tastes."

"Do you want me to cook some for tonight?"

"Maggie's got leftover venison roast we can have tonight, so maybe tomorrow."

They walked onto the porch as Tom and Maggie emerged from hanging the meat in the smokehouse. Tom lifted the ram's head to show Marissa the impressive display of horns, and then hung it on the porch rafters.

"Smithy is going to go nuts over that," Marissa said.

"Yeah, he is," Tom agreed.

†

After stretching the deer and goat hides for drying, they spent a relaxing evening on the porch, allowing their dinner to settle. Nat and Tom had cleared and set new traps, while Marissa and Maggie checked the pools. They found fish and shrimp to harvest for a future meal, but the lobsters had yet to return.

The full moon rose and reflected on the calm water as Nat carved and the others worked on drilling buttons.

Tom looked out across the water. "It's so beautiful here. I can fully appreciate why you fell in love with this spot."

"It has everything I could dream for," Nat said. "Plenty of game, ocean life, and a family to share it with," she added with a warm smile. "My little slice of heaven."

A cool breeze came in from the water, and Maggie shivered. "I think it's time to take these old bones inside."

"I'm right there with you," Marissa said.

"Let's stoke up the fires and call it a day," Nat said to Tom as she put her knife away. She stood and stretched. "Tomorrow will be another long day."

†

Everyone retired for the evening, and Nat held Marissa in her arms. "It's good to be home."

"I missed you, terribly, my bee charmer," Marissa murmured as she snuggled into Nat's warmth. Her hand slipped beneath Nat's nightshirt, and she felt Nat shiver. Marissa's fingers brushed firm skin as her hand settled between Nat's legs to find her moist in anticipation of her touch. Her fingers slid deep inside Nat as she covered her mouth with a fevered kiss. Nat's hips rose to meet Marissa's fingers as she stroked deep into her lover. Nat's desire peaked quickly, and her body quivered as the pleasure rushed through her body. She broke the kiss to gasp for air and quickly rolled on top of Marissa, sliding her long fingers into her depths to give her pleasure.

As they lay quietly, with Marissa tucked into her body and with their passion sated, Nat stroked her lover's hair. "I love you," she whispered and kissed the top of Marissa's head. Her words disappeared into the silence as Marissa had fallen asleep. She pulled the covers over them and wrapped her arm around Marissa.

†

After a quick meal, Tom and Nat began working on the hides she would send back to town. "These are nice quality," Tom said. "Much better processed than most of what we've seen this season."

"Too many trappers rush through the process, destroying the quality of the fur. I believe you honor the animal by presenting the coat well maintained and the hide oiled to keep it supple.

"Smithy is always excited to receive a shipment from you. He never knows what to expect," Tom explained.

Nat laid a beaver fur on the table. "I take whatever nature has to offer me, and sometimes I'm even surprised." She poured a circle of oil on the skin and began massaging it into the hide. "The blubber from the whale that washed up provided me with gallons of rich oils to use and strong bone to use in carving."

"It seems like Mother Nature sends gifts if you just know what to look for," Tom said. "The honey tree was a great find, and I don't know of anyone that puts a set of antlers to so many different uses like you and Maggie."

Nat smiled at her young friend. "We were both raised to use every gift an animal has to offer. Most animals provide useful materials in many different ways, rather than just meat for nourishment."

"A porcupine," Tom challenged. "What can you use that for?"

Nat laughed. "Most people run away from a porcupine, and for a good reason. Those quills are painful, but the meat is delicious, and you can use the quills that cover the body for various things, from needles to jewelry. The quills accept dyes for coloring and are valuable in many tribes as currency for trading or purchasing goods."

"That's interesting. I would have never thought of that," Tom admitted.

"There are several thousand quills on a mature porcupine, so if harvested correctly, it can bring a good profit."

Tom took a bite of jerky and chewed on it while digesting the information Nat was sharing with him. Nat finished the last pelt and added it to the stack Tom would take back into town. "Are you up for a walk?"

"Sure. Where are we headed?"

"I'd like to walk the beach to see if anything of value has washed onto the shore."

"We can check the pools, too, can't we?" Tom asked.

"Yes, we can. Are you as hungry for lobster and shrimp as I am?"

"I got spoiled last year," Tom admitted.

Nat plucked her rifle from the porch and rested it on her shoulder. "Ready?"

"Just waiting on you." Tom smiled back.

Maggie appeared at the door at the sound of Nat's voice.

"Where are you two off to?"

"We thought to take a stroll down the beach to see if anything interesting had washed up," Nat responded. "Is there something you need before we go?"

"Just curious," Maggie smiled. "I'll add more wood to the smokehouse and check the spit to see how that goat meat is coming along."

"I can add the wood before we go," Tom offered.

"No, it will give me a chance to stretch my legs a bit," Maggie replied. "Don't forget buckets for anything you find in the pools."

Tom picked up two buckets. "I think we're all eager for the lobster to return."

Maggie nodded. "My mouth waters every time I think of it."

"Maybe today will be a good day." Tom lifted his rifle to his shoulder and joined Nat.

Gyp and Luna trotted ahead of them, and when they reached the beach, the dogs raced after waves and enjoyed the unique smells of the seashore.

"Do you want me to wade out to the pools?"

"I won't argue with you," Nat said. "That water is still cold."

Tom handed Nat his rifle and bent to start unlacing his boots. "If the lobsters have returned, it will be well worth braving the cold."

Nat waited until he had finished and handed him a bucket. "Good luck."

She glanced down the beach and smiled as she watched the dogs chasing sea birds. The sun glistened off the sand, and the gentle waves lapped at the shoreline. *So very peaceful.* When she turned back to check on Tom, she was excited to see him bent over inside a large pool. She saw his hand plummet into the water, and he raised his hand in triumph. He turned back to her and showed her the lobster he had caught. He dropped his captive into the bucket and retrieved two more before wading back to shore.

"They aren't the biggest we've ever caught, but they are the first of the season." Tom tipped the bucket so Nat could see the lobsters.

"A few more of those, and we can have a feast before you head back to town." She could see the excitement on the young man's face. "Let's hit a few more of the pools."

Tom picked up his boots and the empty bucket. "Let's fill them up."

Tom's bare feet squeaked in the wet sand as they walked down the beach, but after raiding three more pools,

Tom had filled the buckets with lobster. "We are going to have some happy women folk when we return," Tom said as he put his socks and boots on. "That sure feels better."

"Thank you for doing the harvesting. It takes forever for my feet to get warm again." The loud squawking of sea birds down the beach caught Nat's attention. "Let's check what has everyone excited," she said as she pointed her gun down the shoreline. A flock of gulls was swooping down onto a large dark form.

"Should we leave the buckets?" Tom asked.

Nat nodded. "They'll be safe. Just move them away from the waterline."

Tom secured the two buckets in the soft, dry sand and joined Nat, taking the rifle she handed to him. Gyp and Luna ran ahead and the gulls scattered in flight, noisily complaining about the interference of their feast.

When the birds flew away, Nat could see the carcass of a large animal, and as she moved closer, she saw that it was a seal. The birds had begun to tear at the thick outer coat, but Nat found why the animal had died. She frowned and pointed to a gaping hole in the animal's neck. "A careless hunter left this animal to waste," she told Tom. "It's hard to tell how long he's been dead or what direction he came from, but a gunshot was what caused his death."

"Why would you shoot something you did not intend to harvest?" Tom asked.

"For sport most likely." Nat scowled.

Tom shook his head. "What can we harvest so the animal doesn't go to waste?"

Nat examined the carcass. "Most of the hide is intact. The birds have just begun to attack. There will be fat we can use for oil, and we can take some of the meat for the dogs. The rest we can leave for the birds and other scavengers."

Nat knelt next to the animal. "I'll start skinning if you'll take the lobsters back and bring back the small sled and several large buckets to use for the fat."

"I'll be back soon." Tom turned back toward the cabin.

"Hey, Tom." Nat waited for him to turn back to her. "Ask Marissa to give you the skinning knife we made for you. It'll come in handy slicing the blubber from the pelt."

"Got it," he replied and set off at a brisk pace. He stopped after several steps. "You made me a knife?"

Nat nodded. "Go, so you can see for yourself. It will get broken in good today."

†

Nat and Tom continued working on the sealskin and making oil from the fats while Marissa and Maggie finished making supper.

"If it tastes half as good as it smells, we'll be in great shape," Nat told Tom when Maggie pulled the meat from the spit and walked past them into the cabin.

He looked up from the pot he was stirring. "It's got my mouth watering. It smells much better than this fat."

"That's for sure. That will make great oil once it separates from the water. Are you about ready to start straining it?"

Tom nodded. "I think most of the water has cooked off."

"Let's see what we've got." Nat secured a burlap bag over a cooking pot and guided Tom to pour the liquid through the fabric. "Good job. I think you're right. Most of the water has escaped, so now it's a slow boil to break down the oil before we can transfer it to storage tins."

Nat looked up when she heard footsteps on the porch. Marissa had leaned against the porch railing. "Are you two about ready for a supper break?"

Nat smiled at Tom. "We thought you'd never ask. Give us a few more minutes to get the fat back on the fire, and we'll wash up and come in."

"How much longer do you think this will take?" Tom asked as he lifted the pot back over the fire.

"We'll check on it after supper. It should be close by then." Nat stretched the sealskin across the railing.

Tom cocked his head. "What will you do with that?"

"I won't do anything, but I'm sure Maggie will have a few ideas. Sealskin is very watertight. Maggie works magic with all kinds of things." Tom shuffled his feet. "What do you think she could make with that ram hide?"

Nat shrugged. "Many things, I'm sure. Why don't you ask her about it?"

"I will. Over supper. I'm starving."

"I could eat too," Nat replied. "We've got a lot done these last few days. I hate to see you leave, but I know you will bring goods with you when you come back."

"Maybe we could ride down together and check on the bison?" Tom asked.

"I planned on that," Nat said. "Let's go."

Tom followed her into the house. "It smells so good in here." He stopped to wash his hands in the basin.

"Maggie has fresh bread cooking to slice to make sandwiches tomorrow for lunch before we have a lobster feast. I don't think we'll make a big dent in the roast, even with your appetite Tom," Marissa said and began serving plates. "It did surprise me by how tender it cut."

"You also had a very sharp knife," Maggie reminded her.

"If it tastes even half as good as it smells, it will be wonderful. The smell has been torturing Tom and me for an hour." Nat passed Tom the vegetables Maggie had put in a bowl.

"Any food rarely goes to waste around me," Tom smiled as he took the bowl from Nat. "I was willing to try some seal, but Nat wasn't sure if it was safe."

"Better to pass unless you know it's fresh or you might be in the privy for days," Maggie warned.

"That's what she told me. I don't think I'll make that mistake. By the way, I love my new knife, ladies. I forgot to tell you earlier. Nat says it was a team effort."

"It fit his big paw perfectly," Nat said with a laugh.

"I hated to get it dirty, but it worked well on that seal."

"Keep the blade honed, and there's no hide it won't cut through."

"Yes, ma'am," he nodded to Maggie. "Nat and I were talking earlier about the seal and ram hide. What would you make with those?"

Maggie's brows knit in concentration. "The seal skin is very waterproof. You could make water flasks or even a riding cape to keep your upper body and saddle dry in the rain. If you had more than one or a larger piece, it would make a full rain cape."

"What about the goat hide?"

"With that heavy coat, it would make a great blanket. Is there anything that you need?" Maggie looked at Tom. "If you plan to travel often by horseback in the winter, they would make some thick chaps to keep your legs warm."

"That's a thought. You don't think I'd get laughed out of town for wearing those?"

"You would be the one with the last laugh with warm legs to boot," Nat replied. "I guarantee there is no one in town that would have anything like them."

"In the winter, it would also help to camouflage you, too," Marissa added.

"That's true, the white coat would blend right in with snow," Nat agreed.

Maggie looked at Tom. "Chaps then? I could start working on them once the hide cures."

"Let me think on it," Tom replied. "The winter is months away."

Maggie nodded. "No rush. I will wait until you decide."

Tom looked at Nat. "Do you mind if I keep the goat in the smokehouse?"

"That's not a problem. You might consider taking a quarter to Smithy, though. I bet he'd love to try the meat."

"That's a good point."

"I'd love to see his face when you show him that goat head," Nat replied.

"You could ride into town with me?" Tom offered.

"I could check with the general store and see what items they need and pick up a few things," Nat replied. "Are there things we need for us?"

"I'm sure we can come up with a list of things tomorrow," Marissa said.

"This is tasty," Tom said after swallowing a bite of the meat. "I was afraid it would be chewy and taste gamey."

"I'm afraid it would be if you didn't simmer it all day. It was a guess for our first time cooking it, but I think it came out well," Marissa said with a nod to Maggie.

"I think the dogs would agree with you," Nat said, pointing to the two dogs licking the inside of the bowls. "Gyp even ate the carrots."

"That's a miracle," Maggie chuckled. "How is Shine doing?"

"Good. Shine's almost as big as Luna, and I swear Smithy has her so spoiled. She stays in the office during the day with him and Blue while I work. Gosh only knows what he feeds her in there."

"I don't suppose you spoil her at all?" Nat teased.

"Me? Heck no," Tom smirked.

"Bring her out with you on your next trip. We'd all love to see her," Marissa said.

"I will. Do you ever see the wolf?" Tom asked.

"I catch a glimpse of him now and then. He spent a few nights in the barn this winter," Nat replied. "Gyp doesn't sneak out much to run with him anymore. I think she's content with having Luna here."

"I don't know what I did without her before," Maggie said. "She's such a good footwarmer and a great companion."

Gyp came to sit beside Nat. "I always knew you'd make a good mama." Her hand slipped a piece of meat to Gyp, and then Nat patted her head. "I think that was her only litter."

"Like the rest of us, she is getting long in the tooth," Maggie said.

"She's not a pup anymore, but she can still put Luna in her line, when necessary," Nat slid her hand down Gyp's side. "Can't ya, girl?"

Marissa watched Nat's hand go to her neck and touch the bear claw necklace.

"There were times after my father died that I think her love is the only thing that kept me going." Nat looked up at her friends. "Then I met y'all."

"You have to admit we make a good team," Marissa said and laid her hand over Nat's.

"That we do. When I get back from town, do you think you could bake one of your apple pies? Do you still have jars left?"

"I think I may find one or two tucked away for a rainy day." Marissa smiled. "I'll have one ready for when you get home. Do you plan on taking Gyp with you?"

"If she wants to go," Nat answered. "You want to go to town?"

Tom smirked. "That dog will follow you anywhere."

"Yeah, I believe she would." Nat bent down and kissed the top of her head. She looked up at Tom. "Since you will be taking Rusty back to town, will you get the blacksmith to trim his hooves and put new shoes on him? I'll pay him when we arrive."

"Yes, that's not a problem."

"One more round of the trap lines tomorrow, and then we can load the wagon for the trip to town. After a lobster feast, we can call it an early evening and head to town first light."

"You and Gyp are more than welcome to stay at the cabin with me," Tom offered. "You can get up with the chickens and be back here before lunch."

"He's got a good point. I don't cherish the thought of you traveling after dark," Marissa replied.

55

"Fine with me. We can eat at the hotel, and I can tell your old boss how tasty the lobsters will be this year. That will get him eager for seafood."

"That's mean, but I love the idea," Marissa laughed. "Why don't you two enjoy the fresh air on the front porch while Maggie and I straighten up in here?"

"Don't mind if we do," Nat said. "C'mon, Tom."

Nat sat in one of the chairs and stretched her legs out in front of her. "That was a great meal."

"Yes, it was. No matter how hard I try, I can't replicate Marissa's cooking."

"It takes years of practice. Have you not found a young woman to cook for you yet?" Nat teased.

"There is a young woman I've got a shine for," Tom said. "Her name is Ruth, and I'd like you to meet her. Her family returned from the gold rush and decided to settle in the town. She works a few days a week for Smithy."

"Is she a hard worker?"

"Very much so," Tom said. "I've had dinner with her family a few times, and they seem like good people."

"I'd love to meet her." Nat cocked her head. "Do you ever think of going back to California?"

"No, not at all. My brothers will be farmers, but I've never experienced life as I have here."

"It gets in your blood, doesn't it? This way of life."

"Yes. I've experienced more in the last year than I had in my entire life to this point."

"No regrets for not following through on your dream of the gold rush?"

"None whatsoever. The stories I've heard from people traveling back have made me realize staying here was my gold mine. Very few of them found enough gold to make it worth the risk of dying from the elements or the competition."

"I am glad you stayed. You've been a great help to us here, and I know Smithy likes the way you work. He's thanked me dozens of times for introducing y'all."

"He's been like a father to me. Taught me things I'm not sure my real father knows."

"Smithy is a good man and a great businessman. He's been a part of my life for a long time."

Marissa stepped onto the porch. "We're all wrapped up in here. Maggie's gone to bed, and I'm not far behind her."

"We'll bring in some wood to feed the stove, and I'll be there in a few minutes."

"Goodnight, Tom. I'll see you for breakfast in the morning."

"Goodnight, Marissa."

"Let's take a few armfuls of split wood in and hit the sack."

"Sounds good to me. It's been a long day."

"Thanks for all your help, Tom," Nat said as he filled the stove. "See you in the morning."

"Night, Nat."

CHAPTER FOUR

Nat packed her saddlebags with a few items she would take with her, and when the sun rose the following day, she and Tom headed into town. Gyp trotted alongside Nat, eager to smell the scents on the trail ahead. Now and then, she would catch a fresh scent and run ahead of them but would return moments later to trot beside them.

"It's turned into a beautiful morning, hasn't it?" Nat asked Tom.

"Yes, it has. Spring is definitely in the air." He looked up at the sky at a hawk searching for breakfast. "The next few weeks should stay busy as trappers return to the woods and travelers heading to or from the Yukon pass through town."

"That won't stop you from making a delivery in two weeks, will it?"

Tom shook his head. "Heaven's no. Smithy has made it abundantly clear that your orders remain a top priority. He's like a kid at Christmas every time I bring a load back."

"I can't wait to see his face when he sees the ram's head. I bet his eyes pop out of his skull." Nat smirked. "The meat should be ready when you return and you can take it back to town with you."

The jangling sound of the harness attached to the wagon was making Nat sleepy. "Let's pull over at the creek ahead and water the horses. Rusty's harness is about to lull me to sleep."

"I know. It can get so rhythmic. I find myself nodding off, too, until Rusty hits a bump and jars me awake. I swear he does it on purpose sometimes."

"Good thing he knows the route well. He can make it home with you asleep."

"That's true. Some days I think he's smarter than me. He was a good purchase."

"He's a great workhorse. I haven't found anything he can't pull."

Tom pulled the wagon to a stop and grabbed a bucket from the back and Buck's reins. He walked to the creek, dipped the bucket into the cool water, and carried it to Rusty as Buck and Hardy drank freely. Gyp took a deep drink as Nat filled her canteen. She took a long sip and handed it to Tom.

"This is some of the sweetest water," Tom said as he wiped his mouth and handed Nat the canteen.

"Yes, it is. I never mind stopping off here for a refill."

"Only an hour's ride from here to town, right?"

Nat nodded. "You eager to get back and see a young lady?"

Tom's blush answered her question. "I've been thinking. If Ruth and I were to get married, would you mind having us for neighbors someday?"

"I would love that," Nat replied. "Have you been thinking about a spot?"

"The lake sure is pretty. Close, but not too close to crowd you, Marissa, and Maggie. I like the idea of stepping off my front porch and shooting or catching something for dinner." Tom answered.

"Maybe after we hunt bison, we can start collecting some logs for a cabin," Nat suggested. "We can pick out a spot when you deliver goods next trip."

"I'd really like that. You know I wouldn't be surprised if Smithy considered doing the same. He's talked about selling off his business and living off the land."

"It wouldn't be the same in town without Smithy, but he's earned a right to make those choices. With the profits from selling the business, he could afford to have someone build for him whenever he's ready."

"Don't be surprised if that conversation comes up when we hunt bison," Tom replied. "He gets kind of misty-eyed when he talks about your place."

"There is plenty of room for several families," Nat said as she looped her canteen over her saddle horn. "Especially you and Smithy. You're both like family to us already."

Tom tied Buck to the back of the wagon. "You all mean the world to me, and even if Ruth is not interested in me, I may just move out on my own."

Nat punched him in the shoulder. "If she's smart, she'll take you up on your offer. I look forward to meeting her. Maybe she can join us for dinner tonight."

"I will ask her as soon as we hit town." Tom climbed onto the wagon bench. "Shouldn't be too much longer. We can unload our goods, and I'll drop the wagon off at my place and bring Rusty back to the blacksmith for new shoes."

"There's no rush. You have two weeks," Nat reminded him.

"If I get them done and Smithy decides we can leave earlier, then I don't have to wait on the blacksmith." Tom picked up the reins. "Let's go, Rusty."

†

As they rode past Marissa's cabin where Tom now lived, Nat let out a low whistle. "Someone has been busy splitting firewood."

Nat surveyed the property. "The place looks good. You've been taking good care of things. That is a large pile of wood."

Tom looked up at Nat. "I had to make some repairs to the chinking this winter, but overall, the place is in good shape."

As they topped the last hill before entering the town, Nat pulled Hardy to a stop. It had been months since she had last visited. "This place is starting to grow."

"Yes, more people are moving in. It's good for businesses, but it feels like it's beginning to get crowded."

Nat saw the frown on Tom's face. "It may be a good time to move into the wild with us. I'll talk to Marissa and see if she wants to sell her place in town."

"With all the new people, I don't think she would have any problem. I don't want to cause her any hardship."

"It's no hardship. We could always keep it to stay when we come to town if Marissa's not interested in renting it out or selling it now."

Gyp saw Shine, Blue, and Smithy outside of the store and ran ahead to greet them. Smithy turned and smiled when he saw them approach. "Well, look what dragged into town," he said to Nat.

"I missed you, too, Smithy. I couldn't resist seeing your face when Tom gives you a gift."

"A gift? Oh, goody," Smithy replied, rubbing his hands together. "What did you bring me?"

"Something I guarantee you've never gotten before. Tom got it on his own and wants to give it to you," Nat teased.

"Show me," Smithy pleaded.

Tom hopped from the wagon and walked to the back. He lifted a blanket to reveal the ram's head.

"Oh, my goodness. A mountain goat," Smithy purred. "You got him?"

"Yes, I did. I had to climb a mile straight up to fetch the beast, too," Tom teased. He knelt to give Shine some attention. "Did you miss me?" Shine covered his face with kisses.

Smithy reached into the wagon and pulled out the head. "This is amazing. What did you do with the hide and meat? I've never eaten wild goat."

"I kept the hide so Maggie could make me something. We tried some of the meat and put the rest in the smoker. I'll bring some back with me next trip."

"What's Maggie going to make from the hide?"

"Dunno. We haven't decided yet." Tom looked up when a dark-haired young woman stepped onto the loading dock.

Nat followed his eyes and watched a smile grow on the woman's face.

"I thought I heard your voice. Welcome back," she said.

"Thanks. Ruth, I'd like for you to meet my friend, Nat. Nat, this is Ruth."

"Nice to meet you, Ruth," Nat replied.

"Likewise. Tom talks about you all the time," Ruth said. "It's a pleasure to meet you; however, I thought you'd be at least nine feet tall."

Nat smiled. "Not even close. Would you and Smithy like to join us for dinner at the hotel later?"

"That would be grand," Ruth said.

Smithy nodded. "You know I'm always up for someone else's cooking."

"I've got some errands to run, but they won't take long. Tom, are you good for unloading the pelts?"

"No problem, Nat. You need me to carry that honey and jelly for you?" Tom offered.

Nat shook her head and picked up a box of honey. "Nope, I'm recruiting Smithy for that."

"Let's go then," Smithy said. "Take the ram's head into the office for me, please. I can't have anyone walking off with my prize."

"You got it," Tom said. He picked up the head and carried it inside, with Ruth following closely behind him.

"She's pretty," Nat said when they were out of hearing range. "He seems very smitten by her."

"The feeling is mutual. Ruth has moped around here ever since he left," Smithy told her.

"Do you think she would survive out in the wild? Tom wants to build a cabin at the lake eventually."

"She's pretty hardy stock. Ruth isn't afraid to work hard either. She puts some of these guys to shame."

"Maybe things will work out for our young man. How have you been?" Nat picked up a box of jelly, and they started walking toward the general store.

"Doing well, and business keeps growing along with the town. Mostly a good thing, but a few bad seeds come through from time to time. Thankfully they have moved through quickly so far."

"Maggie and I were blazing a trail down to where we will soon hunt bison. Tom showed up in time to be a big help. We're all set with shelter, fire pits, and plenty of firewood."

"I can't wait. I've always wanted to hunt bison but never had the opportunity."

"I would wager within a month you will have your chance. I told Tom we'd ride down and check for them when he comes out in two weeks to bring supplies."

"How did the goat meat turn out?"

"Marissa roasted it all day, and it wasn't bad at all. I think we were all afraid it would be tough and taste wild, but it didn't. It'll be interesting to see how it tastes smoked."

"Did Tom have to work hard to get it?"

"It wasn't quite a mile, but it was a tough climb to reach the fallen goat. A mountain lion watched Tom the whole way, but he didn't know it until I pointed her out to him when he returned."

"I bet you were holding your breath watching that."

"I was ready to shoot if she made a move toward him, but she was just curious about what he was doing."

"What else do you need to do after the general store?"

"I'm going to see the blacksmith about new shoes for Rusty after placing an order for supplies. Do you need something?"

"No. I just wanted to spend some time with you catching up. I know you won't stay in town long, and it seems like forever since I've seen you."

Nat smiled at the big man. "I won't be a long time. I'll meet you back at the store. I want to see what the competition is bringing you, too."

"Nothing compared to your quality, but you can judge that for yourself."

"See you soon, then."

Nat set the case of jelly on the counter.

"You are a sight for sore eyes, Nat. I am running low on everything," Jacob announced.

"I've got a dozen bags of jerky for you and a couple of smoked deer quarters. I'll have Tom drop those off to you."

"My prayers are answered. The people here love your jerky. They have been griping for weeks about getting more in stock."

"We've set up a second smokehouse, so this spring I will get you loaded up."

"Smithy says you're also going to hunt bison, is that right?"

"Yes, I hope in the coming weeks. Are you interested in some of the smoked meat and jerky?"

"I'll take all you're willing to sell. I want to ask a favor too," the owner said in a hushed tone. "We have a wedding anniversary coming up, and I'd love to have one of the hides to give the missus for a present." He looked at Nat. "I know Smithy probably wants them all, but I'd be willing to pay top dollar for a cured hide big enough for a bed covering."

"I will make that happen. We will be making more jellies and pick fresh berries once they start to ripen. Is there anything else you would like to have?"

"Has Maggie been making buttons? I'm down to a handful."

"She and Marissa have plenty to send to you. Tom is coming out in two weeks to bring supplies, so I'll send them back with him and anything else we have ready. Do you see a market for smoked fish? We've got a fair amount of those I could send, too."

"I'll try anything. There are so many new folks in town that are always asking for new things. I'll let you know how they sell."

Nat pulled out a list of the items she would need Tom to deliver. "Is there a problem with anything on the list?"

"No, I don't think there is anything I don't have in stock. Just tell Tom to give me a day before he's ready to go, and I'll have the order pulled."

"I'll be in town until the morning, but I've got a few things I need to take back with me." She handed him another list. "I'll be back for these and to settle up for the order later if you'll be ready."

"You've got a healthy credit, and I'll add the jelly, honey, and meats to it, so if there's a balance, it shouldn't be much."

"Fine, I'll be back later to pay for my order." Nat shook his hand and walked down the street to the blacksmith.

She paid him for a new set of shoes and ordered a dozen knife blades so she could continue making knives.

Nat walked across the street to the gunsmith and entered the store.

"Hi there, Nat," Bill, the owner, called out from behind the counter. "What are you looking for today?"

"Something small for Marissa," Nat replied. "Easy to load and conceal."

"I've got just the thing." Nat watched him pull out a small pistol. "Holds two rounds, but for the size, it'll pack a wallop. Won't take a bear down, but it'll knock a man to his knees or some other vermin."

"That's perfect. I'll take it and two boxes of shells for it. I also need three boxes for my rifle and one for my colt."

"Give me a few minutes, and I'll have you all set. Feel free to look around to see if there's anything else you like."

"That's always dangerous, Bill," Nat teased.

She browsed the selection of rifles and picked up a gun with a lever action. She lifted it and looked down the barrel.

"You've got great taste. That's a brand-new model that I was only able to purchase two of from back east. It's a Henry repeating rifle. It holds sixteen rounds of forty-four magnum shells."

"It's a beauty," Nat said, placing it back on the holder.

"I'd be willing to sell it to you at a discount. There's not a big market for repeaters yet due to the cost. I'd be ready to sell that one to you for thirty dollars. I'll even throw in three boxes of shells."

"That's a healthy price for a rifle, but it is an excellent piece. I've heard stories of how it turned the tide in the Civil War once the Yanks received them."

"This gives a shooter a definite advantage to the single-shot and reload rifles."

Nat picked it up again.

"For you, I'll drop it to twenty-five with shells if you'll bring me six jars of your honey," Bill told her.

"Sold," Nat said. "I'll send the honey with Tom in two weeks." She pulled out money from her pocket and paid for her purchases. "This will be perfect for hunting bison."

"Oh, most definitely," Bill replied. "Bring me a smoked hindquarter, and I'll keep you in shells for years. That is some of the best meat I've ever eaten."

Nat reached out her hand. "Add two more boxes of shells as a down payment, and you'll have your quarter when it's ready."

Bill shook her hand. "You drive a hard bargain, young lady." Bill stored the pistol and ammunition in a box and looked up at Nat. "Hang on a second." He walked into the back room and returned carrying a leather case for her new rifle. "This should work well," he said and slid the gun into the supple leather. "Fits like a glove."

"How much?"

"On the house with dreams of a nice bison dinner," Bill answered.

Nat smiled back at him. "Much appreciated. I'll be seeing you." Nat slung the case over her shoulder and picked up the box.

†

When she arrived at Smithy's, Tom had several people gathered around him as he retold the story of shooting his first mountain goat. He picked up the head and told them about having to climb halfway up the mountain to retrieve him after the animal was down. Tom looked up to see Nat enter. "Then when I get back down the mountain to where Nat was waiting, she pointed out a mountain lion, not more than a hundred yards from where I'd been climbing."

Nat walked by headed to Smithy's office. "He'd surely have soiled his britches if he'd seen her stalking him."

The group, including Tom, broke out in laughter.

She entered Smithy's office and sat her box on his desk.

"What ya got there?" he asked.

"I bought a small pistol for Marissa, some ammunition, and a gift for myself," Nat said as she pulled out the rifle and handed it to Smithy.

"Damn, that's one fine piece," he said, pulling the gun up to his shoulder. "Sixteen shots, right?"

"That's correct. I did a bit of bartering with Bill, but I'm sure I came out on top. He has one more, just like it."

Smithy's eyes sparkled with excitement. "It would be a fine gun for hunting bison."

"My thoughts exactly. I've been working hard, so I thought I would splurge when I saw it, and Bill kept on until I couldn't say no."

"What did it cost ya?"

"He dropped the price to twenty-five from forty, threw in several boxes of shells and this nice case. He wants a bison dinner and said if I'd bring him a hind quarter, he'd keep me in shells for years."

"I should probably notify the sheriff because you robbed Bill," Smithy said and broke out laughing.

"I think I bargained pretty well," Nat said as she sat and propped her feet on a stool.

"Damn right you did." Smithy marveled at the rifle before handing it back to her. "I may have to go see him, too."

Tom walked into the office and let out a soft whistle. "That's nice," he said and reached for the gun. "A repeater?"

Nat nodded. "Sixteen rounds."

"That's fantastic." He handed the gun back to her. "I'm going to take the wagon back to my place, and then I'll bring Rusty back to the blacksmith for his shoes."

"Why don't you let Ruth ride out with you?" Smithy suggested.

"Don't mind if I do," Tom said. "We'll be back shortly. Do you want me to take Hardy and put him in the corral?"

"Sure, you can take this box and the rifle. I think the guns will be safe."

"I'll hide them well," Tom promised.

"I will be ready to close up and head to dinner when you get back," Smithy said.

"We'll see you soon then." Tom raced out of the room in search of Ruth.

Smithy looked at Nat. "You know, Tom's not the only one itching to get into the wild with you. Town's getting a bit crowded. I've thought it might be a good time to sell this place and enjoy the rest of my days."

"We would love to have both of y'all for neighbors. When Tom told me of his plans, it got me thinking. We cut some trees that would make good cabin logs when we blazed the bison camp trail. When Tom comes out to deliver supplies, we could spend a few days bringing them closer to begin preparing for builds. If you could spare him for a couple of extra days."

"That does sound like a good plan. Harvested trees wouldn't go to waste, and they have already started curing." Smithy ran his hand through his dark hair. "Maybe I can come help as well. I'll send out a two-person saw with the first load of supplies."

"Do you have any idea where you would like to build?"

"Tom's dream is the lake area, but I'd rather be by the ocean. I know it will be colder in the winter, but I love the view and the sound of the water."

Nat looked up at him. "I think I know the perfect spot, not far from ours. When you come out, you can take a look for yourself." Nat noticed the shine of excitement in Smithy's eyes. "I can't wait to tell the ladies we may have neighbors."

"I don't want to infringe on your space. A small cabin, smokehouse, and barn. Maybe a corral, too, for my horse."

"I think we should consider a corral down by the lake. There is plenty of sweetgrass for grazing and access to freshwater. Tom, and hopefully Ruth, could tend to them for us." Nat smiled.

"I'm not a young man any longer, but I think there will be a lot of things I can do to help. I can skin, help tan the hides, maybe run a line or two myself, and keep smokehouses running."

"That would be a huge help. With two extra hunters, we can bring in enough meat to sell and still have full bellies."

"I'll start putting some plans in place for the store. I may talk with Ruth's father. He seems a capable businessman, and I may decide to let him manage the business, and if it continues to do well, he can buy it outright."

"You will still be close enough to travel in to see how things are going, and if you need to stay awhile until he learns to grade pelts, we can keep things going for you at your homestead." Nat was enjoying the conversation. "We will continue to bring in pelts and other goods to sell as well, so you'll have ample opportunity to be in town."

"Speaking of pelts, I had a Canadian trapper come through a month ago who wanted to sell his traps. They are high quality and in good shape. Are you interested in them?"

"I'm always interested in a good deal. Send the traps out with Tom and take the price from my inventory. Why was he selling out?"

"He said he was tired and wanted to go home and put down some roots."

"I understand that completely. Trapping is hard work and lonely if you don't have good companions." Nat looked around the room. "Speaking of which, I wonder where Gyp got off to."

"She was napping by the fire earlier. I bet Tom took Gyp and Shine out to the cabin for the night."

"That would make good sense. Tom's grown up so much since he arrived."

"He's like the son I never had," Smithy said. "I almost forgot, there's something else I traded for that might be of interest to you. Come on, and I'll show you."

Nat followed Smithy into the back of the store. In the corner was an odd-looking device. "This is a foot-powered grinding device. I thought it would do well to sharpen knives, and if you're still making knives and blades, it will make things much faster. You sit on the stool and pump the levers with your feet. I bet Maggie would be perfect at this."

"Only one way to find out. I've still got plenty of whalebone left to try out, and carving it takes forever. The blacksmith is making me some blades that I can finish and hone down to a nice edge."

"Heck, I might even try my hand at that," Smithy replied.

"Send it on out then," Nat said.

"Will do, and anything else I think we can use," Smithy said.

Tom and Ruth walked in. "We're all set," Tom said. "The blacksmith will get his new shoes on in the next few days."

"Thanks, Tom. I appreciate you doing that." Nat looked at Smithy. "You about ready to close up? I'm getting hungry."

"Lock us up, Tom, and we'll go get a table," Smithy said.

"Will do, boss."

†

Nat enjoyed teasing Randall, the hotel owner, with comments on how sweet the lobster would taste this year while waiting on food.

"I sure hope you can start bringing in a delivery soon," he said. "The town is hungry for your seafood."

Smithy grinned at Nat. "Should we tell him what else we are planning?"

"Sure, go ahead, Smithy."

"As soon as the herd arrives, Nat, Tom, and I are going to be hunting bison."

"No kidding. I'd be happy to buy some of that meat. I've only had it once, but it is one of the best steaks I've ever eaten. When do you think they will arrive?"

Smithy looked at Nat to answer. "I think they will return within a month. If the herd is half the size of last year, I think we can count on at least a dozen or more animals."

"Count me in for three if you can."

"You got it," Nat answered.

"You think we can get twelve on the first trip?" Tom asked.

"I think so. Rusty can pull that much weight, and Quincy should be able to haul the pelts. Maggie and I will stay at the homestead to start working the hides and smoke some meat of our own if you and Tom bring the rest of the meat to town."

Smithy nodded in thought. "We'll need an ample supply of salt to treat the meat until we can get it back. I'll get an order in at the general store tomorrow."

Nat took a sip of her drink. "That's a good plan. If the first hunt is a success, we can return in a few weeks to see if the herd is still grazing there and take a smaller load back. I don't want to cull too many or keep them from returning next year."

"It would be nice to have them return every year," Tom agreed.

Nat turned to Ruth. "So, tell me about you. What do you like to do? What are your dreams?"

Ruth sat up straight. "I like to hunt and fish, and I'm not afraid to get my hands dirty. I think I'm a hard worker, and I like to grow things."

"Do you consider yourself a town girl, or would you prefer living out where everything is wild and free?" Nat asked.

"Living in a town is all I've known, but I'd like to have someplace where I could grow a big garden and raise a few kids without someone living right outside my window."

Nat liked what she heard from Ruth. She sounded like she would make a good match for Tom. "What have you hunted?"

"Mostly small game. Rabbits, squirrels, but I'd like to hunt the bigger animals like deer, moose, and elk."

"I'd like you to visit sometime. Maybe you and Tom could ride out for a day. You could stay with the three of us women, and we'll put Tom out in the barn if that will sit better with your parents."

Ruth's eyes lit up. "I'd like that. Tom talks of your place like it's a fairy tale, almost too good to be true."

"It's no fairy tale. There are many dangers and even more hard work to make a go of living off the land, but we do pretty well for ourselves. I don't think we go without anything we need."

"I'll talk it over with my parents and let Tom know. I really would like to see your place and the ocean. I've only seen it once."

"Prepare to fall in love. I fell in love with the spot the first time I laid eyes on it. I had trapped all my life with my parents until they died, and I lost the desire to be out in the woods alone and lonely."

"Smithy tells me you're a bit of a legend when it comes to trapping and treating pelts. Says that you bring in the best of anyone in these parts."

"He does, huh?" Nat shot a wink to Ruth. "I suppose you know he's a great storyteller, too."

"Maybe so, but these two adore you. I can see why though, now that I've met you myself."

Tom was smiling as he listened to his two favorite women. Smithy, too, had a wide grin on his face.

"I think pretty highly of them, too. Darn near shot Tom the first time I met him, all starving and skinny. He taught me quick how hard he could work in exchange for food and a warm place to sleep. I thank my lucky stars every day the smoke from my cabin brought us together."

"I'll have to second that. I don't know what I did before Tom came to work for me. He's been a godsend to me too." Smithy took a long drink to hide the emotion on his face.

"Well, we're starting to sound pretty sappy. I think that's my cue to pay the check and head home for the night," Nat announced.

"Dinner is on me," Smithy said. "You gone at sun up tomorrow?"

"Yes, I've got lots of work to do. Lobsters and shrimp to catch, fish to smoke, jerky to make," Nat replied. "I'll see you in two weeks, right?"

"I reckon I'll ride out with Tom. After we unload, we can go down and check for bison, can't we?"

"If you get there early enough, we may let Maggie and Marissa unload, and we'll head down the trail. On horseback with no load to bear, we could make it just after nightfall if we ride hard. If not, we can stay in the mid-trail shelter."

"That sounds like a good plan. We can pack jerky and maybe some of Marissa's biscuits and be good for two days," Tom said.

"It was very nice to meet you, Ruth, and I hope to see you again soon. Smithy, I'll see you in two weeks. I'll see you when you get done walking Ruth home," she said to Tom.

"Do you want me to walk out with you?" Smithy asked.

"I've made that walk many times. But thank you for the offer." She hugged Smithy tight. "Thanks for a wonderful dinner."

†

When Nat stepped outside, the night had fallen, and the farther she walked, the more brilliant the sky lit up with stars. The conveniences of town could have their benefits, but there was nothing that moved her soul more than an open night sky, except for Marissa. She was the love Nat had felt was missing from her life. One more day and she'd be back in Marissa's arms, snuggling in their warm bed.

Nat opened the door to the cabin to let the dogs out and sat in a familiar rocker on the front porch to watch them play. The moon had risen, and the beams shimmered against Shine's coat. A cool breeze had also sprung to life as Nat enjoyed the relaxing early evening. Her eyes gazed around the yard where she and Marissa had shared so many memories. She wouldn't dream of changing anything about their life together at the shore, but this cabin and the town would always hold a cache of special memories.

The rocker had nearly lulled Nat to sleep when Gyp and Shine raced to the edge of the property. She looked up to see a figure moving through the darkness. Tom had returned home, and the dogs welcomed him with yips and barks as they nipped at his heels.

"Welcome home," Nat said when Tom arrived and sat on the porch steps.

"Thanks. It's turned into a beautiful night."

"Yes, it has. I didn't expect you home so soon," Nat teased.

"I figured you'd want to be up and gone early in the morning, and I wanted to talk with you. What do you think of Ruth?"

Nat was surprised at how valued her opinion was to Tom. "What would you think if I didn't like her?" Nat tried to keep a straight face.

Tom frowned. "I'd be worried that you see something in her I don't."

Nat immediately felt bad for teasing him so. "It's a good thing I like her then. I think she will make the perfect partner for you."

Tom let out a big sigh. "That's a relief. I thought you didn't like her for a second."

"I'm sorry, that was mean of me, but I couldn't resist. I like that Ruth has some of the same dreams as you."

"Yes, she does. I do hope her father will consent to her marrying me, and we can start a life together near you."

"You were right about Smithy. He and I talked about him moving out, too, in the future. He's thinking about talking to Ruth's dad about managing the store with the potential to buy it if things go well and Smithy is ready to sell."

"I think he would jump at the offer. He seems like a smart man. He doesn't know much about furs, but if Smithy can teach me, he can teach anyone."

Nat shook her head. "Don't sell yourself short. You are an intelligent young man and a hard worker. If marriage is not an option, Smithy would probably put you in the position until you're ready to build your place."

"I know I could handle it, but I hope I don't have to take that option."

"Have you planned to speak to her father about a proposal?"

Tom blushed. "I thought after we come back from the bison hunt."

"That would be good. Maybe invite Ruth's father to dinner at the hotel and talk to him about your plans." She smiled at Tom. "He probably already knows you're a good man and would be a wise choice for Ruth."

"I hope so," Tom said and knocked the dust off his boots.

"I also talked to Smithy about having you stay behind a few days after your deliveries. I reckon we cut enough large trees blazing the trail to build several nice buildings, but we'll have to use muscle and Rusty to bring them up to the lake."

"I reckon I need to start drawing up a plan for a cabin," Tom said. "Did Smithy mention where he wanted to live?"

"He wants to be on the coastline, and I think I know of the perfect spot for him. I think we should build a corral and a barn and let the livestock stay with you and Ruth. They could graze the sweet grasses in the meadows during the day."

"Me and Ruth." He smiled. "That sounds good to my ears."

"Mine too," Nat said. "Oh, he's coming out with you to make the delivery, and we're going to make a fast trip down to the bison camp to see if they have arrived."

"I can hardly wait. I'll put your new rifle and box of shells and the pistol on the table. I reckon you can store them in your saddlebags."

"Yes, everything should fit."

"Ruth helped me put linens on the bed in the spare room, but you can have the larger bed if you'd like."

"I've slept on the ground and pallets for so long it doesn't matter to me. Once I lay down, I usually go to sleep quickly. But thank you for the offer."

"I usually have oats for breakfast, but I can make anything you want," Tom said.

"Oats are fine with me. A little butter and sugar, and I'm good to go."

"I've got both of those, so we're all set."

Nat stood and stretched. "I think I'll call it a night then. It's going to be odd not to have Rufus wake me in the morning."

"If it helps, I'll stand outside your door and crow for you," Tom teased.

Nat nodded. "Yes, I want to see if you're half as good as he is."

"You know I've got one final question for you."

"What's that?"

"There is a small lumber mill just outside of town now. If I check on the price, do you think I could use Rusty to bring some logs into town to mill for flooring?"

"Of course, you can. You may find it cheaper, to go ahead and buy directly from the mill, but check into it," Nat said.

"I will go out tomorrow before I go to work. Is there anything you need tonight?"

"I have a full belly and a clean bed. I think I'm good to go," Nat smiled as they walked into the cabin. "I'll see you in the morning, Tom."

"Goodnight, Nat."

†

The following morning, Nat nearly jumped out of her skin when Tom kept his promise to crow outside her door. "Good grief, you're as obnoxious as Rufus," Nat called out to him.

"The coffee is on, and I've got water heating for the oats. I'll go saddle Hardy and bring him around while you get ready."

"Thanks, Tom. Will you bring my saddlebags in when you come?"

"No problem," he answered.

Nat sat up on the bed and pulled her breeches and boots on. She buttoned her work shirt and tucked it into her breeches and made the bed. The covers were barely ruffled, so she must not have moved much during the night. Nat smiled and picked up her hat before walking into the kitchen. She was pouring a cup of coffee when she heard Tom's boots clunking on the porch.

He came through the open door and laid her saddlebags on the table beside her hat. Gyp's cold nose touched her hand. "That's a chilly nose, Gyp. It reminds me I better hit the privy before I add more liquid to my stomach. I'll be right back."

"I'll check on the water for the oats," Tom said as he moved to the fireplace.

When Nat returned, Tom set a steaming bowl of oats in front of her. "I'm glad you stayed here last night. I've missed seeing you."

"Hopefully, it won't be long before we are neighbors," Nat said as she picked up a spoon. "These are hot."

"Yeah, I think I left the water on too long. If you want, we can load your saddlebags while they cool."

Nat nodded and took the first few boxes of shells, tucked them away, and then stored Marissa's pistol. "I hope she can get used to carrying this around with her," Nat said.

"Do you worry about her safety?" Tom asked.

"Not generally, but the signs we found of someone else possibly being in the area has me worried. Maggie is there, so one of them will have a pistol in their apron. Now they both can have one."

Shine laid her head on Tom's lap as they talked and loaded her saddlebags. "I bet Luna would be a fierce protector. I know these two would be."

"Yes, Luna has more of the wolf in her and would die to protect Maggie and Marissa. I pray it never comes to that. Still, if Ruth isn't a good shot, you need to prepare her for protecting herself when you're out and about."

"She's actually a good shot and has hunted with me before and taken down a large buck," Tom said proudly. "She's got some grit, that's for sure."

"Ruth will be a great partner for you. I look forward to cleaning up for a wedding soon."

"I don't think it will be a grand event, but the folks that count will be there," Tom promised.

"If we can get those trees pulled up to the lake, Maggie and I can start notching your logs. That way, when you have some time to come down, we can start building walls. If you get your floorboards milled, that will give you a good start."

"I'd like a place about this size with a top floor loft. What do you think?"

"That would be perfect for a young couple with a potential for a family," Nat answered.

Tom blushed. "I wouldn't mind a couple of kids."

"That would be great to have some little ones running around. Just don't feel like you have to rush into making a family. Enjoy the time you have with Ruth while you can. Get your home established and when the time is right, start making babies."

Nat tied the saddlebags closed and picked up her spoon. She tasted the oats and nodded. "These are just right."

"What are you planning to send back to town when I come out with the delivery?"

"I hope to have lobsters, shrimp, and live fish in the barrels. More pelts, jerky, and smoked fish, and all the buttons Maggie has ready."

"You're going to be busy then, eh?"

"Never a dull moment." Nat sipped her coffee. "The days are growing longer, so I can get more done. Maggie will help me, and Marissa will tend to the garden and smoker."

"Y'all work very well together. Like well-oiled machines," Tom added to his compliment.

"Smithy is sending out a pedal grinder when y'all come. I can use that for sharpening blades, making knife handles, and many other uses that will save time."

"I hope you will teach me how to make knives in the future," Tom said.

Nat looked out the window to see the sky beginning to lighten. "I'm sure we'll have lots of new things to learn in the coming years. Thank you for letting me stay over with you. This place holds some great memories."

"I bet it does. I enjoy that bathtub you put in for Marissa often. I will plan on one for the lake cabin."

"I will see you soon," Nat said as she stood and put her hat on and picked up her rifle and saddlebags. "Hardy and I need to get a move on."

"I'll be out as fast as I can," Tom promised. "Travel safe, and I'll see you soon."

Nat tightened up the girth strap and secured her rifle and saddlebags before mounting Hardy. She smiled and nodded to Tom, then turned Hardy toward home and urged him into a soft canter.

†

An hour later, she stopped at the creek to water Hardy and took a short break. Gyp was the first to reach the water and had a long drink before trotting over to sit next to Nat. The sun was burning brightly in the sky, and the smell of blooming plants filled the air. Hardy took advantage of Nat's break to graze on the sweet grass growing near the creek. Nat listened to the sounds around her. The insects were buzzing, birds sang in the distance, and she could hear a mama fox barking for her pups. Nat marveled at how alive the world was outside of town.

Nat stood up and called to Hardy. "This ain't getting us home," she said as she mounted him. They walked at a brisk pace as Nat enjoyed the incredible morning ride. Gyp trotted along beside them, occasionally racing ahead following a scent, but she eventually returned to trot beside Hardy. Just a few short hours, and they would be home.

†

Nat could smell the faint scent of the ocean salt in the air, and she knew she was drawing close to home. She relaxed and enjoyed the rhythmic plodding of Hardy's hooves on the packed earth when shots exploded in the air. First one sounding like a rifle, and a second, the minor sound of a pistol. Gyp started growling and raced ahead as Nat kicked Hardy into a full gallop. Nat's heart pounded wildly in her chest as the seconds seemed an eternity. When she reached the final hill before home, Hardy slowed due to the climb, and Nat could hear hoofbeats in the distance. Gyp was growling as she circled the cabin, her nose to the ground. As

Hardy skidded to a stop, Nat flew out of the saddle and never missed a stride as she bolted through the back door, her rifle in hand. No one was inside, but the front door was open. She raced through the cabin to find Maggie and Marissa on the ground with Luna. Crazed by confusion, Nat rushed over to them.

"What the hell happened?" She could see the river of blood pouring down Maggie's face.

Marissa looked up from tending Maggie's wounds. "I am so glad to see you."

Nat kneeled and removed the towel Marissa used to hold pressure against Maggie's head. It didn't look like a deep cut, but drying blood covered the left side of her face. Nat replaced the rag and looked at Maggie. "Are you going to be, okay?"

"Yes, as soon as the blood stops, I'll make a poultice and wrap the wound. It's never as bad as it looks, but my head will hurt for a day or two."

Nat looked at Marissa. "Are you okay?"

Marissa nodded, with tears running down her face. "Yes, I'm fine."

Luna whined as Gyp licked her leg. "I think he may have broken her leg," Maggie said as she reached out to stroke the dog's head. "You did a good job of protecting us."

"What happened?" Nat repeated her question.

"Luna and I were working in the garden, and we didn't hear anyone walk up. When Luna heard Maggie cry out in distress, she raced into the cabin and latched on to the bigger man's arm and wouldn't let go. He pulled a gun to shoot her. Maggie blocked his arm, causing the shot to go high, but his boot stomped her left leg, and the butt of his rifle struck Maggie in the head." Marissa paused to wipe her tears. "I pulled Maggie's pistol from my apron as I ran into the cabin, and when the man raised his arm to strike Maggie, I shot him in the belly."

"He dropped to his knees like a sack of stone. When Marissa cocked the gun for a second shot, the other man got his partner to his feet and guided him out the door. They must have walked in on us, but they left in a hurry on horseback."

"We need to get you both into town. Can you drive Quincy to Doc's?"

"Yes, of course, but what are you going to do?" Marissa asked.

"I'm going to track those mongrels down so they can't hurt anyone else."

Marissa recognized the growl in Nat's voice and the anger flashing in her eyes that could not be mistaken for anything short of rage. She had never seen Nat so incensed.

"I'm going to hitch Quincy up and pull him around. Then I'll help you get Maggie and Luna in the wagon and off to town."

"I don't like you going off alone after those men," Marissa said.

"I won't be alone. I'll have Gyp with me," Nat answered as she walked away. Nat stopped long enough to tie Hardy to the hitching post, then ran to the barn to take Quincy out of his stall and hitch him to the wagon. "You've got to hurry this time," Nat whispered to him. Quincy began trotting beside her as she pulled the wagon around the front.

She carefully laid Luna on a blanket in the back of the wagon and looked at Maggie. "Do you feel like sitting up?"

Maggie looked from Marissa to Nat. "I want to be in the back to comfort Luna if I can."

"I think that's a wise decision," Marissa said.

Nat helped Maggie into the back and positioned some blankets around her for comfort. She handed the wagon reins to Marissa, who had climbed onto the driver's bench. Then she gave Marissa the pistol.

"What's this?"

"A pistol I should have already bought you," Nat said. "You did well with Maggie's, but now you will both have protection." Nat looked into Marissa's eyes. "Quincy has promised to hurry today to get you into town to see Doc. I want you both armed along the way. I won't know until I start tracking them which way they went, but if they headed back to town, they would be well ahead of you. Get medical attention for these two and stay with Tom. I'll come for you as soon as I'm able."

Marissa had tears in her eyes as she pleaded, "Can't you just let them go?"

"You know I can't. What if the men hurt someone else? I couldn't live with myself knowing I had a chance to stop them. I promise to be safe, and I'll hopefully see you sometime later tonight. Let Smithy and the sheriff know what happened."

"I will worry until I see you again. I know you'll be safe, but these are bad men," Marissa said.

"More the reason I need to hunt them down and bring them in for justice." Nat swung into the saddle. "I'll walk with you down the road to make sure they didn't head into town."

When they reached the split in the path leading toward the beach or town, Nat was relieved to see the tracks heading in the opposite direction.

"They are headed down the coast, which should make it easier to track them." She leaned over and kissed Marissa. "I'll see you soon." Nat turned to Maggie. "Keep your eyes open in case they double back."

"I will. You be safe."

Nat nodded and headed down the path toward the beach. Gyp stopped in front of her, getting a blood scent, and she pulled Hardy to a stop. "Good, both those bastards are bleeding. The one with the gut shot won't last long at this rate. Stay close, Gyp."

Nat scanned the shore ahead of them and saw evidence of the hoofprints but no humans were in sight as they trotted down the beach.

†

Quincy trotted along, and when they reached the watering spot, he instinctively walked toward the creek. Marissa jumped down from the bench and used a bucket to bring him cool water.

"Good boy, Quincy," she praised as he took a long drink. "How are you two doing back there?"

"As good as we can," Maggie answered. "Would you bring a bucket for Luna?"

"Yes, I will. Nat set a canteen in the seat too that I will fill with some cold water for us."

Maggie smiled. "She thinks of everything."

"Yes, she does. We are lucky to have her in our lives. I'll be right back," Marissa said and took the bucket and canteen to the creek.

When Marissa handed Maggie the bucket, Maggie cupped her hands together and filled them with water for Luna. The dog drank the water and two more offerings from Maggie.

"We should keep the bucket full," Maggie said.

Marissa handed Maggie the canteen. "You need to drink, too. How is your head?"

Maggie took a long drink. "I feel like Quincy kicked me in the head, but the bleeding has stopped. We've only got about an hour until we get to town, so we'll make it before sundown."

Marissa took a drink and climbed back onto the bench. She handed the canteen back to Maggie. "Keep sipping on this. It might help." Marissa steered Quincy back to the road, and he picked up his pace to a smooth trot. He had made good time pulling a wagon, and she would make sure he got a special treat tonight.

†

The sun beating down on the sand sent shimmers of heat ahead of Nat as she continued down the shore. The span of the hoofprints decreased, telling her the rider's pace had slowed. She pulled out her rifle and made sure there was a round in the chamber. Nat kept her right hand on the gun as it lay across her lap. She would be ready to shoot in an instant if the need arose. Nat hoped her confrontation didn't end in violence, but was prepared to shoot to defend herself and her loved ones. Something in her gut warned her these men would not go easy, especially at the hands of a woman they found so inferior, but she would give them that option if allowed.

A bit farther down the beach, Gyp started to growl, and Nat could make out a dark figure in the sand. "Ease up, Gyp," she commanded, and Gyp slowed her pace to move beside Nat.

Nat pulled Hardy to a stop and watched the figure from a distance, but there was no sign of movement. She turned Hardy to the left to approach the figure from behind and twenty yards away; she pulled him to a stop and slowly dismounted.

"Stay, Gyp," she commanded. Gyp complied but whined at being left behind as Nat crept up behind the man propped against a rock. The man was ghostly white from blood loss, and the sounds of her approach did not alarm him. She held a steady aim on his head just in case he was not dead. Nat used her booted foot to push his shoulder, and the man toppled to the sand. The evidence of Marissa's shot filled his clothing and the surrounding sand with bloodstains.

"This one won't be bothering anyone any longer," she spoke aloud. Nat noticed the man's gun and horse were gone, probably taken by his partner after he collapsed on the beach. She could see drag marks where he was pulled off the shore and propped on a rock.

"At least he had that much decency," Nat growled. "I should drag you out and let the waves turn you into fish food." Nat contemplated that last thought and turned, certain he was dead and walked back to Hardy.

Nat picked up the trail and started Hardy loping down the beach. No longer burdened by an injured rider, the other man had picked up speed. Nat was wary of rushing ahead too quickly, but the tide would be rising soon, and she didn't want to lose the trail. If the waves washed the tracks away, there would be no way to determine if the rider stayed on the coast or worked his way inland. A glance at the sky told Nat all she needed to know. She'd be lucky to have three hours of daylight to track down the remaining rider. *It's now, or never,* she thought as she urged Hardy faster.

†

When Marissa pulled the wagon into town, Tom was out on the loading dock, and she called out to him. "Bring Smithy and meet us at Doc's."

Tom was startled by her appearance for a few seconds, then he jumped into action and raced inside for Smithy.

Doc was sitting inside his office when Marissa pulled Quincy to a halt outside his door. He rushed out to meet them when he saw Maggie in the back of the wagon.

"Looks like you're a bit worse for wear, Maggie. What happened? Did this old mule kick you in the head?"

"It feels like it, Doc, but no, it wasn't Quincy. I'll be all right, but I need you to care for Luna. I think she's got a busted leg."

Tom skidded to a halt with Smithy hot on his heels. Marissa had to hold in a laugh at the sight of Smithy running. She didn't think Smithy had it in him to move that fast.

Maggie looked up at Tom. "Will you carry Luna inside so Doc can fix her up?" she pleaded with tears in her eyes.

"Yes, I will." Tom climbed up in the wagon and cradled Luna in his arms, stepping down as gently as he could to prevent further pain. Smithy reached out for Maggie and helped her from the wagon bed as Marissa stepped down and tied Quincy to a hitching post.

When they all made it inside, Doc looked at them. "What happened?"

"Two men arrived at the cabin and caught us all off guard this morning. Luna rushed in to protect Maggie, and one of the men got a good bite on his arm, but Maggie got a nasty cut on her head when she kept him from shooting Luna. The man stomped on Luna, and I think, broke her leg."

"Are you okay?" Smithy asked.

"Yes, I arrived just in time to get a shot off and hit one of them in the belly. After that, the bastards decided we weren't worth the effort and took off."

"Damn, I'm glad you were armed and didn't get hurt. Where's Nat?" Smithy asked.

"Nat heard the shots and was not far away. She rushed to us and made sure we were on our way here before going after the men," Marissa said.

"Alone?" Tom screeched out.

"You know Nat. I have never seen her so mad before." Marissa said. "She's going to track them down and told us to stay with you until she comes for us."

"Like hell," Tom said. "Which way did she go?"

"Down the coast," Marissa said.

"I'm gone. See that Maggie and Marissa make it to my place and have something to eat. I'm going to find Nat," Tom said to Smithy.

Smithy grabbed him by the arm. "Be careful. Nat knows how to track the worst of critters, but this is new for you."

"Yes, sir," he said and bolted toward his house.

93

Marissa looked at Smithy. "Will you take Quincy out to the cabin and unhitch him? Give him some molasses if Tom has any. I promised him a special treat for getting us here so quickly."

"You know I will, but I think we should wait until Luna and Maggie get fixed up."

"Dang. You're right. I sure don't want to carry Luna that far," Marissa said.

Doc looked up at Smithy. "Can you run get me four pieces of kindling I can use for a splint?"

"I sure can. I'll be right back."

Doc looked at Maggie. "It is broken. Luna is young and healthy, so if we can keep her still for a few weeks, she should heal just fine." He carefully removed the bandage from her head. "You, on the other hand, it's good you have a hard head. I would cause more damage by stitching it, so I'm going to clean it well, put some salve on it, and wrap it up. You need to change this every day and put some of this on it." He handed a jar to Marissa. "I'll give you plenty of bandages. Four or five days should be enough, but you need to lie low like Luna."

Maggie started to protest, but Marissa interrupted her. "I will make sure they both take it easy."

Doc handed Maggie a pill. "This should help with your headache. She can take a couple of these a day as needed. Watch out for redness or drainage that would show infection."

Smithy rushed back in with the splints and Ruth on his heels. "Will this work?"

"Those will be perfect. Hello, Ms. Ruth, how are you?"

"I'm fine, Doc. How are the patients?"

"They'll both live but need to take it easy for a while."

Marissa smiled at Ruth. "Tom's Ruth?"

Ruth's face lit up in a blush. "Yes, ma'am."

Marissa reached out for a hug. "I'm Marissa, and this is Maggie and Luna."

"Tom talks about you ladies all the time," Ruth said.

"We've heard much about you too," Marissa smiled. "Tom is a good man, and I'm happy to call him family."

Smithy helped Doc put the splints on Luna's leg. She whimpered in pain a few times but allowed them to tend to her.

"Is there anything I can give her for pain?" Maggie asked.

"Sure is. You taught me about this," Doc said as he went to a shelf and pulled out some roots. "Grind these up and make it into a tea and let her drink it. It's one of the best pain relievers I know. Only give it to her if she seems to be in great pain or to help her sleep. An animal needs to feel a little pain to keep them from hurting themselves worse by doing too much too soon. You can drink some, too."

Maggie smiled, then grimaced from the pain of stretching her facial muscles. "I'm glad you remembered. I have some of this back home I can use for her. Me, too, if the ache doesn't go away."

"What do we owe you, Doc?" Marissa asked.

"Word says y'all are going on a bison hunt soon." He kept adding bandages and supplies to the bag. He turned and handed it to Marissa. "I think two fine steaks would be a fair trade."

"That sounds like a deal too good to pass up," Marissa said.

Smithy agreed. "I'll make sure you get your steaks."

"Oh, I do hope to see you two again soon, but for a social call instead of an emergency."

"We will make it a point to come in soon. We have lots of goods to barter," Marissa pointed out.

The door to the office opened, and the sheriff walked in. He nodded to Marissa and Maggie. "I heard you ladies had a terrible scare today. Do you mind telling me about it?"

"Would you mind walking with us out to my old place?" Marissa asked. "I want to get these two comfortable for the night."

"I will give you a few minutes to settle in and come out," he promised. He tipped his hat and walked out the door.

Smithy walked over to pick up Luna, then carried her out and laid her gently in the rear of the wagon. "Thanks for everything, Doc," Marissa said.

"I'm happy the consequences weren't any worse than what they are. That must have been terrifying."

"Now that I can think about it, it was, and we were lucky. I won't be snuck up on again if I can help it."

"Be careful, Marissa. There's a lot of people moving through the area. Stay armed and keep one of the dogs with you. I hope everything is well with Nat, but if you need me, bang on my door."

"Will do, Doc. Let's go, Maggie."

†

Marissa and Ruth walked beside Smithy as he led Quincy from town. "Is there anything I can help with?" Ruth asked.

"Can you go to the hotel and pick up six meals for us?" Smithy pulled out several coins from his pocket. "Something hardy, like their fried chicken."

"I can do that," Ruth said and took the coins from Smithy. "I'll bring it out as soon as it's ready."

"Thanks, Ruth," Smithy answered.

When they reached the front of the cabin, Smithy pulled Quincy to a halt. "I'll carry Luna in and place her in front of the fireplace. I doubt Tom took Shine since he planned to ride full speed to find Nat. I'll care for Quincy and get the fire stoked when I come inside."

"You care for Quincy. I'll get everyone settled and tend to the fire. I'm still quite capable of starting a fire," Marissa said with a wink.

"I know you are," Smithy said. "Sit Maggie at the table so she can start grinding the roots. You can put some water on to heat as soon as *you* get a fire started," Smithy teased back with an emphasis on the word you.

When Marissa opened the door, Shine yipped anxiously and danced around Smithy, who carried Luna. He placed her gently on a rug in front of the fireplace and moved to allow Shine to inspect Luna. Shine sniffed her broken leg and then curled up beside her. Blue had also accompanied the group out to Tom's cabin and sat at Smithy's side.

"Good dogs," Smithy said and patted each one on the head. "You should be proud of your sister, Blue and Shine. Luna protected these ladies well today." He straightened and stretched his back. "I'll be back in a few."

Maggie sat down at the table and pulled out the roots Doc had given her to begin grinding them to a powder. "I'm happy he still had these on hand," she said to Marissa.

"Me, too," Marissa replied as she stirred the warm embers in the fireplace and added small logs to feed the fire with a handful of kindling. Tom had stored in a bucket. "I hope they work for both of you."

"The pill Doc gave me has taken away most of my pain," Maggie replied. "I think we'll both have a good dose before bedtime to help us sleep."

"That's not a bad idea. You will both need plenty of rest. Do you want some water to drink?" Marissa picked up a water pail to head outside.

"Yes, that would be good. My mouth is dry," Maggie answered.

"I'll be right back." Marissa opened the door and walked outside. The sun was beginning to fade as she pumped the water from the well. She picked up a dipper and took a long drink of the cold, sweet water. "That is good."

When Marissa returned, she poured a cup for Maggie. Maggie took a long drink. "Thanks, that was good."

"You're welcome," Marissa answered, refilled her cup, and took water to heat for Luna. Both dogs looked up at her with sad expressions. "Everything is going to be fine soon," she promised them.

When the sheriff arrived a few minutes later, Maggie and Marissa retold the story of the assault by the two men. He was concerned that Nat had gone after them alone, but he would ride out that way to see if he could locate both Nat and Tom before sunrise. He left just as Ruth returned, carrying a box with hot food.

"Something smells wonderful," Smithy said as Ruth set the box on the counter.

"Fried chicken as you requested," Ruth said. "A few extras are thrown in by the owner when I told him what had happened."

"Thanks, Ruth. Will you stay and join us?" Marissa asked.

"I should be heading home to help Mama. I hope to see you again before you leave."

"We will make certain of it," Marissa promised. "Thanks for your help."

"You're welcome. I hope everyone has a restful evening and Tom and Nat make it home safe."

"I'm sure they will," Smithy said. "Do you want me to walk you back to town?"

"No, sir. I can make it fine, but thank you. I'll see you tomorrow at work."

"Thank you, Ruth," Smithy said and walked her to the door. "Don't worry about Tom. He'll be fine. Nat will make sure of that."

†

Nat saw that the hoofprints had grown closer together, indicating the rider had slowed his pace and hoped that he felt confident that no one was in pursuit. She reined in Hardy and kept a vigilant eye on the shoreline ahead. Nat smiled when she saw droplets of blood on the sand. *You did good, Luna.* She rode on until she saw the plumes of smoke rising ahead just in the tree line. The rider had stopped and built a fire. Hoping she remained undetected, Nat guided Hardy toward the edge of the beach and dismounted, tethering him to a small tree.

"This is it, Gyp. We need to be very careful. Stay close." Nat double-checked her rifle and crept into the wooded area with Gyp stalking beside her.

†

Tom had pushed Buck as fast as the horse could gallop. He reached the cabin and allowed Buck to rest for a few minutes and drink some cool water. Tom filled a dipper for himself and stepped into his friend's home for a couple of slices of Nat's jerky. He knew Nat wouldn't have thought about food in her rage, and he wasn't sure how long the pursuit would last. He filled his canteen, mounted Buck and trotted toward the beach. Buck had caught his second wind, and they cantered down the shoreline. Tom's eyes scanned the sand to read the hoofprints. Nat had been moving fast through this area, and when her tracks slowed, Tom reined in Buck. Minutes later, he understood why she had reduced speed. He saw the body of a dead man propped against a large rock. The massive stain on his clothing and the sand around him indicated this was the man Marissa had gut shot. "One down, one to go," Tom said aloud, as he turned away from the body and urged Buck into a canter. Nat was running again, and he hoped he would find her safe before the darkness fell.

†

Nat's life spent in the wild prepared her for a stealthy pursuit. For years she had stalked wild game on foot, and this man was no different. She hoped his arrogance and overconfidence would dull his senses from picking up any sound she might accidentally make. The smell of the fire filled her nostrils as she approached, and Nat saw the two horses tied off together. At first, Nat did not see the rider, but several minutes later he emerged from the woods adjusting his clothing from relieving his body. Nat saw a bloodied rag on his left forearm where the rider had attempted to treat his wound. She watched as he sat near the fire, several feet away from his rifle. The rider still wore a sidearm, but Nat was loaded and ready for any aggressive movement he made. She would not hesitate to pull the trigger if needed.

Nat aimed the gun at the man's chest as she stepped from the cover of the trees. "Hold it right there, you coward," she growled.

The man's head spun toward her in shock. Gyp bared her teeth and braced for an attack.

"Who the hell are you?" he spat back, trying to seem unconcerned that he had a rifle pointed at him.

"You broke into my home this morning and injured my family," Nat replied through gritted teeth. "Your low-life partner got what he deserved, and now it's your turn."

The man's eyes grew wide as he looked up at Nat and he tried to gauge her ability to shoot him. Nat could see his confidence wavering as he looked from her to Gyp.

"We was just gonna have some fun with that pretty little one. The old Indian and the dog just got in the way."

"Your mama should have taught you better how to treat a woman," Nat said with a snarl. "Now, you have a decision to make. I can take you to the sheriff to stand trial for assaulting two innocent women, or I can shoot you, and leave you here for the crabs to pick you apart, or some other creature to scatter your bones in the woods or ocean." Nat shrugged. "Makes no difference to me."

Nat saw his hand inch toward his gun. "I know you have a sidearm. You won't be faster than the bullet going into your chest, but if you insist, go ahead and try."

"I ain't going to sit in no jail cell," he growled back at her. "If you think you got it in you to shoot me, go ahead."

Nat's eyes met his, and she could see the fear in them and felt her rage pouring out at him through her own gaze. "You are a terrible poker player," she said. "Your bluff ain't no good, and next, I'd expect you to soil your pants," Nat taunted him.

Nat waited until his hand had reached the handle of his gun before firing. One shot straight into his wicked heart and the man slumped forward. Nat pulled the lever to clear the shell and reload the chamber. She bent down to retrieve the spent cartridge and looked at the burly man. Gyp sat down beside her. "As much as I'd like to leave him here, I know I can't. Even someone as despicable as these two deserves a pauper's grave."

†

A rifle shot in the distance broke through the wind, and Tom's heart pounded in his chest as he raced forward. Being so near the water, it was difficult to tell from how far away the shot came, but he prayed it wasn't miles ahead. Buck was tired from such a long run, but he seemed to sense the urgency in Tom and raced down the beach at full gallop.

†

Smithy got Marissa to sit down long enough to attempt to get food into her and Maggie. "You both need to eat to keep up your strength. You've had a long, difficult day, and it may be well into the night or tomorrow before Nat and Tom return."

Marissa nodded. "I'll put on some coffee."

"Good, I'll stay here with y'all. I wish you'd try to get some rest. I promise I'll wake you the moment Nat and Tom return."

"Smithy, you know I won't be able to sleep." Marissa looked at Maggie. "I do wish you would finish drinking the tea and try to get a little rest."

Maggie looked at Marissa with a weak smile. "I don't think I will have any choice. I'm already feeling sleepy from the tea."

"That's probably the best thing for you right now," Smithy replied. "Sleep off that headache. I've done it a time or two in my life."

"Go ahead and lay down. I'll pick up here and try to keep the food warm for when Nat and Tom return," Marissa said.

†

Nat removed the gun from the man's hand and tucked it under her belt. She leaned against a rock contemplating how she would get the big man across his saddle to take him back to town when she heard a rider fast approaching down the shore. She grabbed her rifle and waited for the rider to appear. Nat trained the sights on the rider as a precaution but sighed in relief when Tom and Buck came into view. Buck's sides heaved for breath, and sweat lathered his body from the long run.

"You two are a sight for sore eyes," Nat said as she stroked down Buck's face. "You must have run like the wind to get here so fast," she told the horse. "Do you have some water for him?"

Tom's eyes were fixed on the dead man. "What? Water, yes I do." Tom dismounted and loosened the cinch on his saddle, allowing Buck to breathe easier. He removed the canteen and twisted the top.

Nat walked over to the fire and picked up a small pot, and carried it to Tom. "He won't be needing this anymore."

"I don't reckon he will," Tom replied and started pouring water for Buck. "What happened here?"

"When I caught up with him, I gave him a choice to go back to face charges or draw on me and take his chances. Damn fool chose to draw, and now he's dead just like his partner."

"He probably didn't think you had the nerve to shoot him."

"That was his last arrogant mistake. The first was hurting my family. Is everyone okay?"

"They were on their way to Doc's to get patched up. Smithy will bring them out to the cabin, get them fed, and settled in for the night."

"Thanks for coming. I could use some muscle to get these two tied across their saddles to go back to town. As much as I'd like to leave them here for the vultures or crabs, I just can't do it, even to them."

"That's no problem. I'll get the horses and get the bastard loaded while Buck rests a few more minutes. Where is Hardy?"

"He's back in the tree line about thirty paces. I tied him off there so I could come in stealthy."

"I'll go get him first so that he can have a drink."

"We can stop by the cabin to let them have some feed and water before we go the rest of the way. They've had a hard day."

Tom smiled at Nat. "I think Buck enjoyed running wide open. He doesn't get too much opportunity to do that in town."

"Probably so. Check the men's canteens for water. Their horses could probably use a drink as well."

"Will do." Tom walked swiftly to retrieve Hardy and handed Nat the full canteen.

She took a drink and offered some to Tom. "I'm good. I'll get the other horses."

Nat emptied the contents of her canteen into the pot for Hardy who took a long drink.

"Not much here," Tom said, shaking the canteens.

Nat handed him the pot with the remainder of her water. "At least they can have a little drink until we get back to the cabin."

Tom nodded and poured the contents into the pot. "You will get your fill soon. Nice looking horses. What will happen with them?"

"I reckon the sheriff will give them to the undertaker for payment to bury these two," Nat said. "Do you want them?"

Tom stroked a horse's neck. "They would be an excellent addition for when we move out here."

"I'll tell the sheriff to have them delivered to you and give him a couple of dollars to cover the pine boxes."

"I can pay that," he offered.

"It would probably be better coming from me," Nat suggested.

Tom nodded. "He'd probably charge me more."

"Yes, he would." Nat returned his smile. "Let's get this rascal on his horse and head back for the other."

Tying the man across his saddle was no problem with Tom's help, and they were soon on their way down the beach. They had just finished loading the second man when the sheriff reached them.

He looked at Nat. "I see you've saved me some work."

"This one died from the gut shot Marissa gave him, and the second refused to be taken into jail and chose to draw on me instead."

"Understandable. I wouldn't want to sit in a jail cell, and the man probably underestimated you as a woman. Damn, fool," he chuckled.

"I'll pay the undertaker for the boxes and burial in exchange for the two horses and gear," Nat offered.

"Not necessary if they have a few dollars on them. I'll check through their gear when I get them to the undertaker and have the horses sent out to Tom's."

"If they don't have money, tell him I'll pay. Even bad people deserve a burial," Nat said.

"I'll let them know," the sheriff said and reached for the reins.

"Would you mind stopping off at our place for some water and feed for the horses? We didn't have much water to give any of them."

"No problem. I want to see what all you've been doing since my last visit," the sheriff replied.

"We've been busy. Added a second smokehouse, a couple of chicken coops, and Maggie and Marissa have extended the garden plot. Did you see them before you left town?"

"I did. I stopped by Tom's to talk to them to find out what happened. Maggie's got a bandage on her head, and the dog has a splint on her leg, but they will both be on the mend soon."

"That's good to hear. I was only a few minutes away from home when all that happened. I was too late in arriving to prevent it from happening."

The sheriff could sense Nat's feeling of guilt. "I think Maggie and Marissa did an excellent job of protecting themselves, given the situation. There will always be some jeopardy in living remotely, no matter who you are. I think they have learned a good lesson about being armed."

"I was bringing home a pistol for Marissa to use. I will make sure they both stay armed moving forward," Nat replied.

"That would be a wise decision."

When they reached home, Tom took control of feeding and watering the animals, while Nat showed the sheriff around the homestead.

"This is very impressive. It looks like you have become extremely self-sufficient out here."

"We don't lack for much, and want we don't have, we can usually get in town," Nat told him.

"Me and the missus are looking forward to a lobster dinner at the hotel. Are they getting close enough to harvest yet?"

"They should be in the next few weeks. I hope to send a batch in with Tom soon. I'll ask him to give you a head's up so you can get reservations. If y'all would like to ride out one day, I can show you how to catch them, and you can take some back. Just bring a couple of large buckets."

"I'd really like that. I'll let you know. Thanks."

"No problem. You are welcome any time."

They were sitting on the front steps when Tom brought the horses around. "I think we're all set. I filled everyone's canteens, and I raided your pantry earlier for some jerky," Tom smiled as he handed out strips of the dried meat.

"You've got me addicted to this stuff," the Sheriff said.

"You and half the town. I can't get it into the general store fast enough."

"Even with the second smokehouse?" the Sheriff asked.

"I might need to build one for jerky alone," Nat said.

"We could do that," Tom said. "We'll build a huge one at my place when I move out."

"You're coming out this way?" the Sheriff asked Tom.

"Yes, sir, I'd like to. I plan to ask Ruth to marry me after we get done hunting bison, and I'd like to build us a place down by the lake."

"Bison, huh? I hope they show up this year. I've been reading of mass slaughtering going on down in the plains. Hundreds of carcasses laying on the ground rotting after hunters took only the hides and heads."

Nat shook her head. "A sad waste. The meat is delicious and would feed many hungry families. They left the most valuable part to rot under the sun. People can be so stupid."

"I sure hope it wasn't the herd that travels through our area," Tom said.

"Me, too," Nat sighed. "Should we head back to town?"

†

"You're going to wear out the floorboards," Smithy teased Marissa. "Pacing isn't going to make them return any faster."

"I know. I can't help but worry about Nat. Tom, too, now that he went after her."

"You should know by now that Nat is more than capable of taking care of herself. Growing up in the wild, Nat learned many skills that most people couldn't even dream of having."

"I won't rest easy until I see her walk through the door." Marissa plopped down in her chair. "Do you want some coffee and some of the cake that Ruth brought?"

"May as well. It will help pass the time." Smithy laughed.

Marissa cut slices of cake and poured them both a coffee before sitting across from Smithy. "Tell me about Ruth. Tom seems pretty taken with her."

"She and her family moved to town about six months ago. She and her father work for me at the store, and they are both hard workers. Like Tom, Ruth loves being outside and likes to hunt and fish. I do believe our young Tom plans to propose to her when we return from the bison hunt."

"She sounds like she'd be a good partner for Tom," Marissa replied.

"I think so, too. Tom and Ruth could carve out their place in the world together. He's excited to build out by your lake."

"It would be a beautiful spot to live. Maybe a little warmer in the winter than where we are on the coast. I still wouldn't give up our view for anything."

"I'm with you. I love the view and the sound of the water," Smithy agreed.

"I know you've mentioned joining us before. Is that something you are ready for?"?"

"I am giving it some serious consideration. Ruth's father seems a capable businessman, and I'm considering putting him in as manager with the possibility of selling him the store. It's getting too crowded for me here."

"You know there is plenty for you to do in the wild."

"I think I'd enjoy learning how to trap and finish pelts the way Nat does. I've always admired her products. Her father taught her well. He was a great man."

"Did you know her parents well?"

"I never met her mother, but Nathan was one of the finest trappers I've ever met. He doted on Nat and couldn't have been prouder of a child. Nat is so much like him."

"I wish I could have met him," Marissa said.

"You would have liked him. He was a rugged man, full of the wild, but he was also a family man."

†

Nat and the others were fortunate to have moonlight to make it back to town. When they approached Tom's cabin, the sheriff said, "Thanks for taking out these two critters. I'll get them taken care of, and have the horses and gear sent to Tom tomorrow."

"Thanks, sheriff."

"I'm sorry your friends had to experience these awful men, but I'm glad the outcome was what it was. There's no telling what else these two could have done."

When they arrived, Nat and Tom dismounted. "Go on in, and I'll take care of the horses."

"Thanks, Tom. I'm too tired to argue with you."

The cabin door swung open, and Marissa rushed out to Nat. "I thought I heard voices," she said as Nat enveloped her in her arms.

"I'll help you with those horses," Smithy said and walked with Tom to the barn.

"I am so glad you made it back safely. Smithy swears I'm wearing out Tom's floorboards."

"I hoped it wouldn't be so late, but we finally made it."

"Come inside. I have dinner warming for you and Tom." Marissa took her hand and led her inside.

"Wow, that smells good."

"Smithy had Ruth go to the hotel for dinners for us."

Nat knelt to check Luna. "How's Maggie?"

"She's got a headache, as you would expect. She's trying to get some sleep."

"I feel much better," Maggie said as she walked into the room.

Nat hugged her friend. "I hope we didn't wake you."

"No, I was dreaming of some cake," Maggie told her. "Did you take care of business?"

"Yes, I did," Nat answered. "You don't have to worry about those two any longer."

"Good," Maggie said.

"Why don't you two get something to eat and get some sleep?" Marissa said when Tom and Smithy walked through the door.

"I'll take mine to go. I'm going to stay at Smithy's tonight," Tom announced as he leaned Nat's rifle by the door. "I'll be out tomorrow morning after we've all had some sleep." He looked at Nat. "I assume you'll want to head home tomorrow?"

Nat looked at Marissa and Maggie. "Do you want to spend a day in town since we're here?"

"We could," Marissa replied.

"Stay as long as you like," Tom replied. "I'll see you in the morning."

"Thanks, Tom. Thank you, Smithy, for taking care of our family," Nat said.

"My pleasure," Smithy answered. "It's our family, too."

"Yes, it is," Nat said and hugged the large man. "We'll see you in the morning."

"Goodnight, ladies," Smithy tipped his hat.

"Goodnight," Nat and Marissa replied.

Nat took a seat at the table. "I'm starved. What smells so good?"

Marissa laughed and began serving a plate for Nat. She poured them both a cup of coffee and sat with Nat while she ate.

"Now that you're home and safe, I'm going back to bed," Maggie said and left the kitchen.

"Goodnight, Maggie," Nat called to her between bites of food.

"Did everything go as expected?" Marissa asked.

"I was hoping for a better outcome, but that wasn't his choice. You won't ever be harmed by those two again."

"I'm sorry," Marissa said and laid a comforting hand on Nat's arm.

"You have nothing to be sorry for; those bastards attacked you and Maggie."

"I know. I just hate that you ended up taking a life you hadn't planned. It's hard on you."

"They made the decision. I did what needed doing. If I had my way, they'd both be sitting in a jail cell."

"I'm glad you are back unharmed, and we can go home safely soon. I would enjoy spending the day in town tomorrow."

"We all deserve a break," Nat said.

Logs shifted in the fireplace, and Luna and Shine startled awake.

"I'll put some logs in, and they will doze back off." Marissa looked at Gyp. "You need to join your babies and get some rest."

"She needs to eat first," Nat said. "She had a hard day too."

"I'm sorry, Gyp. Let's get you something to eat." Marissa dropped a second log in the fireplace and walked into the kitchen.

Gyp danced around Marissa's feet as she put together food in a bowl and set it on the floor. "There you go, Gyp. Eat up."

Nat ate her fill and then fed Gyp the remainder of her food. "I am stuffed and ready to lay my head down," Nat told Marissa.

"Let's go then," Marissa smiled and reached for Nat.

They stripped down to their undergarments and curled up together in bed. "Now I am home," Nat whispered and kissed Marissa softly.

"Yes, we are," Marissa answered and snuggled deeper into Nat.

CHAPTER FIVE

Nat woke late the following day and found Marissa's side of the bed empty. She slipped into her clothes and discovered Maggie and Marissa on the front porch drinking coffee and talking with Smithy. Tom walked around the end of the cabin as Nat stepped outside.

"Well, there she is," Tom said. "Smithy and I walked the new horses out and thought we'd treat you ladies to an early lunch."

Nat wiped her face with her hand. "I've barely gotten my eyes open, and you're talking of food already." She smiled. "That sounds like a good plan." Nat turned to Marissa. "Let me wash my face and hit the privy, and I'll be ready."

Smithy held out his arm to Maggie. "Would you like to accompany Tom and me to town? We can go ahead and get a table to wait for these two."

Maggie smiled up at Smithy. "I'd like that." She turned to Nat. "Don't take long. I'm hungry."

"I am, too, so I'll hurry," Nat promised and disappeared inside the cabin.

"Go ahead and order. We'll take whatever the hotel has on special today," Marissa told them.

"Pork chops and the fixin's," Smithy said.

"Perfect," Tom said. "Let's go."

Marissa watched her family disappear over the hill while she waited on Nat. Gyp sat beside her, and Marissa stroked down her neck. "We'll go home soon, pretty girl, and you can follow Nat everywhere again."

When Nat returned, she looked at Gyp. "Stay inside and guard the babies," she told Gyp, who trotted inside, and Nat closed the door.

Nat turned and found Marissa smiling. "You do realize both babies are much larger than mama, right?"

"Gyp may be smaller, but she's got my bet if she had to take on someone to protect her babies."

"You got that right. Gyp has made a good mama." Marissa stood. "Ready for pork chops?"

"Oh, heck yeah," Nat said. "Let's go." They held hands until they reached the top of the hill. "What do you want to do in town after we eat?"

"I'd like to see what new things they have at the general store. I bet Maggie will want to look, too. What about you?"

"I'm going to check in with the sheriff, and then I'll visit with Smithy. Maybe we can eat dinner in town and be ready to go home early in the morning."

"That will be good. I'll be ready by then. I've got lots of things to catch up on when we get home."

"Like what?" Nat asked.

"Laundry for one," Marissa teased. "The garden, the pools, the smokehouses. Do I need to continue?"

"I will help you with everything but the laundry. I hope we have lobsters and shrimp when we get home. I want to get as much fish as possible to smoke and maybe see if I can get a moose or elk for the smokehouse. The jerky supply in this town is dwindling," Nat said with a chuckle. "Check for jars at the store. I bet Maggie could start cooking her chowder and selling it there."

"I'll mention that to her. We could use more antlers for buttons, too. Maybe you and I can take a walk in the woods when we get home," Marissa suggested.

"I'd like that," Nat said as they entered the town. "I see the sheriff. I'm going to catch up to him. I won't be long."

"I'll keep Tom away from your chops," Marissa teased.

"Please do." Nat walked over to the office where the sheriff was sitting outside enjoying his pipe. "Hello. I just wanted to make sure we are square with the undertaker before I head back home tomorrow."

The sheriff stood to greet her. "All square with some coins left over. Rightfully they are yours," he said.

"Will you do something else with them?" Nat asked.

The tall man nodded. "What did you have in mind?"

"If you see a family needing a bit of extra help, make sure they get it as long as the money lasts?"

"That's an easy request. I can do that with no problems. That's very generous, especially since you don't know the amount."

"I don't care how much it is. I want nothing more to remind me of those men," Nat said.

"Understood, and I promise you I'll use it wisely."

"Thanks, sheriff. Have a good day."

"You too, Nat."

Nat stepped off the sidewalk and started toward the hotel. Her entrance to the dining room was well-timed as the staff served food plates on the table.

"That was perfect timing," Nat said.

"Marissa said you were worried about me eating your chops," Tom joked.

"Is that so? She told me that she'd guard my plate to keep you away from them," Nat said with a laugh.

"Let's eat," Smithy said no sooner than Nat had taken her seat.

†

"Will you take a walk with me out to the sawmill?" Tom asked Nat after they finished lunch.

"Sure will. I need to stretch my legs after that meal," Nat answered. "That was delicious as usual," she told Smithy. "I can see why you eat here so often."

"Much better than my cooking." Smithy smiled.

"When you move out with us, you can eat with us every day," Marissa promised.

"I'll be there tomorrow," Smithy teased. "I'll sleep on the porch."

"Soon enough, we will have our little community," Nat said.

"I can't wait," Tom said and stood from the table. "Ready?"

"I'll be waiting for y'all at Smithy's." Nat looked at Smithy. "Dinner is my treat tonight."

Smithy raised his arms. "I won't argue with that."

"Let's go, Tom."

Nat pulled her hat on when they walked out into the sunny afternoon. "Such a beautiful day. So, how do you want to handle this?"

"I was thinking of inquiring about the price of milled floorboards if he has them, or if not, how much he would charge me to mill the logs we brought to him."

"You might want to see if he would mill them for some of the logs. We have plenty already cut. It would be a matter of getting them into town."

"What would be a fair trade for the milled lumber?"

"I would tell him what types of trees you can offer since we have a variety. Then suggest one log for every two he mills for you. It would be best if you had some cedar boards for closets and pantry space. The scent helps to keep insects away and your clothes smelling fresh. Also great for shingles."

"What about the flooring? What would work best?"

"Either the fir or thicker planks of pine or cottonwood. Let's play it by ear and see what the mill owner is hungry for," Nat replied. "I don't think he gets much of the black cottonwood here."

"Ten-foot planks? I'd like a twenty-foot first-floor base."

"Yes, those would be great. We can haul logs a bit over ten feet. Any planks bigger than that will be difficult to work with," Nat said. "You've got this in your head, don't you?"

"Yes, I've been thinking of the plan a good bit lately. Maybe you and Smithy can help me draw it out?"

"We should have time until the ladies get back from the store. They will be like kids in a candy shop," Nat teased.

†

Nat appeared to be inspecting the milled lumber as Tom and the mill owner negotiated. The boards he had milled were not the thickness or quality Nat would use on a cabin. She listened closely to Tom's bargaining and smiled when she heard the man's voice rise in excitement when Tom mentioned black cottonwood. Tom had him right where he wanted him. The owner agreed to cut three fir logs for each cottonwood log Tom could bring in exchange. Nat turned and saw them shake on the deal, and then Tom walked over to her.

"I think I did well. One cottonwood for three fir logs."

"I couldn't have done better myself," Nat praised. "We've got work to do." As they started walking back to Smithy's, Nat turned to Tom. "I think we should have a couple of the black cottonwood milled for us, too. I bet they would make a beautiful table."

"We certainly have the trees for it," Tom said. "I am so ready to get started."

"We need to concentrate on pulling logs for your walls, and then when we have enough to get you started, you can deliver sections to town for the flooring. Maggie and I can begin notching your logs."

"I don't want to pull you off your chores," Tom said.

"We can do chores during the day, and while Marissa cooks supper, Maggie and I can sneak down to your place to notch a few."

"Are you worried about her security after yesterday?" Tom asked.

"I will always worry whenever she's not in my eyesight, but that's no way to live. I've bought her a new pistol, and she knows how to use it. I will make sure one of the dogs is near when Maggie and I are not at home."

"Maybe some latches on the doors, too?" Tom suggested.

"I will think about that. If someone intends to come in, they will find a way, but a latch may make enough noise to alert one of us or a dog. Good idea. I'll see what they have at the general store."

"Smithy has some that just came in not long ago. I'll put them up for you when we come out."

"You have a deal." Nat slipped an arm around Tom's shoulders. "Let's see if Smithy can help us with a drawing."

Smithy was finishing with a customer when they returned. "We have a project we need your help with," Nat said. "Young buck here turned a great deal with the mill owner on milling some boards in exchange for black cottonwood logs."

Smithy smiled. "Good job, Tom. What do you need help with?"

"I've got the cabin up here." He tapped on his temple. "I need help drawing it so I can determine the number of logs and floorboards I'll need to have cut for two stories."

"Two stories?" Smithy asked.

"Well, one main and a loft upstairs." Tom corrected himself.

Smithy pulled out a sheet of white paper. "Let's start with the dimensions of the first floor."

Nat sat back in a chair and watched the two men bent over a table, carefully plotting out the dimensions for Tom's cabin. Smithy did some math and turned to Tom.

"You're going to need about forty logs at twenty feet for the first floor alone. Depending on the size of the logs for the floorboards, that will determine how many ten-foot floorboards you can get from one section." Smithy scribbled more math on the paper. "Count on needing forty to fifty floorboards for the downstairs." Smithy looked up at Nat. "Notching logs?"

"Yes, I figure that's the most efficient," Nat said.

"You'll need square head nails for the flooring and windows and door hinges. We can start picking those up as you can afford them," Smithy said.

Nat found it hard to tell who was more excited between the two.

"If you bring some logs up for me, I'll cover the cost of your hardware and windows, as long as you don't go crazy with windows," Smithy added.

"That sounds like a pretty good deal. What size will you need?" Tom asked.

"I'm thinking that sixteen feet by sixteen feet, single story, will be plenty for me," Smithy said. "I'll work on the calculations for mine later, once you've got your logs pulled." Smithy smiled at Nat.

"So, you're going to do it?" Nat asked.

"Yes, I am. There's no time like the present to start making changes. Ruth's father is interested, so I thought I'd give him some opportunities to prove himself. Starting next week, Tom and I will be at your place if you don't mind us sleeping on your floor."

"We what?" Tom said.

"You and I are going to start hauling trees while Nat gets a load of goods ready for town. If we start early, I don't see why the two of us can't put a dent in the logs for your home and maybe a load or two for the mill."

"That sounds fine with me," Nat said. "I'll help out when and where I can."

Tom's eyes filled with tears. "Are you sure we can take time off now?"

"I'm the boss. Besides, things are a bit slow right now—nothing they can't handle without us."

"You say the day, and I'll have Rusty and the wagon loaded with supplies. We can't forget the items from here, too."

Smithy smiled and looked at Nat. "Are you good with us coming out and unloading late Saturday? The store is closed on Sundays anyhow."

"Saturday is perfect. I'll try to get as much of my tasks done as possible before then." Nat spotted some red ribbon on Smithy's shelf. "Do you mind if I take some of that?"

"Take it all. I won't need it any longer," Smithy stated.

Nat tucked the ribbon in her pocket. When she looked up, she saw Marissa and Maggie entering the store. "This looks like trouble." She nodded toward the two smiling women. "They look like they are up to something."

Smithy and Tom looked up, and Tom turned back to Nat. "Yes, they do."

"Reckon we're about to find out," Smithy said.

"You all look like you've been busy," Marissa said, looking at the drawings and figures.

"We've been drawing out Tom's cabin and figuring the boards and logs he will need," Nat said.

"We've been busy, too," Marissa said. "We've been bargaining with the general store."

"Dare I ask for what?" Nat asked.

"Well, since you didn't stop in today, Jacob hit us up with a proposition. He's just received a meat grinder that makes link sausages. He said he would provide the machine and the casings if we provide the meat and smoking. He'll pay top dollar, too."

"What do I need to go hunting for?" Nat asked.

"Venison," Marissa answered, "but he'll take moose or elk too."

"I guess my list just grew. I'll still be ready by Saturday," Nat said with a wink to Tom.

"What happens Saturday?" Marissa asked.

"You will have two more mouths to feed. Tom and Smithy are coming out with a load of supplies and will stay for a week to start pulling logs for Tom's cabin."

"That's terrific news. Maggie and I can handle most everything around the homestead so that you can help them. I know you'll want to be right in the middle of things."

"You know me too well. I can get the majority of my chores done and maybe bring in a deer or two for you to try your hands at making sausage. Is the owner providing the spices too?"

Marissa nodded with a bright smile. "Yes, I told him he could get everything together, and we'd stop by tomorrow before we leave town."

"It sounds like we have another business to try out," Nat said. "It's going to be a busy spring and summer."

†

"I'll be out early in the morning to hitch up Quincy and get him ready to head for home after a stop at the general store," Tom said as they walked out of the hotel. "I'm going to stay with Smithy again tonight so we can finalize our drawings and materials list."

"We'll see you in the morning. You know I'm capable of hitching Quincy, right?" Nat teased.

"I know, but I enjoy doing things to help you out," Tom replied. "You do so much for me. Any little thing I can do to help, I will."

"It's not necessary, but I won't deprive you of helping where you can. You have no idea what kinds of hard work I have planned for you," Nat warned. "We'll see you in the morning."

†

Nat, Marissa, and Maggie returned to the cabin and settled in for a relaxing evening. Marissa surveyed Tom's pantry. "I can make some breakfast in the morning, so we start for home with a full belly."

"I'd never turn down one of your breakfasts," Nat replied. She kicked back on one of the porch chairs pulled her knife from her pocket, and picked up a chunk of wood she'd spotted earlier.

"What ya making?" Maggie asked as she settled in beside Nat.

"No clue yet," Nat answered and started smoothing the raw wood. "I reckon it will come to me."

"Usually does," Maggie said and sat quietly watching the sunset. "It will be good to get home. I feel lazy without something to do."

Nat looked up at her. "We will be busy until next fall and maybe after that. With new neighbors moving in, it will be up to us to make sure they prepare for a winter in the wild. It's much harder than living in town."

"I can check for seafood and harvest some clams to make chowder if you need to check your traplines. We should be home by midafternoon, right?"

Nat set her knife to the wood and cut off a small section. "I would think so. It won't take long to pick up the goods from the store, and we can be on our way."

"Good. If you allow me to use your old rifle, I can help hunt for deer to turn into jerky and sausage."

"Maggie, you are more than welcome to use anything I have. It would be nice to have a hunting partner. Marissa doesn't enjoy it as we do."

"Maybe she can hunt for antlers then and still join us in the same area."

Nat nodded. "That's a good idea, Maggie. We can send her back for Quincy when we bring in some animals. She gets queasy around the butchering." Nat smiled.

"It's a good thing she doesn't mind slicing the meat for jerky. That can be tedious at times, but Marissa doesn't mind it at all."

"That frees me up to do more hunting if y'all can process," Nat said. "I may even try for a moose down by the lake. That will keep us busy for a while."

"Would you mind if I block off a section of the back porch to contain Luna until she heals? I don't think I can keep her cooped up inside, but if she could watch us in the garden or elsewhere on the grounds, I think she'll be fine."

"That's an excellent idea. I'll help you put up some boards if needed," Nat offered.

"I think I'm good. I'll set it up when we get home tomorrow and then head to the beach to check the pools."

"I'll run my traps and be back as quick as I can," Nat replied.

Marissa stepped onto the porch. "Are you two already plotting out chores for tomorrow?"

"Several days after, too," Nat said. "We have lots of plans to work on."

"That sounds interesting. Would y'all like some coffee, and you can share your plans with me?"

"Coffee sounds good. You sit with Nat, and I'll make some," Maggie said.

"I won't argue with you," Marissa replied and pulled a chair next to Nat. "What are you working on?"

"Dunno yet. I'm just shaping right now."

"I think we're all a bit excited to get home, don't you?" Marissa asked.

"Yes, I feel too idle here in town. Even though we got things done, it's not the same," Nat replied.

"It was a nice break and good to see some old friends," Marissa said. "That's a beautiful sunset, but not near as nice as the ones we see from home."

"That's true. There's nothing like the view from home."

Maggie returned with steaming mugs of coffee. "Here we go," she said as she passed the cups around.

"How are you feeling?" Nat asked.

"My head is a bit sore to touch, but the headache is gone. A few more days of wearing a bandage and I should be good as new." Maggie smiled.

"That's good to hear," Nat replied. "When we get home tomorrow, I'm going to run my traplines while Maggie checks the pools and harvests some clams for chowder. You can store the goods from town, and if we finish with daylight left, Maggie and I plan to hunt for deer. If you would join us, you can look for antlers, and if we're successful, you could bring Quincy out with the wagon."

"I can do that. I'll check on the garden and smokehouse, too. When I finish, I'll see if Maggie needs my help. I do hope the lobsters have arrived."

"Even if they haven't, we still need to prepare the barrels by hauling seawater up the hill on the pulley line. Not a lot of water, but enough to dampen the insides after being stored all winter."

"I know we can handle that job," Marissa said and turned to Maggie. "If you fill the buckets, I'll pull them up the hill and dump them."

Nat smiled. "I'll bring three barrels out of storage and place them near the front porch."

"I reckon it's a good thing the days are starting to get longer." Maggie laughed.

"Lots to do," Nat replied.

"Are you excited with the news Tom and Smithy gave you today?" Marissa watched Nat for her answer.

"I'm delighted they will be joining us, but there is so much to do. At least we will have more hands to help get the work done."

"It will be great to have them nearby," Marissa said.

"Are you worried about another unwelcome visitor?" Nat asked.

"Not really. I think we will all be more prepared in the future. I'll be honest, I miss Tom and Smithy. I didn't realize how much until now."

"If it were anyone else besides those two, I'd be less excited. We have always made a good team, and I don't see that changing."

"They are both good men," Maggie tossed out. "We may be surprised by Ruth. I think she will fit right in with our group."

"I like what I've seen so far," Nat said.

"Me, too," Marissa agreed with a nod. "I like the possibility of having some little ones around too. They will be fun to spoil."

"Did you ever want to have children?" Nat asked.

"I thought so when we were first married, but in hindsight, I'm thankful it never happened."

"You would have made a great mother," Maggie stated.

"I think so, too," Nat said.

Marissa sighed. "I'll have to be satisfied with four-legged babies until Tom and Ruth start having little ones."

"Here we are planning on children, and he hasn't popped the question yet." Nat smirked. "I think that's one of the reasons he wants to build a cabin so bad."

"You do realize that you will have your work cut out for you teaching Tom and Smithy to trap, right?" Marissa asked.

"I have no doubt they will both pick up the skills quickly. I may let Tom run my lines while I concentrate on tanning the hides. That's a skill not as easily learned."

"I'm sure he would love that. He enjoys being outside," Maggie said.

"You can't blame him for that." Nat grinned.

Marissa stood and stretched. "I think I'm going to call it a night. I'll be up early to cook some breakfast. Don't stay up too late," she told Nat.

"I won't. I feel like I'm still a few hours behind on sleep. Maggie, are you ready?"

"I will be after I hit the privy."

"I'll go ahead and stoke the fire and put on a few fresh logs. You will have good coals in the morning," Nat told Marissa.

Nat entered the bedroom and undressed. Marissa was already under the covers and toasty warm when Nat slipped in beside her. She leaned over and blew out the candle. "I can remember some cold nights when we first met, but the bearskin kept us warm all night, even when we were skin to skin."

"We don't have our bearskin, but I'd love to be skin to skin with you tonight," Marissa said.

It only took Nat a moment to lose the rest of her clothing. "Anything for you," she whispered as her lips covered Marissa's in a fevered kiss. Nat rolled on top of Marissa, and their bodies began moving together as their desire blossomed. Nat's hand moved between their bodies and slipped into the wetness between Marissa's legs. Her groans filled the room with the sounds of their pleasure, and she snaked her hand between Nat's legs.

Nat's body welcomed Marissa's fingers with deep contractions as they held her fingers deep inside as their bodies continued their rhythm. Nat could feel her body begin to quiver, and she kissed Marissa hard to cover the sound of her climax. The sensation of Nat's release sent Marissa's passion tumbling over the edge of release. Nat moved to lay beside Marissa and softly laughed. "I hope we didn't keep Maggie awake."

"You would think she's used to hearing our loving by now," Marissa said as she snuggled into Nat.

"Maybe so," Nat said as her lips kissed Marissa's neck. "I certainly enjoy the sounds we make together."

"Me, too," Marissa whispered against Nat's ear. "I love you."

"I love you, too," Nat replied.

CHAPTER SIX

The sunrise the following morning was glorious. Tom arrived early and hitched Quincy to the wagon while Nat saddled Hardy. She inspected the two new horses. "With some feeding and new shoes, they should make good horses."

"I was thinking of giving one of them to Marissa," Tom surprised Nat. "I don't need more than two, and I'll be honest, I've grown attached to Buck, but if you want him back, I'd understand."

"I think my father would be proud of how well you care for Buck. The mare is a little smaller, and she may be easier for Marissa to handle."

"I'll fatten her up some and get some new shoes on her before we come out. Would you mind if it stays our secret for now?"

Nat smiled. "Not at all. Your gift will tickle Marissa."

"Thanks," Tom said. "Are you ready to go home, Quincy?"

Quincy tossed his head. "I think that's a yes," Nat told them. "You know he's going to feel left out when Rusty starts hauling those logs. What do you think about putting smaller logs in the wagon for him to pull?"

"Do you think he could handle an eight-foot log or two?" Tom asked.

"For the flooring? Yes, I believe he could," Nat answered. "He may be small, but he's a hard worker." They started walking to the front of the cabin. "Once you and Smithy get a load ready to bring into the mill, Quincy and I can continue with some of the smaller logs."

"I'll need plenty for a barn and smokehouse," Tom agreed.

"Yes, you will. The trimmings you can use to start your woodpile for firewood. It's never too early to start on firewood."

"Do you want me to carry Luna out to the wagon?"

"Let's see what these two have dished up for breakfast first," Nat suggested.

†

"How come your cooking always tastes so much better than mine?" Tom asked Marissa.

"I've had much more practice," Marissa replied as she washed the last of the dishes. "There, all set."

133

"Let's get Luna loaded up and get our goods from the general store," Nat said. "I'm itching to get home."

Tom helped load the goods and helped Maggie up to the bench beside Marissa. "I'll see you in a few days," he told them.

"We'll be as ready as we can be," Marissa promised.

"See ya, Tom," Nat said, and they started for the trail home. Nat turned as they topped the hill and waved at Tom, who returned her wave and then bolted toward Smithy's.

†

They had finished watering the animals at the creek when Gyp's ears perked up. "Yes, I see him ahead."

Nat motioned for Marissa to pull Quincy to a stop as she retrieved her rifle. A ten-point buck was frozen in the path ahead, staring back at them. Nat aimed and dropped the deer with one shot.

"That's one we won't have to work hard for," Nat told Maggie. She turned to Marissa. "Pull the wagon ahead on the trail, and Maggie and I will prepare him for travel."

"Thanks," Marissa answered. She was glad Nat could understand how difficult it was to watch an animal gutted and bled. Marissa knew it was the only way to process wild meat safely, but Marissa still couldn't watch. She waited until Maggie made it to the ground before easing Quincy ahead out of sight.

Maggie looked at Nat. "We better hurry before she decides we have to walk home."

"This won't take long. We can skin and quarter the buck once we make it home, and Marissa's busy inside the cabin."

"He has a nice hide," Maggie mentioned. "Time for a new pair of buckskins for you?"

"Not a bad idea. Some of mine are getting a bit worn in the seat." Nat smiled.

"I should get at least two pairs from this buck. It'll give me something to work on before I go to sleep at night."

"What about a pair of your own?" Nat asked.

"Because you are so tall, I can use yours and add some fresh hide in worn spots and have new pants that you have already broken in for me," Maggie explained.

"There is that," Nat said and heaved the carcass off the ground.

It didn't take them long, and Nat and Maggie loaded the deer into the back of the wagon as Gyp danced around them. "You two will have to wait for scraps," Nat told Gyp and Luna, who were licking their lips at the scent of fresh meat.

"That was almost too easy," Nat said as Maggie crawled back onto the wagon bench.

"Take every small blessing you can. There will be plenty of times ahead that will be much more difficult." Maggie took a drink from her canteen.

Nat rode beside them as Marissa and Maggie discussed how they would use the deer to grind up for sausage. She couldn't help but smile at the excitement in their voices as they discussed a new project. Hardy plodded along, and Nat felt her body relaxing with every step he took away from town. She smelled the fresh blossoms on the breeze and felt the warm rays of sunshine on her skin. She took a sip of the water from the creek and marveled at how sweet and cold the water was. Yes, this was home.

†

Gyp raced ahead when they could smell the salt from the ocean and was sitting patiently on the back porch when they arrived.

"Show off," Marissa mocked as she eased Quincy to a stop in front of the cabin.

"I'll hang the buck by the smokehouse and will be back to carry Luna inside if you and Maggie will unload the goods. Maggie can help with the skinning, and you can unhitch and feed Quincy. Once the meat is quartered and hung in the smokehouse, I'll start on my traplines, and you two can get to work around here."

"Don't forget to bring the barrels out before you go," Marissa called to her as she carried a load inside.

"Yes, ma'am," Nat answered with a chuckle.

Nat and Maggie made quick work of the skinning, and Nat made deep cuts to quarter the buck. "He's got a lot of meat on him for this early in the spring."

"Plenty for some roasts, chops, jerky, and sausage," Maggie said as she salted the meat.

"I'm looking forward to tasting your sausage," Nat said as she hung a heavy hindquarter in the smokehouse.

"It will be a fun and interesting project for us," Maggie said. "Something new to learn."

"I have no doubts that it will be great tasting and become a big hit in town."

Maggie nodded. "I believe you are right on that. Go ahead and start your trapline. I'll take care of Hardy and help Marissa get things started around here."

"Thanks. Do you need help to get the hide on the table?"

"No, Nat, I can handle that."

Nat pulled her rifle from the sheath. "I'll see you later then."

†

As Nat began walking toward the first set on her line, she noted the small game evident in the area. Gyp too enjoyed following the scents, and Nat saw tracks for a variety of creatures. Nat skirted the lake and saw several moose grazing in the soggy meadow. *I hope you will be around later.*

Nat's traps harvested several martens and a wolverine. She was thankful the wolverine wasn't still alive. They could be highly aggressive and were one of the area's top predators for their size. Nat started a trail for home and watched Gyp take off after a rabbit that had bolted off in front of them. Several moments later, she heard a sharp cry, and Gyp caught up to her with a giant rabbit in her mouth.

"I know what you and Luna are having for dinner." Nat took Gyp's offering. As Nat reached a clearing, she could see Marissa walking through the garden, occasionally stopping to check a plant as Maggie rolled the large barrels around the front of the cabin. Gyp ran ahead to let Marissa know they were home. When Marissa's head lifted in search of her, Nat smiled at the most beautiful sight in her world.

"Are you ready to go down to the beach?"

"Yes, I will be in a few minutes," Marissa answered.

"Let me stash these, and I'll be right back," Nat said, holding up the string of animals she had trapped.

Maggie had moved the last barrel and was walking around back when she saw Nat.

137

"Grab a few buckets and your rake. Let's see what mother nature has to offer us today." Nat picked up four buckets, leaving two each for Marissa and Maggie. She looked at Luna, snuggled into a pallet on the back porch. "We'll be back soon. Rest and get better."

When they arrived on the beach, Nat sat down and began removing her boots and socks. "If you two want to dig some clams, I'll check the pools."

"Fine by me," Maggie said. "That water is too cold for these old bones."

Nat rolled up her breeches. "Yes, but it's the only way we can check for lobster."

"I would wade through it for lobster," Maggie replied. "Nothing else, though."

"Cross your fingers," Nat said. She stood and picked up two buckets and walked into the frigid water. "Oh, heck yes," she said as she neared the first pool and saw lobster, shrimp, and some good-sized fish. The contents of the first pool were an excellent start to her harvest. Nat set one bucket on a rock and stepped into the pool. She began filling the bucket with lobsters she carefully plucked from the bottom. Nat was able to load both buckets with lobster before picking them up to wade back to shore.

"Marissa, I need you to go back up top, so you can take these and place them in a barrel. I've got two buckets, and there are more to come."

"Hand those to me, and Marissa and I will get them up the line while you collect more," Maggie said. She took the two buckets from Nat and pointed to two empties. "Those clams aren't going anywhere. Use them all if you need."

Nat returned with three buckets and quickly harvested the remaining lobsters. She chased down three large fish for the final bucket before carrying them to shore. Nat secured the buckets onto the pulley line.

"Do you have a fish trap handy? That sure would make catching the shrimp easier."

Maggie nodded. "Yes, there is one on the back porch. I'll get Marissa to toss it down. Do you want to check out the next pool while she gets it?"

"Might as well." Nat picked up three emptied buckets and walked down to the next pool. Her eyes grew wide with surprise to see it filled with spiny brown lobsters. Nat began quickly plucking them from the cold and added water to fill the bucket. When she finished, she carried the buckets to Maggie.

"Maybe we should leave home more often," Maggie teased. "You've already made quite a haul with several pools left to check."

"Head's up down there," Marissa called out, then tossed the fish trap down the cliff.

Nat caught it quickly and smiled up at Marissa. "Thanks." Nat inspected the trap and smiled when she saw that Maggie had added a piece of string long enough to secure the device over her shoulder. "This should work perfectly."

Nat walked back to the first pool and used the fish trap to scoop the shrimp from the water. She laughed at how much easier this was than chasing them around the pool. Nat dumped the final scoop into the bucket and nearly had it filled.

Nat carried the shrimp to Maggie. "Your fish trap works perfectly for shrimp. You may need to make a few more of these."

"I will," Maggie smiled.

Nat returned to harvesting and filled bucket after bucket with lobster, shrimp, and fish. "I think that's enough for now," Nat told Maggie. "I'd like to clean those fish and get them in the smoker."

"I can help with that," Maggie replied. "I'll finish digging some clams and be up shortly."

"Do you need help?"

"Take a rest for a few minutes, Nat. You've probably walked several miles today. Get some cool water, too. You look a bit flushed."

"Yes, Mama," Nat answered and danced away from the playful swat Maggie aimed her way.

Nat picked up her boots and socks and started on the trail home. Marissa had emptied a bucket of shrimp and blew her hair away from her face as Nat approached. "Welcome back."

"Thanks," Nat answered. She inspected the contents of the barrels. "We made a good haul today."

"Yes, we did," Marissa agreed. "What would you like for dinner?"

"How about I filet some of these fish to fry to go with Maggie's fry bread. What vegetables do we still have canned?"

"Corn and a few carrots," Marissa replied. "Those would go well."

"That sounds good. I'll prepare the fish to fry for dinner and then dress the rest for the smokehouse. I need to skin my catch from the traplines, too."

"Go, do what you need to do, and I'll handle dinner. Maggie can help with the fish and skinning, right?"

"Yes, after she brings up her clams and shells them."

Nat sat on the porch steps to brush off her feet before putting on her socks and boots. "I have one more request for dinner."

"What's that?" Marissa asked.

"Gyp caught a rabbit, and I promised her she and Luna would have it for supper."

Gyp's ears perked up at the sound of her name as she sat near Marissa.

"She did? Well, Gyp, fried or stewed rabbit?" Marissa asked.

"I think a good stew would do them both good," Nat answered for Gyp. "Maybe toss in a few of those carrots and any potatoes you may have leftover."

"I think I can handle that request. Bring the rabbit first, so I can get it cooking."

"Yes, ma'am," Nat answered and walked to the back of the cabin.

†

Nat had just finished skinning the rabbit when Maggie walked over. "Do you want me to take that to Marissa?"

"That would be good. Thanks," Nat said. She walked with Maggie and took a long drink from their spring water.

Nat was busily fileting the fish for dinner when Maggie returned. "I'll finish the fish and get the others hung for smoking if you want to work on the pelts."

"Good enough for me," Nat said. "Did you shell your clams?"

"Nope, Marissa is doing those. She's very good at that."

"Yes, she is. Tom and Smithy will be out in two days. Do you think we should wait on them for lobster?"

"I think we can handle another day or two. We may need to free up a barrel, though," Maggie added.

"I think I could suffer through two meals of lobster. Let's see how tomorrow's harvest goes."

When Maggie returned, they worked together in comfortable silence. Maggie prepared the fish for smoking and then took the buckskin to stretch it, and salted it down after scraping off any loose fat.

Nat skinned the wolverine and cut up the meat for future meals for the dogs. She was working on a marten when Maggie walked over to her.

"That wolverine has a beautiful coat," she said as she brushed her hand through the thick fur.

"Yes, he does. What would you do with the pelt?"

"So many things are possible. Warm winter gloves and hats for starters."

"That sounds good. When the wolverine is tanned, he's all yours," Nat said.

Maggie looked up at her. "You know, Smithy would give you top dollar for that quality."

"I know, but there are some things we need to keep for ourselves. We don't go without, and if today's harvest is any indication of how our season will go, we won't lack for anything."

Maggie nodded and kept working on the hide. Nat finished skinning the martens and carried the fresh meat to the smokehouse. "The dogs will love that meat, but I'm not fond of eating it," Nat said.

Maggie nodded. "Not my favorite either when we have so many options to choose. Do you want to start trimming one of the deer quarters for jerky and sausage?"

"Might as well. We've got daylight left." Nat walked to the smokehouse and carried out a hind quarter and set it on the table. "I'll cut a few roasts for us, and the rest we can use for jerky and sausage."

Maggie started trimming from the leg upward as Nat carved out two roasts and carried them to the smokehouse. She sliced a few larger sections into strips and dropped them in a bucket of seasonings. Nat would allow them to soak before stretching them across a shelf in the smokehouse.

"We'll need to cut more wood for the smokehouse soon," Nat commented as she continued trimming meat and tossing scraps to Gyp.

"I can work on that in the morning if you have something else you need to do."

Nat paused for a moment. "I'd like to run my other trapline, and if the moose I saw earlier at the lake are still present, I'll get a bull. So, if you hear a shot, hook Quincy up and head my way."

Maggie nodded. "I'll already have him hooked up for hauling some firewood, so that won't be a problem. I told Marissa we'd hunt for antlers, too."

"When do you want to set up the meat grinder and sausage machine?"

"Maybe tomorrow afternoon, especially if you get a moose."

"Be sure to add some of this fat to the meat for sausage," Nat recommended. After stripping the hindquarter, they had three large containers of meat for sausage. Nat had cut a nice pile of jerky strips as well. "Do you want to get your meat into the smoke tomorrow? I'm going to put the jerky in and see if there is some to take out."

"I've already cleared you a nice section," Maggie said. "I can set the container of meat in there, too, until we start grinding and spicing tomorrow."

"I'll finish and clean our workspace if you want to go make your chowder and help with dinner," Nat offered. "I'm going to get a saw and split the leg bone between the dogs. They could both benefit from the fresh marrow."

"Especially, Luna. She needs meat to help her heal. I've got a few meat scraps I'll give her on my way to the cabin," Maggie replied.

"See you in a bit then," Nat said, and carried the first container of meat to the smokehouse. Nat removed the strips of deer that were soaking and laid them across the shelf for smoking. She looked at the three remaining quarters. They would provide enough meat for them to eat and still allow for sausage and jerky. Nat added wood to the fire and checked the smaller smokehouse. Fish hung from poles soaking in the flavor from the fire. If she cut more saplings for racks, she could increase the number of fish they could smoke. The fish would be in ample supply throughout the spring and summer, and possibly late into the fall. Nat cut the leg bone and took a section for Luna, and gave it to her. Gyp took her section and laid down next to her pup. They were gnawing on the bones while Nat rinsed their worktable. Nat sat on the steps near the dogs to rest for a few minutes. It was a busy day, but they had managed to accomplish many of their chores once they arrived home.

Nat was still sitting on the steps, drinking cool water when Marissa stepped out of the cabin and sat beside her. "A penny for your thoughts?" Marissa said.

"I was thinking about how much we got done today and what a remarkable team we make."

"We did manage to do a lot of work today," Marissa said. "We've got a bit of time until supper is ready if you want to sit out here and relax."

Nat looked at Marissa. "Do you remember where you put that spool of red ribbon?"

"Yes, I'll go get it. What are you planning to use it for?"

"I thought I'd take a walk and mark out the plot that I think will be good for Smithy since I have some time before we eat."

"I'll be right back then," Marissa said and returned inside. When she handed the spool to Nat, she kissed her softly. "Don't get lost in daydreams out there, or supper will get cold."

"I won't be long." Nat stood and hugged Marissa. "I know the perfect spot."

"Hurry home to me," Marissa said.

"I will." Nat waited until Marissa was inside and began her walk through the woods. She passed many small saplings she would cut for the smokehouse to clear a path to Smithy's. When she reached the spot envisioned in her mind, Nat walked to the cliff's edge and looked out across the ocean. It had a nice view. One she was sure Smithy would enjoy.

Nat paced off twenty yards from the cliff face and used a branch she had broken off as a stake with the red ribbon attached to it. That would be the boundary for the front porch. Nat continued marking until she had an ample-sized space marked for the cabin Smithy wanted to build. She stood back and surveyed the spot.

145

"Nice stand of trees to the north to block the wind, and another small clearing with minimal work could hold a barn and smokehouse. Perfect."

As she started for home, Gyp and Marissa were coming down the trail. "Here you are," Marissa smiled.

"I was just admiring my choice and was about to start home. Do you want to see?"

"Of course, I do. Smithy is going to be our neighbor," Marissa said as she walked with Nat.

Nat gave her the general layout and looked for Marissa's opinion.

"I think this will be the perfect spot for Smithy. Close to us and eventually Tom, but enough distance between for privacy. You did great, selecting this location. I bet Smithy will love it."

They began the walk back to the cabin. "Before I do anything else tomorrow, I'm going to cut these saplings to clear a path and use them in the smokehouses for fish."

"I can help you with that. If you cut the trees, I'll trim the branches, and we will finish in no time," Marissa said as she looped her hand around Nat's arm.

"You have a deal, my lady," Nat said. "I'm hungry."

"The dogs have already had a good portion of the rabbit stew. Maggie gave Luna another dose of root tea. She's been standing trying to wobble out to relieve herself, so Maggie and I carried her. She's sound asleep near the fireplace now."

"Good. We all need a good night's rest so that we can get up bright and early tomorrow."

"Another big day ahead for us." Marissa squeezed Nat's arm. "This is all so exciting."

✝

After the meal, they all decided to turn in early. Nat stoked the fire and joined Marissa in the bedroom. She slipped out of her clothes and crawled into bed.

"Leave those clothes on the floor and start fresh tomorrow. I'll light the fire while Maggie and I grind meat and throw them in the washpot."

"Maybe if we have time, we can have a nice soaking bath tomorrow night? I think I'm well past due," Nat stated.

"I think it would do us both some good," Marissa said. "I'm feeling a bit stiff from pulling the rope with the heavy buckets up the cliff."

"I can do that if it's too heavy," Nat offered.

"No, but thank you. I need to build up my strength," Marissa said as she snuggled into Nat's warmth. "Love you, my bee charmer," Marissa whispered.

"I love you, too. Goodnight."

CHAPTER SEVEN

Nat felt energized the following day and woke before Rufus had the pleasure of waking her with his crowing. She crept from the bed and dressed in clean clothing and walked to the kitchen to put on her socks and boots.

Maggie was sitting at the kitchen table drinking a cup of coffee. "Good morning. Are you ready for a cup?"

"I've got a chore I'd like to take care of after I hit the privy. I shouldn't be gone long," Nat answered.

"How about some eggs and flapjacks?"

"That sounds perfect for a busy day. If Marissa wakes, tell her I'm cutting saplings, but don't wake her, please."

Maggie nodded. "I'll come to get you if you haven't returned by breakfast."

"No hurry. Finish your coffee first. Do I need to collect some eggs?"

"Nope. I got a couple of dozen already this morning." Maggie smiled.

"I'll see you soon," Nat said and walked outside. She entered the privy, and when she came out, Rufus was on his perch, ready to start wailing. She grabbed her ax and hatchet and started down the path to Smithy's. Nat barely made it ten steps before Rufus let loose with a blood-curdling crow. Nat shook her head and kept walking.

Nat started cutting the saplings from her cabin toward Smithy's, downing a sapling with her ax and then trimming the branches with her hatchet. She stacked the saplings and made a pile of small wood they would burn under the wash pot. With only four left to cut, Marissa arrived.

"Why didn't you wake me?"

"Because you were sleeping so well, I didn't want to disturb you."

"Maggie says to start back this way. Breakfast is almost ready. I hope you're hungry. She cooked enough to feed a small army."

"Let's go then. We can finish after we eat. Do you mind grabbing a few of the saplings?"

"Not at all," Marissa answered and picked up three cut saplings.

"You are getting stronger," Nat said as she picked up five.

"Show off," Marissa teased. She followed Nat to the smokehouse, and they propped the saplings next to the building.

Nat washed her hands and followed Marissa into the cabin. Gyp and Luna were curled up at the fireplace, waiting for their breakfast.

"Everyone is hungry today," Maggie said as she spooned eggs and bits of flapjacks into the dogs' bowls and set them on the floor.

"Those look good," Nat said as Maggie placed a stack of flapjacks on her plate with several eggs.

"Do you want honey or syrup?" Marissa asked from the pantry.

"Butter and honey for me, please," Nat answered.

"Sounds good," Maggie said as she poured mugs of coffee.

Nat wasted no time digging into the pile of eggs Maggie had served her. She used a flapjack to soak up the runny yolk. "These flapjacks taste good," Nat said as she stuffed a bite in her mouth.

"Slow down and enjoy them. I promise no one will take the food away, and if you want more, I'll cook more," Maggie replied.

"I didn't realize how hungry I was until I sat down," Nat replied as she slathered butter and drizzled honey over the flapjacks.

"Eat your fill. You'll need all that energy for all that you have planned for today," Marissa said.

"It will be a busy day. Hopefully as productive as yesterday was. I'll start on my traplines if you two want to hunt for antlers."

Maggie nodded. "We'll hitch Quincy and head your way when we hear a shot. I hope the big bull moose are at the lake again today. One of those will practically fill the small smokehouse."

Nat swallowed and nodded. "I was thinking of sending a few extra logs to be milled for another smokehouse. If we manage to get bison, we will need the room."

"I think that would be a wise decision. We never seem to have enough space." Marissa looked at Nat. "Adding the extra saplings for fish will help, but I agree we need a bigger smokehouse for larger game."

"If you plot it off, I can work on digging a smoke pit and holes for poles. Once we get boards, it will go up fast," Maggie offered.

"I can do that later today. I'll also look for some good poles to use," Nat said.

"How many more saplings need bringing to the smokehouse?" Maggie asked.

"Only about six. I can get those if you and Marissa use the wagon to bring the branches in for the wash pot. We have decided it will be a good night for a bath."

"That does sound good. Maybe I'll take one when you two finish," Maggie replied. "If I'm still awake."

Nat took her last bite. "You two settle on supper tonight. If you want lobster and shrimp, I'm good with that. Anything else is okay too," she said as she stood and kissed Marissa. "I'm going to hang the saplings, and then I'm off to the trapline."

"We'll catch up with you later," Marissa said. "Be careful."

"Always. Gyp, you coming?" Gyp ran to catch up with Nat. She slung her rifle over her shoulder and walked out the back door. Nat rested her gun against the wall and opened the door of the smokehouse to carry the saplings inside.

"That was darn near a perfect fit," she told Gyp as the left to pick up the last saplings.

When Maggie emerged from the cabin to hitch Quincy, she saw Nat disappear in the trees, heading to her trapline. with Gyp trotting along beside her. She smiled and walked inside to get Quincy who was stomping his feet, eager to leave his stall and do some work.

"We are all eager to work today," Maggie told him as she opened his door and led him outside.

Marissa joined Maggie on the path, and they were able to collect all the branches in one big load. "Let's drop these and get to huntin' some antlers," Maggie said.

As they headed deeper into the woods with Quincy, Nat had reached her first set of traps. She collected a nice-sized beaver and a second farther down the line. "It looks like we'll be making an early trip home, Gyp," Nat told her companion. "These guys are too big to be lugging all over the woods." Nat collected several dark minks and started for the cabin.

She set her catch on the table and got a drink of water. Nat filled Luna's bowl and watched her struggle to her feet. The injured dog whined but laid back down after drinking. "You will be running again with us soon. Rest and get well," Nat said with a pat to her head.

Nat finished running the line, collecting several more minks before starting toward the lake. As she crept along the tree line, she could see several large bulls grazing on the sweet meadow grass. She secured the minks in the crook of a tree and knelt to study the bulls. Two of the bulls were younger and not as fully developed as the third, who carried a massive rack of antlers. Nat watched for several minutes and finally decided on the older bull, who showed a bit of struggle in walking. She aimed and took her shot. The bull staggered a few steps and collapsed to the ground. The younger bulls took off with speed, heading for the cover of nearby trees.

"Now, the work starts," Nat said. She collected her minks and walked to the edge of the lake. Nat used a rope to drag the bull from the knee-deep water onto dry land, struggling with his immense size. "He will for sure fill the smokehouse," she told Gyp through gritted teeth. Nat began field processing, bled, and gutted the moose by the time Maggie and Marissa arrived with Quincy.

"I think I will have to skin and quarter him here. I don't think the two of us can get him into the wagon," Nat told Maggie. "Will you take Marissa and Gyp back to the cabin, unload your antlers, and come back here? I'll do what I can to skin him. Bring the bone saw with you."

"I'll be back in a bit," Maggie said. "With a couple of buckets. too."

†

It took Maggie and Nat over an hour to prepare the moose for travel, and when they finally hung the quarters in the smokehouse, Nat was ready for a rest.

"Let's see if we can find something to eat and take a break. That bull wore me out."

"He was a big animal, no doubt," Maggie said. "I'll rinse the wagon and put Quincy away."

"Rinse the cart, but I'll take him down on the shore with me to check the pools while you and Marissa start on sausage. He won't have any trouble carrying buckets in the sand."

"Do you mind me using some of the moose for sausage too?" Maggie asked.

"Not at all. I'm interested to see how this process turns out," Nat answered. "Come inside when you get done."

Nat stepped onto the back porch, and the aroma of baking apples filled her senses. She walked into the kitchen and hugged Marissa from behind. "You've got this place smelling heavenly."

"You didn't get the apple pie I promised you, so I thought I'd bake one with fresh bread."

"Is the bread cool enough to eat? I'm starving." Nat kissed Marissa's neck.

"It should be. I've got some cheese I could slice for you as well," Marissa answered.

"That'll do. I'm going to eat and rest for a few minutes, and then Quincy and I will check the pools while you and Maggie start making sausage."

"I'm looking forward to that. Maybe we can try some at breakfast tomorrow. We still have eggs from this morning's gathering."

"You've got my mouth watering already," Nat said. She walked to the pantry for the block of cheese and cut several large slices while Marissa sliced the loaf of bread. "How much longer for the pie?"

"At least another hour. You can have a snack when you get back from the pools. It will have cooked and cooled by then."

Maggie walked into the kitchen. "I smell apple pie," she said while drying her hands on a towel.

"Yes, you do," Marissa answered. "Are we having lobster and fried shrimp tonight?"

"They both sound great to me," Nat said. She took a bite of bread with cheese. "Hopefully, the pools will be fruitful again today. I may walk farther down the shore in both directions to search for other treasures."

"We haven't been north at all," Maggie said.

"I may try that way today to see what it may offer," Nat said.

"Nat said we could use some of the moose for sausage too," Maggie told Marissa.

Marissa smiled at Maggie. "I'm excited to see how this goes. We should fashion a couple of tables to use on the front porch. We can both work and enjoy the beautiful day. I'll volunteer to grind if you want to try your hand at stuffing the casings."

"I've seen it done before, so I think I may have an idea," Maggie replied.

Nat smiled at the enthusiastic exchange between her two favorite people. It was hard to tell who was looking forward to the project the most. "Do y'all need me to do anything before I go?"

"Thanks, but I think between the two of us we can manage," Marissa said.

"Wait, before you go," Maggie said and disappeared into the cabin. She returned carrying a small bundle and handed it to Nat. "I made these for you."

Nat opened the bundle and smiled at Maggie. "I know you get tired of pulling off your socks and boots to explore the pools. I used one of your beaver tails to make you some simple moccasins. Much easier to kick them off and then slip back into them."

"These are perfect," Nat said and started removing her boots. "I bet they are warm too."

"They should be," Maggie said.

Nat stood and hugged the much smaller woman. "Thank you, my friend."

"You are most welcome, and I hope you enjoy wearing them."

"I already am, and they are very comfortable and fit perfectly." Nat picked up her boots. "I'll see you both later."

Nat dropped her boots on the back porch. She filled her canteen and secured her rifle in the holder attached to the wagon bench. Maggie had filled the wagon with empty buckets and a fish trap. She smiled and walked up to Quincy. "Let's get to work."

†

Nat harvested their usual tidal pools and had filled over half the buckets with lobster, fish, and shrimp. Instead of turning up the trail to return home, Nat led Quincy farther down the shoreline to the north. The beach was much narrower yet still wide enough for the small wagon to pass. The trees near the water had grown twisted from withstanding the strong winds that whipped the coastline in the wintry season. It didn't take Nat long to locate the first tidal pool, and she kicked off her shoes to wade into the water. The pool was deeper than those close to home and had captured curious-looking long-legged creatures that Nat had never seen. She approached them cautiously and carefully plucked one from the water.

"I have no idea what you are, but I hope you taste good." Nat removed six of the spiny creatures and found eight lobsters. The fish trap worked great on the shrimp, and with the trap and two full buckets, Nat waded back to the wagon. She dumped the shrimp into a nearly full bucket and placed the lobsters and the other creatures in the wagon bed.

"They are some strange-looking things," she told Quincy as they resumed their walk on the shore. With only three empty buckets, Nat planned to locate one more pool.

A cry from the top of a dead tree alerted Nat to an eagle in the area. She watched as the bird took flight and skimmed the water, then emerged with a large fish in its talons before flying away. A large pool surrounded by an outcropping of rocks was up ahead. When Nat waded out to it, the water churned with large fish. She quickly filled her two buckets and walked back to Quincy.

"This was a good trip, Quincy," Nat told him as they turned to start for home. As she got closer, Nat could hear the laughter from Marissa and Maggie like sweet music floating across the air.

She pulled Quincy to a stop in the front of the cabin. "It was well worth a trip north. They have some different creatures up there."

"Like what?" Marissa asked.

Nat's comment also sparked Maggie's interest, and they walked out to look at Nat's catch. "Like this," Nat said and pulled up one of the spiny-legged creatures.

"Those are crabs," Marissa said. "Tastes similar to lobster, just a bit harder to eat.

"What about those?" Nat pointed to the buckets of large fish.

"Salmon," Maggie said. "Those will be good for the smoker."

"They are big, and there were a lot of them," Nat said. "I ran out of buckets to fill, so we came back." She turned to look at the porch railing covered in strings of sausage links. "You two were busy, too. Do you want to add those to the wagon to take back to the smokehouse?"

"It would save us a bit of walking," Maggie agreed.

"Oh, I also found this," Nat said as she picked up something that looked like a rock. "It spits water from under the sand like a clam, so I dug one up. Is it a clam?"

Marissa nodded. "It's called a butter clam for its sweetness. Delicious eating."

"The size of this one, makes ten of the ones we get here," Maggie said as she examined the clam. "How far away?"

"A short walk from here. Do you want more?"

"Yes, but I'll go get them in the morning so we can try them with Smithy and Tom. It'll be a nice surprise."

Nat nodded. "I know it's only been a few days, but I'll be glad to see them."

"I hope the four of you won't work your fingers to the bone while they are here, and you take some time for some fun," Marissa said.

"I'd like to send Smithy back to town with a load of logs to bring back as milled boards. Tom and I can work on hauling shorter logs and start notching them for his walls."

"I can do that while you concentrate on the hauling. I assume you will stagger the lengths for strength," Maggie said.

"Yes, Tom and I will cut them eight, twelve feet after a base of twenty. Quincy won't be able to haul the base logs but can do the rest in low numbers."

"He will pull hard all day for you." Maggie smiled. "Better give him some molasses or honey in his feed to keep him strong."

"He's been a great partner. I don't know what I would have done without him," Nat said as she stroked down the mule's face. "Let's get you unloaded so you can rest and eat."

Marissa and Maggie dumped the lobsters, shrimp, and crab into barrels while Nat carried the fish to the cleaning table, then started hanging strings of sausage on the new saplings she had suspended earlier.

Maggie started a fire under the washpot and carried fresh water to heat for the laundry.

Nat finished dressing the fish she now knew as salmon, stored them in the smokehouse, and then dropped the remains in the garden. After washing the table, Nat began carrying freshwater buckets, dumping them in the bathtub for later. While Maggie and Marissa started supper, Nat worked on the moose hide and nailed it to the barn wall to cure. She walked inside the barn to feed Quincy and Hardy and emerged with a bucket of chicken scratch. She called to the brood and teased them back to the coop with the feed. Rufus, who sat on top of the henhouse, watched her every step. He waited until she left the enclosure to jump down for his share of grain.

Nat sat on the steps next to Gyp and looked over at her boots. The shoes Maggie had made her were so comfortable she had forgotten she was still wearing them. She pulled one off and examined it more closely. Maggie's stitching skills were impeccable, and the use of the beavertail for the sole was a great choice. They were much lighter than her boots and perfect for wearing while doing chores around the homestead. Nat slipped the shoe on her foot and was surveying the grounds when Marissa stepped outside.

"Are you done for the day?"

"I'm not sure yet. Is there something you need me to do?"

"Just rest for now. After supper, you can help me carry some hot water into the tub. I think you've done plenty for today."

"I'll add some wood to the smokehouses and maybe do a bit of carving on the front porch until it's time to eat." Nat pointed at her feet. "We need to get Maggie to make you a pair of these. They feel so good."

"I'm sure she will if I ask. We've got beavertails left and plenty of buckskin," Marissa answered. "I'll let you know when supper is ready."

Nat tossed several logs in each of the smokehouses and then walked around to the front porch to sit in her favorite chair. The sun was slipping toward the horizon quickly, and darkness would soon be upon them. Her blade sliced quickly through the wood, and Nat smiled when she recognized the shape of a bison forming in her hands.

Marissa walked out and fed her a fried shrimp. "How does that taste?"

"Mm, delicious as always," Nat said with a smile. "Are we close to eating?"

"Maggie will be bringing the lobster and crab in soon. Everything else is ready if you want to come inside."

†

Supper was good, and Nat decided that the sweet crab closely rivaled the lobster. They were a bit more challenging to get the meat from the legs and claws, but Maggie showed her the best way, and she took right to the task. She had a large slice of Marissa's apple pie and then pushed away from the table.

"I will explode if I don't stop eating."

"It was a good meal," Marissa replied. "If you want to carry a few buckets of hot water in, Maggie and I will pick up here. We'll let it cool a bit and take a nice bath before bed."

"I've decided to bathe tomorrow night, so don't feel rushed. Enjoy a nice soak. We've all earned it." Maggie smiled and took a sip of coffee.

"We've had a few good days," Nat agreed. "I hope the next few days are as productive with Smithy and Tom here."

"I bet they arrive before lunch," Maggie stated. "Why don't we have some smoked salmon for lunch? They will have plenty of time overnight to soak in the flavor of the smokehouse."

"Fine with me. I'm eager to taste salmon. We can unload the wagon if you want to make some chowder and fry bread to go with the fish. You and Marissa can store our goods while Tom, Smithy, and I start hauling logs."

Maggie looked at Marissa. "That sounds fine to me."

†

Marissa laid back against Nat's chest in the bathtub as they enjoyed the soak. Nat's arms were wrapped loosely around her waist as they relaxed, and Marissa could feel Nat's breathing slow as she drifted toward sleep. The water had cooled, so she decided to wake Nat to go to bed. "Nat, sweetie, it's time for bed."

Nat jumped when she heard Marissa. "Did I fall asleep?"

"Yes, you did. The bath worked its magic. We're all clean and relaxed. Dry off and climb in the bed while I drain the tub."

"I won't argue with you tonight," Nat said. "I can't believe I fell asleep in the bathtub, though."

"I can. You've worked extremely hard since we've returned. You need a good night's rest."

Nat dried her body and slipped into a long nightshirt before heading to their bedroom. When Marissa finished draining the tub and entered the bedroom, Nat was fast asleep. Gyp was curled up at the end of the bed and didn't twitch when she walked in and blew out the candle.

CHAPTER EIGHT

Nat woke early and rested from the excellent night's sleep. Maggie and Gyp were nowhere in sight. She poured a cup of coffee and walked to the back porch, sat next to Luna, and gazed out at the area she planned for another smokehouse.

"I think I'll cut some poles and get them in the ground this morning, Luna. What do you think?" Luna looked up at her with curiosity. "I think that's a good plan and will keep me close if Tom and Smithy arrive early."

"Who are you talking to?" Marissa asked from the doorway.

Nat turned to see her lover pushing the hair from her face. "Luna and I were discussing the location of the new smokehouse," Nat answered. "I'm going to cut the poles and get them planted while we wait for Tom and Smithy."

"I can work on splitting some wood for the cookstove and fireplace. Where's Maggie?"

"I think she and Gyp are digging clams. I haven't seen either of them since I've been up." She stood and kissed Marissa. "I'll go get Quincy hitched up if you'd like to pour us coffee. I'll drink a cup with you before we start to work."

"Can you break long enough for some breakfast?" Marissa asked.

"I will never pass on your cooking."

"I'll cook up some eggs and sausage to go with the fresh bread. I might as well get a couple of loaves in the stove. I'm sure with two extra mouths to feed, we'll need them."

"That's a good idea. I'll hold off on coffee then and cut my poles and break when you have breakfast ready. I promise I won't be gone long."

"Be careful," Marissa said.

"Always," Nat answered with a smile and walked toward the barn. She had spotted two trees that would make perfect poles and would need to be cleared from Smithy's area, so taking them down served two purposes. She hitched Quincy to the wagon and laid an ax and hatchet in the bed. As they pulled out of the barn, Maggie and Gyp were returning. Maggie carried two buckets filled with the butter clams.

"You got a good haul."

"I thought we might try slicing and frying some of these. I'll use the rest in chowder. Where are you off to so early?"

"To cut two trees for poles for a new smokehouse."

"Do you need help?" Maggie asked.

"No, they won't be large trees. Marissa will be cooking some breakfast for us. You can work on your clams, and then we can break to eat."

"Good enough for me," Maggie said.

Nat nodded and continued up the trail to the trees she wanted. She tied Quincy in a safe spot and began chopping. Nat started to remove the limbs and cut the trunks into nine-foot sections after bringing the second tree down. Then she loaded the logs into the wagon and stored her equipment before making the short trip home.

Maggie was sitting on the back-porch steps, shelling the clams when Nat pulled into the yard. Maggie looked up to see her and smiled, holding out a clamshell. "These are big and very sweet," Maggie cut a slice and handed it to Nat.

Nat took the meat in her mouth. "They are sweet and tasty, even uncooked."

"Welcome back. Are you two ready for a break, and some food?" Marissa asked from the back door.

"I do believe I could eat." Nat tied Quincy to the hitching post and drew a bucket of water for him.

†

"I think I will survive until lunch now," Nat said as she set her fork on an empty plate.

"I'm almost done with the clams. Do you want help digging the post holes?" Maggie asked.

"I'll never turn down help," Nat said. "Thanks for a good breakfast," she told Marissa. "Are you still planning to chop some wood?"

"Yes, it's too pretty to be cooped up inside. I've got bread in the stove, so I'll join you outside."

Nat positioned the poles near to where she would be digging and unhitched Quincy to allow him to graze for a while. She walked to the barn for a shovel and began her first hole. Nat had two holes dug when Maggie joined her.

"Let me grab a shovel, and I'll be right back," Maggie said as she walked by headed to the barn.

Nat nodded as she slid the first of the logs into a hole and began tamping dirt back to secure the post. Maggie returned and began digging as Nat secured the next pole.

Marissa brought a dipper of water to Nat. "You need something cool to drink."

"Thanks." Nat drank from the dipper and handed it back to Marissa before unbuttoning and removing her work shirt. "It's warming up fast today."

Marissa took the shirt and hung it over the porch railing. "Do either of you need anything before I start chopping wood?"

Maggie shook her head. "I think we're good."

The women returned to their tasks, and a rhythmic beat filled the air between the shovels digging into the earth and Marissa's ax splitting wood. The rest of the poles went quickly with Maggie's help, and Nat outlined the firepit.

"I've got the pit if you want to work on lunch," she told Maggie.

"The pit will get done more quickly with both of us digging. The chowder is cooking already. I'll check on it while you take a water break. The clams shouldn't take long. I can cook them while the wagon gets unloaded, so they are fresh."

"That works for me," Nat replied. "Do we want to put the extra soil in the garden?"

"That's not a bad idea. I'll bring the small hand wagon if you want to use it," Maggie suggested.

"That should work good," Nat said as she plunged her shovel into the ground.

"You've got a nice pile chopped," Maggie said as they walked toward the cabin. "Come take a break with us."

Marissa blew a strand of hair out of her face. "That sounds good to me."

Nat dipped out water and handed it to Maggie for the first drink. "Maggie and I are going to dig the fire pit and put the soil in the garden."

"We need some fresh soil," Marissa agreed and then took a long drink.

"We can add some ash from the other fire pits if that will help," Nat suggested.

"That's a project for another day," Marissa answered. "Maybe Maggie and I can work on that while you are hauling logs with Tom and Smithy."

Nat nodded. "If they haven't arrived by the time we finish with the pit, would you like to walk to the pools with me?"

"I'd be happy to," Marissa answered.

"That reminds me. There were more salmon and crab in the northern pools this morning," Maggie said.

"I'm looking forward to trying them smoked," Nat said. "Do you and Marissa want to keep Quincy and go make a harvest while we start hauling logs?"

"It's not too far for us to carry buckets. Keep Quincy to help with the logs," Maggie said.

"We have more than enough large logs to work on first. Take Quincy and let him work so that he won't feel left out," Nat suggested.

"He does get a bit moody," Maggie agreed. "I'll hitch him up and bring him over if you'll round up empty buckets and a couple of fish traps."

"I'm going to start digging," Nat replied.

Maggie brought the smaller hand cart over to Nat and picked up her shovel. When they filled it, Nat pushed it to the garden and dumped it in a corner. "We should get one more load out of the pit," Nat said as she resumed shoveling.

Nat had dumped the last load of soil in the garden when she heard the jangle of Rusty's hardware on the path to the cabin. "Our supplies have arrived," she said, nodding toward the approaching wagon. "We'll place the cabin supplies on the porch and take the rest to the barn for storage."

"I'll finish cooking while you begin storing our goods," Maggie told Marissa.

"Hello," Smithy called from the wagon as Tom pulled to a stop.

"Welcome," Nat called back to them. "Tom, pull up close so we can drop the supplies for the cabin on the porch, and we'll take the rest to the barn and get Rusty fed and watered."

"I hope y'all are hungry. We've got a nice meal planned for you," Marissa said.

"Have you ever known us to not be hungry for your cooking?" Smithy asked as he stepped down from the wagon.

"We've got a few new things for you to try," Maggie said. She turned to Marissa. "I'll cook the frybread and finish in here. Nat, will you bring the fish when you've finished unloading?"

"Sure thing," Nat replied. "Let's get to work, boys. I'm hungry."

Tom climbed into the wagon's bed and began handing items to Smithy and Nat, who had formed a chain to offload the house goods. Marissa started to carry small items inside, and when they finished unloading, Nat looked at Tom. "Will you pull Rusty to the barn?"

As Smithy and Nat walked to the barn, Smithy pointed to the new building site. "A new smokehouse?"

"Yes, we are getting a bit crowded, so I plan to send some logs back with y'all for some boards to build one."

"That sounds good. With all of us working together, we can have it up in no time."

"That's the plan," Nat said as they arrived at the barn.

It didn't take long to offload the rest of the wagon and store the goods. "Will you feed and water Rusty before we start to work later?" Nat asked Tom.

"I sure will," Tom replied. "What's the plan for today?"

"After we eat, you, Smithy, and I will start cutting some logs to length and hauling them to the lake. I'd like to get a couple of loads in and finish the day with a load of logs for Smithy and Rusty to take to town tomorrow to the mill. You and I will continue to cut logs until he returns, and maybe we can haul a few more loads."

"That sounds good," Smithy said.

"While we're working today, Marissa and Maggie will harvest the pools. We've found some new ones that have some different creatures that we'll share with you today.

Tonight, we will feast on lobster and whatever else they plan on cooking."

Tom nodded toward the posts. "Are you making another smokehouse?"

"Yes, that's partially the reason I want to send Smithy with a load in the morning. I hope they can mill enough boards to build it and get your floor done for your cabin."

Tom's face lit up at the mention of his cabin. "Good deal," he said as he poured some feed into Rusty's bucket.

Nat turned back to Smithy. "I think we have some time for a walk. I'd like to show you where I think would be a good spot for your cabin."

"Lead the way." Smithy replied.

As they started up the path, Tom noticed Nat had removed some small trees. "You already cut a path?"

"Yes, I needed some saplings for the smokehouse, and there were several in the way," Nat winked at Tom.

When they stepped into a clearing, Smithy gasped when he saw the view of the ocean.

"I thought your cabin could face the ocean and still have a nice row of trees to the north to break the winter wind. I tried to measure it off to your dimensions," Nat said, pointing at the red ribbons.

When Smithy looked at Nat, she could see his eyes had turned shiny with tears. "This spot is perfect," Smithy said. "A smokehouse and barn can go there," he pointed out. "Maybe a small garden plot."

"Or you can help Maggie and Marissa add on to ours and grow what you want," Nat said.

"This is really happening." Smithy smiled.

"Yes, it is. Let's go to the smokehouse, and we can bring in part of lunch. The rest of lunch should be about made by now," Nat said.

Nat picked up a large pan and opened the door to the smokehouse. "I found some new pools heading north from here, and they held crabs and these fish called salmon. Marissa assures me they will be delicious when smoked." She handed Tom the pan and filled it with several of the fileted fish for him to carry. "We also found a different type of clam we will be trying out today."

"They all sound good to me," Tom said as he carried the pan into the cabin.

Marissa looked up. "Why don't we plan to eat on the porch? We still have the tables set up there."

Nat nodded. "What can we carry out?"

Marissa handed her a stack of plates with utensils and some bowls. "Set the tables. Maggie and I will bring the rest. Smithy can draw us a bucket of water."

"You got it," Smithy said and walked to the pump on the back porch.

†

"That was one fine meal," Smithy said as he patted his stomach. "Folks in town are going to love those smoked salmon and the clams."

"See why we need another smokehouse?" Nat asked.

"I noticed you've got a big moose hide and buckskin hanging on the barn. You've been busy since you came home," Tom pointed out.

Nat nodded. "The buck had the misfortune of crossing paths with us on our way from town. That moose

171

was in your front yard. He was so big, Maggie and I had to quarter him to get him back here."

"You said you had started with the sausage," Smithy said to Marissa. "How did that go?"

"Maggie and I made quite a bit for the smokehouse using the deer and moose. We had some this morning with breakfast. I think it turned out quite well," Marissa said.

"There was none left if that tells you anything," Nat replied. "It was delicious."

"We will cook more in the morning so you can try it yourselves," Maggie said.

"Sounds good to me," Smithy replied.

Tom was starting to get restless. "Are you ready to get to work?" Nat asked him.

"Yes, ma'am. Chomping at the bit." He looked at Marissa and smiled. "I have one more thing I need to do before we start work. Will you come to the barn with me?"

Marissa looked confused. "Me?"

"Yes, you." Tom stood and offered her his hand.

"We'll be back in a few," Tom said.

Tom walked her out to the barn to the stall where he had put the horse that had been tethered to the wagon. "This is Willow," he said. "She's for you."

"What? I thought this was Smithy's horse."

"No, she's yours, complete with tack, so you can ride whenever you want," Tom said.

"I don't understand."

"Nat bought them from the undertaker in exchange for burying the two men who attacked you and Maggie, and I bought them from her. I wanted one for Ruth and the other for you for all that you have done for me."

Marissa hugged his neck. "Thank you. She's beautiful. Did you name her?"

"Heaven's no. I'm terrible with names. Ruth named her Willow due to her coloring, but if you don't like it, you can change it."

"Willow is perfect. Thank you, Tom."

"Thank you."

When they walked back to the cabin, Nat and Smithy had hitched Quincy to the small wagon for Maggie and were waiting for their return.

"Tom brought me a horse," Marissa said. "Now I can ride with you," she told Nat. "Her name is Willow, and she's beautiful."

"We will take a ride together in a couple of days," Nat promised. "We've got Quincy ready to go. We'll work until it starts to get dark, and then we'll head home."

"Maggie and I have already made the cots for Tom and Smithy. Not as comfortable as a bed, but better than the floor."

"I love the cot Maggie made me," Tom smiled.

"We will have a good meal ready for you," Maggie said.

"Be careful. See you when you get home," Marissa told them.

Nat looked at Tom and Smithy. "Let's get to work."

†

Tom drove the wagon with Smithy beside him. Nat chose to walk. She had her rifle slung over her shoulder in case they ran into some game that would be good in the smokehouse.

"What is the rope you have coiled up in the wagon?"

"Smithy measured out sections to match the lengths of logs we will need for our cabins and boards. That way, we know the exact length we are sawing a log for," Tom answered.

"That was a smart idea," Nat said. "That will make cutting much faster. We can mark them and start cutting."

When they reached the trail's head, Tom and Smithy began measuring logs, and soon they began sawing the logs into sections. Nat continued selecting trees and marking them for the correct lengths. With the first load on the way to the lake, Nat continued measuring and moving the trees to a convenient spot. The small sections leftover from cutting the lengths would be suitable for the cookstove and smokehouses. She would plan to use Quincy and the smaller wagon to take them to the cabin later.

The afternoon quickly faded, and they had delivered three loads to the lake.

"We probably have daylight left to get a load for me to take to town," Smithy said.

Working together, they loaded the wagon with logs to mill for Tom's flooring and Nat's smokehouse.

"I think that's a pretty decent load for Rusty," Tom said as they positioned the last log.

"I agree. We can use Quincy tomorrow for some of the smaller logs while we wait for Smithy to return," Nat said. "Do you think the mill owner will be able to turn these around tomorrow afternoon, or will you need to stay in town?"

Smithy shrugged his shoulders. "I'll wait as long as it takes. If I get to town early enough, I may be able to make it back before dark. If I have to stay, I'll be back as soon as I can the following day."

"Don't worry if you can't make it back tomorrow. Tom and I have plenty of logs we can pull to the lake using Quincy. We've barely touched the trees we cut for the trail, so we should be able to get your logs delivered if time allows."

Smithy smiled. "One cabin at a time. If we get my logs, that's fine, but no worries if we don't."

"One more load of logs to the mill and I'm sure we will have plenty for your flooring as well as logs for the mill owner," Nat said as they walked beside Rusty.

They reached the barn, and Tom unhitched Rusty from the wagon. "We did good today," he smiled.

"Yes, we did. I think my body will need a day of driving the wagon to rest up from today," Smithy groaned.

Nat rolled her shoulders. "I think we will all be a bit stiff tomorrow, but we made a good start."

"I know I won't have any trouble sleeping," Tom said. "Get my belly full of good food, and I'll be gone."

"Something sure smells wonderful," Smithy said as they waited for Tom.

"Marissa and Maggie will have a feast ready for us," Nat replied.

†

The meal was incredible, and Marissa surprised them by cooking sausage and fresh biscuits for the morning. "I figured one of the guys would drive a load into town early, so whoever has that duty can take food with them."

"That would be me," Smithy said. "I hope to be back tomorrow night, but there's no guarantee."

"If you have room on the bench, can you drop some jerky, sausage, smoked fish, and buttons off at the general store for us?" Marissa asked.

"I'll deliver it while I'm waiting on the boards," Smithy answered. "Just package up what you want to send. I'll load it on the wagon in the morning."

Marissa nodded. "We can certainly do that."

†

Everyone was up early the following day, ready to get to work. The skies were still dark when Smithy pulled out of the yard heading to town with a full load. Marissa was cooking fresh eggs for their breakfast while Tom and Nat got Quincy hitched and ready to work.

Maggie rearranged the smokehouse after filling a box full of smoked fish. She was emerging when Tom and Nat walked by. "We have room for more fish now," she reported. "Marissa and I will go down to the new pools and harvest what we can. I'll clean them and get them in the smoker, and then I'll come down to start helping you notch the logs."

"That works for me," Nat said.

Marissa filled their plates with eggs, sausage, and biscuits. After everyone ate their fill, the work of the day began.

"I was thinking a nice roast from that buck would be good for supper," Marissa suggested.

"That sounds good. Tom and I will take some jerky with us today to hold us over," Nat replied.

"I've got bread and cheese. I'll send some with Maggie when she comes. I'll work on the garden and get supper on to cook."

"Thanks," Nat said and kissed her softly. "We'll see you tonight." Nat picked up her rifle and walked toward the barn.

†

Tom began loading some of the eight-foot sections while Nat marked others for cutting. When he had as much as he thought Quincy could pull, he turned to Nat. "I'm going to drop this load at the lake."

"I'll have more ready when you return," Nat promised. She watched Tom until he was out of sight, then moved to the following sections of logs to saw. The sun was in full force, and Nat pulled off her work shirt. Her muscles were sore at the beginning of the morning, but the activity had loosened them as she began to break a sweat. Nat counted out the remaining logs Tom would need and measured them accordingly.

When she heard Quincy's gear jingling, Nat looked up to see Tom returning with Maggie walking beside him.

"Time for a meal break," Maggie said as they arrived.

Nat walked over to the empty wagon and accepted a slice of bread and cheese from Maggie. "How did the fishing go?" she asked.

"We don't have empty spaces any longer. I thought you two might enjoy a piece of fish too," Maggie said as she pulled two large pieces from a cloth.

"I have to admit, they sure are tasty," Tom said as he pulled a chunk of fish.

177

"Good for keeping your energy up, too," Maggie said. "Y'all have made a bit of progress today."

"We've got a good stack cut that should finish off Tom's shorter logs. I think Quincy can handle a few of the longer ones at a time. I want to load some of the short pieces for the smokehouse wood. They aren't long enough to use for much else." Nat pointed to a pile she had accumulated. "We can split them later."

"That's always a good project for the end of the day," Maggie said. "With a third smokehouse, we will need the extra wood."

"With a bison or two for our use, it won't take long to fill a new one," Nat said.

"You know we could probably use a few extra barrels," Maggie said. "It would be nice to harvest the fish and crabs as long as they hold out."

"I'll get Smithy to check on some when he makes his next run," Nat said. She looked at Tom. "Let's take this last load of short logs, and we can work on some longer ones. I'd like to place your ground floor logs today if we can."

"Don't we need the twenty-foot logs for that?" Tom asked.

"Yes, we do. Only two of those, though, to have room for your porch. Hardy can pull those if Maggie will saddle him and bring some rope."

"I can do that," Maggie said. "Do you need anything else?"

"No, I think that will do. We'll load the last logs and some of the smokehouse wood and meet you at the lake. Tom and I'll saw the two big poles, and I'll use Hardy to drag them out. You can start notching while we position his base logs."

Maggie nodded. "I better bring a file too then in case I need to sharpen some blades."

"That's probably a good idea. We can measure the notches, and you can get to work." Nat smiled.

"I'll meet you at the lake then." Maggie stood to leave.

"Thanks for bringing us food. My jerky was about gone," Tom told her.

"You're welcome. I'll see you soon."

"Let's get to sawing," Nat told Tom. "I think these two are the best. Nice and straight and about the same size."

They finished cutting the two base poles, loaded the last of the short logs, and had several pieces for smokehouse logs. "Ready to head to the lake?" Nat asked Tom.

"Yes, I'm excited to see this begin to take shape." Tom's smile covered his face.

Maggie had arrived and was sitting on a stack of logs waiting for them. She popped up when the wagon pulled up next to her. "I brought these," she said, holding out two burnt pieces of charcoal. "I remember how well they worked for marking our water logs for the garden."

"That was smart of you to remember. We can mark one, and you can measure from there." Nat chuckled. "I'm glad you are thinking today. That will save a bunch of time and effort." Nat looked at the ground beside Maggie and saw a hammer and a chisel. "Maggie, I have to admit you're brilliant."

"They will help make the notches smooth as a saddle." Maggie smiled at Nat's high praise.

"If you two will start drawing out the notches, Hardy and I will bring the long poles, and we can begin setting your foundation."

"We're on it," Tom said. "I'll follow any lead Maggie gives me."

†

Nat took Hardy's reins and began walking toward the trail. An eagle soared high above the treetops as she walked beside Hardy. A cool breeze had come up, and Nat hoped it wasn't bringing in some rain. Working in a light rain didn't bother her, but heavy rain could make the roads unbearable for Smithy and Rusty. She hoped they had made it to town safely and would soon be on the way back home.

She wrapped the rope around the first pole and tied it to her saddle horn. "Let's go, Hardy." Hardy began walking forward, quickly pulling the long log. He probably could have pulled both at once, but there was no need to overburden him. They had plenty of daylight left.

Tom and Maggie were busy cutting the notches from the logs when she and Hardy arrived.

"We need to determine where these base poles are going," Nat told Tom.

Tom paced out a reasonable distance from the lake and found a level space. "This looks like a good spot."

Nat led Hardy over to where Tom was indicating to position the pole. "One down. Will you use the rope measure and stake out sixteen feet across from here? You can also mark a spot four feet down this pole. That will start the base logs for your cabin."

"Got it," Tom said as Nat rolled her rope and started for the second pole.

"Those are looking good," she told Maggie as she walked by.

"Coming along well," Maggie said.

"I'll be back soon." Nat swung up in the saddle and trotted down the trail. When she tied the second pole to her saddle, she looked back at all the progress they had made. "Plenty of logs left for Smithy."

Tom and Maggie had ten logs notched by the time she made it back, and they quickly set the final pole. "Are you ready to place your first logs? We need to secure three across your main supports to give your floor a good foundation. Once we get the floorboards in place, we can put your walls up in no time."

Tom nodded.

"Let's see if we can handle one of these sixteen-foot logs. We'll start with your first four-foot mark." They each took an end of the log and carried it to the support poles. They rolled the heavy log into place, and it locked perfectly into the notches they had cut.

"I'm almost afraid of how well that fit. If the rest fit that well, we'll be in good shape."

"Did you mark the halfway point at eight feet?"

"After Maggie reminded me." Tom laughed.

"Let's get this next one set then," Nat replied. "Not quite as perfect, but it won't take but a little trim to make a solid fit."

With the third log in place on the end, the cabin began taking shape. "You know, I thought about something when I walked back this time. We should get some river rock to line the edges to keep water from washing out the soil."

"A combination of rocks and those big clam shells should work," Maggie said. "They are pretty solid. I'll save the ones we eat."

"That will work," Nat said. "I think we've made a lot of progress today. Not much else we can do besides continue notching, and the sun is fading. Let's head home and care for the animals." She looked at Tom. "I'll split this wood if you tend the animals, and Maggie can see if Marissa needs help."

"I'll help split, too, when I get done," Tom said.

"If Marissa doesn't need me, I'll stack for you. Then we can all relax. I hope Smithy makes it back tonight."

"I do, too," Nat replied.

†

With the three of them working, it didn't take long to split and stack the wood. Supper was ready by the time they washed up and walked inside the cabin.

Marissa looked up when Nat entered the kitchen. "I have another project for you."

"What would that be?" Nat leaned against the wall to wait for Marissa's answer.

"I want you to build a table we can share meals around in the front yard. We have such beautiful weather, and I'd like to take advantage of eating outside while it's nice."

Nat smiled. "I don't see a problem with that. We can use some of the stumps we cut off trees for seats."

"That would be fine." Marissa walked over to Nat. "Thank you."

"For what?"

"Making my every wish come true." Marissa smiled.

Nat pulled her into a hug. "You have made my life perfect since the day we met. I'm sure we will have some boards left over that we can use for the table."

"I can help with that," Maggie said. "With Tom's help, I can load six large stumps and a few short logs we can use for legs and a base. If Smithy doesn't arrive tonight, we can do that in the morning."

"See, we have a plan already," Nat reported.

"Let's eat on the small tables on the porch tonight then. It is a beautiful day," Marissa replied.

"Earlier, I was afraid we might get some rain, but I don't think it will happen tonight. It may have stayed east of us, so I hope Smithy doesn't get caught in it."

†

Nat and Tom talked out on the porch after dinner when they heard the jangling sound of a horse's harness. "I think Smithy may have returned," Nat said. "Let's go see."

They took a shortcut through the cabin to the backyard. "Smithy's back," Tom said excitedly.

"I'll get him some food warming," Marissa called out to them.

"Welcome back," Nat said as Smithy pulled Rusty to a halt. A look at the wagon found it loaded with more boards than Nat expected. "That was quite a haul."

"That's not even all of them, but I stacked them as high as I thought safe," Smithy said and carefully crept down from the wagon.

"It will be plenty to keep us busy," Nat said with a grin to Tom. "Marissa's getting you some food ready, so come inside. Tom and I'll take the wagon down to the barn and tend to Rusty. He's had a busy day too."

"That sounds good," Smithy replied. "I've worked up an appetite today."

183

"You have a treat ahead of you then. Supper was good," Tom said as he started leading Rusty to the barn.

†

After tending to Rusty, Nat and Tom joined the others on the front porch. Smithy swallowed a bite of the venison roast. "This is fantastic," he told Marissa. He looked at Tom. "The mill owner was impressed with the quality of wood and is looking forward to the next load."

"Do you want me to take a load tomorrow?" Tom asked.

Smithy shook his head. "No, I don't mind. I want you to get as far on your cabin as possible this week, and your young muscle is much faster than mine."

"I want to add another log to the load with a special request for some thicker slabs," Nat told him. "Marissa wants an outdoor table to enjoy in nice weather. I think four slabs, cut three inches thick, will do the trick."

"The black cottonwood made some beautiful boards," Smithy told them. "I'd recommend using one of them."

"We can load an extra one along with the load for payment to the mill owner tomorrow," Nat said. "If there's room, I'd like to start cutting some of your floorboards as well."

Marissa surprised them by asking, "Would you mind some company tomorrow?"

"Not at all. Rusty is a great worker, but he doesn't talk much," Smithy said. "The owner of the general store was excited about the delivery. He tasted the smoked fish as soon as I brought them in and promised to buy every one you can send him."

Marissa smiled. "Maggie and I can box up another round and some more jerky in the morning."

"I'll go down and get more tomorrow since we will have more room," Maggie replied.

Smithy took a long drink. "We won't have as many logs to cut tomorrow at the mill, so I believe we will be back much earlier. I'll ask that he cuts the slabs first while I load the rest of the boards I left today. That should be enough for your smokehouse."

"Tom and I will work on his floor tomorrow. We managed to set his foundation today," Nat said.

"I can hardly wait to see it," Smithy replied. "Ruth caught me in town and said to tell you she misses you."

Tom's face turned scarlet.

"Does she know what you are doing this week?" Nat asked.

"She thinks we're helping you with building projects," Tom replied. "Which is true. I want our forever home to be a surprise wedding gift."

"That will be so perfect," Marissa assured him.

†

Marissa woke them the following day with the smell of sausage cooking in a pan. She and Maggie had found a package of dried blackberries when they unloaded supplies, and they were making flapjacks for breakfast.

Tom pulled on his boots. "Is there anything I can help with?"

"No, I believe we've got this," Marissa said. "Why don't you go hitch up Rusty and Quincy?"

"Yes, ma'am." Tom raced out the back door.

185

"If you have everything under control here, I thought I'd rope Smithy into helping me to box up the fish and jerky for the ride to town," Nat said.

"I've already beat you to it," Maggie said. "After you get Smithy and Marissa off to town, will you or Tom help me with the stumps?"

"We can both help you and get them in place in no time," Nat said. "Maybe if they make it back from town before dark, we can have our table built."

Maggie looked at Nat and Marissa. "Will you be good with smoked fish, fried clams, shrimp, and fry bread for supper tonight?"

"That will be fine with me," Nat said.

"If we get back in time, I can help," Marissa replied.

"I'll hit all the pools then and see what I can round up to eat." Maggie turned a flapjack in the pan. "You might want to pick up some spices and casings for sausage while you're in town. We have plenty of meat to use right now, and that's an easy project for us to make."

"Can you think of anything else we need?" Marissa asked.

"We will need a large amount of salt for the bison. Pick up several bags and some flour and cornmeal," Nat requested. "More cheese, too, if they have some. That makes a good midday meal that's easy and fills us with energy."

"Syrup, too," Maggie said as she pulled the last jar from the pantry to heat.

Nat smiled. "While you're wheeling and dealing, see if he knows anyone who will barter a whole hog for a large hind quarter of moose that's already smoking. It would be nice to have some pork for variety."

"I'd bet Jacob would jump all over that," Smithy said. "He could make some money with the moose meat."

†

It didn't take long to unload the boards and load the wagon with logs for the mill. By mid-morning, Smithy and Marissa were on their way to town. Nat looked at Maggie and Tom. "Let's get the stumps moved for our table." They added four additional stumps of a similar size to use for table legs.

Once that chore was complete, Maggie took Quincy to begin the day's harvest while Tom and Nat started building his floor. The boards fit perfectly into the foundation, and by midday, they had the flooring installed for the interior and the front porch.

"Do you want to stop for some jerky or keep going?"

"Would you mind if we kept going for a bit? I'd like to see some walls go up," Tom replied.

"Not a problem. Let's get busy," Nat said.

Maggie arrived after two rows of logs had been raised. "Since we're getting more cheese, I thought I'd bring you two a snack," she said, and handed them fresh bread and hunks of cheese. "It's coming right along," she said as she reviewed their progress. "You've got a lot of boards left."

"We'll use some of them for the flooring for the loft," Nat said, "but there will be plenty of leftovers."

"I've got the fish in the smokehouse. Do you want me to bring Quincy down and take a load for the new smokehouse? I've got time before I need to start supper."

"Fine with me," Nat answered her. "Will you fill a few canteens and bring them down, too?"

Maggie nodded. "I'll see you soon."

†

"I must be getting tired," Nat said. "That last log was heavier than the rest."

"We're starting to get to a height that makes lifting harder on us," Tom replied. "We may need to use the horses to help soon."

Maggie had returned and loaded boards into Quincy's wagon. Nat called for a water break, and as they sat on a log, Nat could hear pounding in the distance. "It sounds like Maggie has started without us."

"Should we take a break from here and go check on her? We can bring the horses back when we come," Tom suggested.

"Sounds good to me." Nat stood and stretched. She turned to face the cabin. "It's coming right along. We'll need Hardy and Willow to pull some longer poles for crossbeams for the loft and roof."

Nat was surprised at the progress Maggie had made on the smokehouse. She had pulled Quincy's wagon close enough to stand in the bed and had one side complete and was halfway done with the back.

"We should leave you unattended more often," Nat teased. "You are rolling right along."

"This is easy work compared to what you both are doing," Maggie answered.

Tom handed her a board that she nailed to the posts. "Do you want help to knock this out?"

"I can manage this, but I'll need you to cut the door and trim the ends with a saw," Maggie replied.

Nat nodded. "We needed the horses for the next section, and then we'll break for the day. If you finish with the walls, Tom and I will build the door and do the trimming. You've done great so far."

"I may need a few more boards to finish the roof," Maggie said.

"When you're ready, bring Quincy down, and we'll get them loaded." Tom handed her another board.

†

With the horse's muscle, Tom and Nat were able to place the final logs on the first floor. "We can start on the crossbeams tomorrow," Nat said. "I think we're at a good stopping point for today."

As they began walking toward the cabin, Nat did not hear any evidence of nailing boards. "Either Maggie finished, or she ran out of boards," Nat said.

"I bet she's finished and working on supper," Tom replied.

"Well, let's see if we can knock this out and relax for a bit. We got a lot accomplished today."

"You won't get an argument from me." Tom took the reins as they reached the edge of the property. "You go survey the work, and I'll bring the saws."

Maggie had indeed finished the walls and roof of the new smokehouse. Other than building the door, there wasn't much trimming needed. Nat went to the firepit for a chunk of charcoal, then picked up a board to outline the placement for the door. Nat would use a few leftover boards to trim the door and add hinges and a latch.

Tom brought the saws. "Where do you want to start?"

"You can trim the ends flush with the corners while I start on the door," Nat answered as she picked up a board and measured it for trim. After a few minutes, Nat had the door trimmed, hinges installed, and she was working on a latch when she heard Marissa and Smithy returning.

Marissa was shocked to see the new smokehouse was nearly complete. "You've gotten that built today?" she asked.

"Nope, not us," Nat answered. "We've been working on the cabin all day. Maggie did this on her own. Tom and I just added the door and trimmed off excess boards."

Smithy and Marissa both looked at the porch where Maggie had stepped out of the cabin. "You did this?" Smithy asked.

"Yes, I did, and it was fun," Maggie said. "We got a lot accomplished today."

"It sure sounds like it," Marissa said. Nat helped Marissa from the wagon. "Looks like y'all did well, too."

"I think we did good." Marissa smiled.

"Tom, why don't you walk down with them and show Marissa and Smithy the cabin while Maggie and I start offloading supplies," Nat suggested.

"Let's go," Tom said.

Nat noticed how excited he was to show off their work. She turned back to Maggie. "You did an excellent job on that smokehouse."

"That's a good thing. It looks like we need it for a hog," Maggie said, and nodded to the back of the wagon.

"I'll help you up if you will hand things down to me," Nat said. "We can unload the wares for the cabin, and I'll hang the meat. If Tom and Smithy are back by then, they can help me build the table and then drive the wagon to the lake."

190

"Supper should be ready by then. I've got a hearty meal planned for us." Maggie handed her bags of salt, flour, and meal.

"My cheese and bread are long gone," Nat said as she carried the bags to the porch.

When they had finished, Nat led Rusty closer to the smokehouses. "Do we have room in this one?" she asked, Maggie?

"I think they will fit." Maggie held the door as Nat carried the four quarters of pork and hung them for smoking.

Then they pulled the wagon around to the front yard, and Nat removed four large slabs of wood. They were heavy, and Nat scratched her head thinking of how she would attach them to form a table.

"I think you will need this," Smithy said as he walked around the corner of the cabin. He held a hand drill up to show Nat. "I've also got some large spikes to secure them once we have holes drilled. A piece of board across the middle and near the ends can provide some support. Tom has run back for a saw, hammer, and nails."

"I'm glad you've thought this through," Nat replied.

"Why don't you have a seat on the porch and let Tom and I finish this project? I think you've done enough for today," Smithy added. "If we need you to help, you will be handy. Y'all have done a great job on the cabin so far. It looks good."

"I won't argue with you at all, Smithy. I'm proud of what all we got accomplished, but I am tired."

"Relax and drink some cool water. This table project shouldn't take long at all."

Marissa brought her a cup of water and sat beside her on the porch steps. "I bought some lovely fabric that will make good tablecloths," she told Nat. "I'm impressed by the cabin and the smokehouse. I never dreamed you would get so far in one day."

"It was a good day," Nat said as she watched as Smithy guided Tom through the process of drilling holes and securing boards underneath to support the table. "I think you will be pleased with this when they finish. I hope that position is where you wanted it because it won't be easy to move."

"That is an ideal spot," Marissa answered. She watched for a few more minutes. "I'm going to see if Maggie needs my help."

Smithy turned to Nat and motioned her over. "I think you should drive the final spike in your new table," he said and handed her the hammer.

Nat struck the final blow as Tom and Smithy positioned the stumps around the table for seats. "Perfect," she said when she stepped back to look.

"Once the wood cures, you can stain it or just add some of that whale blubber to fill the grain. It will be beautiful either way," Smithy said.

Nat sat down beside Smithy. "This is more comfortable than I thought."

Tom smiled at them. "I'm going to pull the wagon down to the cabin and unhitch it. I'll feed Rusty and put him up for the night."

"Don't be gone long," Marissa warned. "Supper will be ready soon."

"I won't dawdle," Tom promised as he led Rusty away.

Marissa walked out and sat beside Nat. "This turned out beautiful. Thank you all for building it for us."

Nat ran her hand down the board. "We will share many meals around this table."

"That we will. Starting with tonight," Marissa said.

†

Nat could barely keep her eyes open after eating and felt herself dozing off.

"Why don't you call it an early night?" Marissa suggested. "You've been working hard lately."

"I think I will so I can be ready to go in the morning," Nat said. "Goodnight, everyone."

Nat stripped out of her work clothes and into her nightshirt. She blew out the candle and climbed into the comfortable bed, intending to plan the next day's work. Her eyes slammed shut, and Nat fell quickly to sleep.

†

"Is she okay?" Smithy asked Marissa.

"Yes, she's just been working extremely hard for a few weeks. I'm sure after you and Tom return to town, I will try to convince her to take a day off to relax."

"Good luck with that," Maggie said with a smirk as she gathered dishes to take inside.

"I know, but I will still try," Marissa said.

"If we can get a roof on in the next day or so, why don't we see if we can convince her to ride out and check for bison?" Tom suggested. "Heck, we've made such good progress so far; we could go tomorrow or the next day."

"Maggie and I can help you with the cabin if Smithy and Nat want to ride out," Marissa offered. "If you can get the heavy framework in tomorrow, Maggie and I can help with the smaller stuff."

"That's a great idea," Tom replied. "Who's going to do the talking?"

All heads turned to Marissa. She laughed, "Okay, I'll try to convince her tomorrow."

"They could leave by early afternoon and reach at least the first campsite. Riding faster, Nat and Smithy could reach the main site," Tom said.

†

At breakfast the following day, Marissa convinced Nat to ride with Smithy to check for bison. Marissa made them a bedroll to take and packed some food while the group worked on getting the framework for Tom's roof in place.

"We can take it from here," Tom said when they rolled the last support beam into place.

Nat looked at Smithy. "I do believe they are trying to get rid of us."

"Well, we do need to know if the herd has arrived," Smithy said with a shrug. "Let's get saddled up and hit the trail."

"Not you, too?" Nat laughed. "Let's go."

"I've got bedrolls and some food packed in your saddlebags," Marissa told Nat.

"Sounds like we're all set then. Let me grab my rifle and some jerky. You can fill our canteens," Nat told Smithy. She then turned to Maggie. "I'm leaving you in charge of keeping Tom from falling off the roof."

"Got it," Maggie smiled. "I'll go up there."

"No, you won't," Tom said. "We will just take our time and be safe."

Nat and Smithy saddled up and rode past them on their way to the trail. "We'll see you sometime tomorrow."

"Be safe," Marissa said.

"We will," Nat said, and they trotted away.

"Maggie, can you start passing me boards up here?" Nat heard Tom ask.

†

"What are they really up to?" Nat asked Smithy when they slowed to a walk.

"We decided you needed a break from manual labor today, and we do need to check for the arrival of the herd. You've been pushing yourself mighty hard the last few weeks."

"I won't argue that. I was bone-tired last night." Nat took out a piece of jerky and offered one to Smithy.

"We need you for the long haul. The cabin will get done when it gets done," Smithy said. "If you're laid up sick or injured, that doesn't help anyone."

"I get it," Nat said. "So, do you want to try to make it the entire way today?"

"I'd like to, if possible. I'm excited to see if the herd has arrived."

"We'll have to pick up the pace, but it's reachable before it gets too dark," Nat replied. She urged Hardy into a canter.

†

The floor for the loft went up quickly, and Tom decided it was time for some food. "Let's take a food break and plan the next section," he suggested.

Maggie opened a basket with slices of the venison roast from the night before and fresh bread and cheese. "Are you ready to tackle the roof?" Maggie asked.

Tom swallowed a bite of meat. "I think so. Nat talked me through the process of overlapping the cedar shingles. I'll have to take it slow to make sure I place each one correctly."

"I'll climb up to the loft, and Marissa can start handing them up for me to stack. You can take a few at a time and begin securing them. Our job will be much faster," Maggie pointed out.

"It won't take long for us to unload them," Marissa said. "What do you two want for dinner? I thought I'd go down to the shore and check the pools if you don't need me."

"I would never turn down some of the smoked fish," Tom said.

"If you catch some shrimp, we could cook them with fry bread," Maggie said.

"That should be an easy task. I'll take Quincy, and we can harvest all we can find. We need to finish a load of seafood for Tom to take back when they go."

"If you get more salmon, I'll filet them and get them in the smoker," Maggie volunteered.

"Do you want us to dig some clams if time permits?" Marissa asked.

"If you can. If not, I can do that in the morning before we start back on the roof." Maggie looked at Tom. "I don't think we'll finish today, but tomorrow we will be done."

"I can help by running Nat's trap lines, too, if that will help," Tom said.

Marissa nodded. "She hasn't checked them in a few days, so that's not a bad idea. Maybe you should run them later today while we work on the seafood."

Tom nodded. "My back will probably need a break from all that bending by then."

"Walking her trap lines will be a good remedy for that. Do you know where they are?"

"Yes, Marissa, I've gone with Nat before. I'm pretty sure I can find them."

Nat and Tom had made a ladder to the loft, and Maggie climbed it with ease. Tom gathered his hammer and nails and followed her.

"Be careful up there," Maggie warned.

Tom nodded. "I will," he promised and climbed to the first roof support.

"You can start handing them up, Marissa," Maggie called down.

Marissa picked up two of the wooden shingles and handed them up to Maggie. Maggie then handed them up to Tom, who started positioning them on the roof. It didn't take long for the weight of two shingles to begin to tire Marissa, so she started sending them up individually, but the unloading and stacking went smoothly.

"I'm going to head out now. Do y'all need anything before I go?" Marissa asked.

"Hand up the extra bag of nails, just in case," Maggie replied. "We'll see you later today. Don't forget your pistol. Take Gyp with you. too. I think Nat left her behind to help protect."

Marissa smiled and pulled the small pistol from her apron. "Got it."

"Good luck then. Catch us a bunch. I think we'll all be hungry tonight," Maggie said.

"I know I will be," Tom called down in agreement.

"I promise we won't go hungry." Marissa laughed and left the cabin.

Maggie looked up at Tom. "I say we make it through two stacks and call it a day."

"Fine by me," Tom said as he stood and stretched his back. "I'm glad there's only one roof to this place."

"Take your time and do it right, so you don't freeze to death in the winter from leaks," Maggie warned.

Tom and Maggie worked steadily until the roof began to take shape.

"That's good for today," Maggie said with a nod. "Come down carefully, and let's look at what we've accomplished so far."

Tom climbed down and sat beside Maggie on a large log as she gazed at the cabin. "I think it looks good." she smiled.

"It's beginning to look like a forever home," Tom responded. "Look," Tom pointed across the meadow at a pair of moose drinking at the lake. "Yeah, I could get used to waking up to a view like this every morning."

"It's a beautiful sight," Maggie agreed. "How do you visualize your home?"

Tom pointed to an area to the right of the cabin. "I see a barn there with a corral large enough to hold several animals for grazing. A smokehouse, here," he pointed to an area left of the cabin, "with a garden spot here, tucked in away from the north wind."

"That sounds like a good plan. If you mark out a plot, I will begin breaking the ground on a garden plot for you," Maggie offered.

"You don't have to do that, Maggie," Tom answered.

"I know, Tom, but the sooner you can start preparing the ground, the sooner you can do some planting," Maggie told him. "If you expect to have vegetables for next winter, you need to plant before summer arrives."

Tom nodded his understanding. "Maybe I need to ask Smithy to allow me more time out here to prepare."

Maggie smiled up at him. "Let's wait to see what they find today. You may be back here sooner than you think."

"That would be good with me. Are you ready to head home? I'll grab some gear and head out to Nat's trap lines while you help Marissa." He reached down and offered a hand to Maggie.

†

Nat and Smithy stopped at the first campsite for a quick break. After they ate some of the smoked fish and drank water, Nat refilled their canteens and sat beside Smithy. "It doesn't seem as far away from home as it used to," Nat told him.

"You're just more comfortable with the trail, and you did an excellent job of clearing it. There is so much good wood sitting beside the trail. I'm sure the sawmill operator would pay well for some of these logs."

"That's good to hear. I'd hate for all our hard work to go to waste if the bison don't return," Nat said.

"Do you think that may happen?" Smithy frowned.

"If the reports of them slaughtered so needlessly are true, that could be a possibility. I hope not, but only time will tell."

"If they aren't here yet, how long will you keep checking for them?" Smithy asked.

Nat nodded after taking a drink. "If you can allow Tom some extra time when he makes his deliveries, we could ride down to check, and he could bring a few loads of logs back to the lake. We can make a stockpile, and he can begin taking them to town to generate some extra income."

"I was thinking of asking him if he wanted to work a few days a week so that he can work more here," Smithy said. "Once he has his cabin finished, Tom could start working on mine, and I'd keep him on the payroll."

Nat stood and stretched. "I think that would be an offer too good for him to pass on. He'll need to get a garden in and a barn built for the animals before he can work on your cabin, but we can all pitch in to get him going."

"I'll be down as often as I can, too," Smithy said. "I'll take over making the deliveries to town to allow him more time here."

"Good plan," Nat said. "Let's ride so we can get to camp before it gets too dark."

†

Tom shouldered his rifle and headed into the woods to pick up Nat's traplines. As he walked, Tom remembered how scared he had been when he first passed through this area, alone, hungry, and cold. Wandering into Nat and Marissa's home was the best fortune Tom could have found. Nat and Smithy had taught him so much, he now felt confident in his abilities as a young man, and he wasn't terrified of being alone. Tom smiled when he reached the first trap in her line and found Nat had caught a giant beaver. "I'm not sure how many of this size I can carry," Tom said to himself as he pulled the animal from the water and reset the trap. He hoisted the animal into the pack on his back and resumed walking the line. It didn't take Tom long to fill the basket with mink and another smaller beaver, and he walked back to the cabin. Tom put the two beavers and minks on the table and searched for Maggie and Marissa, but they were not home. He shouldered the basket and went back to finish running the line.

†

Maggie found Marissa busy harvesting creatures from a pool. Marissa looked up and waved when she saw Maggie. Gyp sat by the wagon watching Marissa and raced to Maggie as she approached. Maggie pulled out the rake and a bucket to begin digging the sweet clams along the waterline. Gyp walked along with her and used her paws to help explore for clams.

Maggie filled several buckets that she dumped into Quincy's wagon and then waited for Marissa to emerge with a trap filled with shrimp.

"What is left to harvest in the pools?" Maggie asked.

"Probably a dozen salmon," Marissa said. "I've already gotten the crab, and these are the last of the shrimp." She dumped the trap into a small barrel.

"Do you want some help with the fish? Then we can go home for the day and start working on this catch," Maggie suggested.

"I haven't even checked our normal pools yet," Marissa said. "These were loaded today."

"I'll get the fish in the smoker, and you can dump the rest in the barrels. By that time, Tom should be back, and he and I will check the other pools." Maggie pulled off her boots and socks. "Let's go get some fish."

†

Tom was placing the remainder of the line's pelts on the table when he heard Maggie and Marissa coming up the path. When they arrived, Maggie surveyed the table. "We have work to do," she told Tom. "Take these buckets of fish to the skinning table and help us unload the rest. Marissa will start on some supper for us while you and I do some skinning and then check the other pools if there is daylight left."

"It looks like you made a good haul, too," Tom said.

"The new pools Nat found were packed with good things to eat. I haven't even made it to our normal pools yet," Marissa answered.

"Let's get to work then," Tom suggested, and picked up several buckets from the back of the wagon.

†

When Nat and Smithy arrived at the main camp, they tied off the horses and walked to the hill. As they crested the hill, Nat sighed when her eyes fell on an empty meadow. She saw the disappointed look on Smithy's face as well. "It may still be too early for them to arrive. I was hoping they would be here, but it was later in the early summer months that I saw them before."

202

"We can check again in the morning," Smithy replied as they began walking back toward camp. "It was a nice ride out here with good company."

"You may not think that after a night on the ground," Nat teased him. "I'll get a fire started if you tend to the horses. There's a nice creek behind our campsite. They can graze until full dark, and we'll bring them closer."

Smithy unsaddled the horses, and Nat surveyed the saddlebags to find more of the smoked fish and some slices of venison. She would skewer the venison to warm over the fire while they ate the smoked fish. She smiled when she opened a final flour sack and found ham biscuits with a small jar of honey. Marissa had provided well for them, and the food would be enough to hold them over until they returned the next day.

†

Maggie talked Tom through the process of skinning the two beavers while she fileted the fish and hung them in the smoker. Then she skinned the mink, placing their carcasses in the firepot to be boiled for the dogs.

"Is beaver good to eat?" Tom asked.

"It's not the tastiest meat in the woods, but not the worst either. We can hang them in the smokehouse to use for future food for Gyp and Luna. They seem to enjoy the taste," Maggie said as she tossed a scrap to Gyp.

With the last of the pelts stretched on boards to dry, Maggie turned to Tom. "Will you rinse the table while I go check on Marissa?"

"Sure will. I'll get the buckets loaded back into the wagon, too," Tom answered.

"I'll be right back," Maggie said and walked to the cabin. She found Marissa inside cleaning the shrimp she had caught. "Those will be tasty," she said.

Marissa jumped when she heard Maggie speak.

"I didn't mean to startle you," Maggie apologized.

"I guess I was just too deep in thought," Marissa said.

"Are you good?" Maggie asked.

"Yes, I was thinking how different it will be with neighbors," Marissa said.

"Different, yes, but at least it's people we know and love. There is plenty of room for all of us, and our businesses won't diminish with Tom, Ruth, and Smithy close. If anything, they may flourish even more."

"It would give us more hands to help with the work," Marissa agreed. "I know Nat is excited to have them here."

"It will be good for her to teach both men how to trap and prepare pelts. Neither of them has much experience on this end of the business, and it will lighten her workload."

Marissa smiled. "She works so hard. I would love to see her relax a bit more."

"Maybe she can relax more in the future. Tom especially is young and eager to learn, and it sounds like Ruth is a hard worker, too." Maggie tilted her head. "Smithy, well, he's an old dog, but I bet he can learn new skills."

Marissa burst out laughing at Maggie's assessment of Smithy. "Maggie, that was too funny but true. I see the excitement in his eyes when Smithy talks about being out here."

"Yes, I see it too. Tom and I have finished the pelts, so we'll go to the other pools. Are you good here alone?"

"Gyp will stay with me unless you need her to dig clams," Marissa said.

"That was fun to see her excited, and she was a big help," Maggie said. "We'll be back soon."

"Get some lobster if you can, and we'll have another feast tomorrow. I'm sure Nat and Smithy will be ready for a good meal when they return."

Maggie nodded. "Will do."

†

Smithy and Nat finished their meals and stretched out their bedrolls. They sat on the logs around the fire as the evening sky filled with stars. "It sure is beautiful out here," Smithy commented. "I can see why you loved trapping with your father."

"It was hard work, but our time together was priceless. To sleep under a blanket of stars when it was warm enough was so fun." Nat fell silent.

"I miss Nathan, too. He was a great man, and he'd be so proud of you," Smithy said as he placed a comforting hand on her shoulder.

"His time was cut too short," Nat said.

"Yes, it was," Smithy replied. "Are we getting up at first light?"

Nat nodded. "Marissa packed us some ham biscuits, so we can eat as we ride back."

"Sounds good to me. If you don't mind, this old man is going to turn in," Smithy said with a grin.

"I won't be far behind you," Nat replied. She watched the passing of the clouds across the moon and then dropped another log on the fire before searching out her bedroll.

†

Tom and Maggie cleaned out three pools before darkness began to set in for the night. Tom unloaded several buckets of lobster, shrimp, and fish, while Maggie went inside to check on Marissa.

"We will be feasting tomorrow night again," Maggie said. "The lobsters were in all three pools."

"That sounds delicious," Marissa replied. "I've almost finished with the shrimp if you want to cook the frybread. I've got the pan ready."

"I'm on my way," Maggie replied. She rinsed off her hands and joined Marissa at the cookstove. "We had a good day, didn't we?"

"Yes, we did. I think Nat will be pleased with what we got done. Maybe we can all break early tomorrow and share a nice meal outside again."

"That is nice, isn't it?" Maggie asked. "I don't think she will have any argument to that. Tom is hoping to finish his roof tomorrow. Don't be surprised if he starts sleeping there."

"I would be surprised if he didn't. Do you think you, Nat, and I could make Tom and Ruth a bed for a wedding present?"

Maggie nodded. "I don't see why not. I may need a few more geese shot for the mattress, but the other supplies are readily available."

Marissa smiled. "I can make them a heavy quilt and can buy material for linens from the general store."

"Let's talk with Nat about it tomorrow, but I'm sure she'd like the idea." Maggie was about to make another suggestion when Tom walked inside. Instead, she smiled up at him. "Hey Tom, do you think you can shoot me a few geese tomorrow?"

"I'll do my best," Tom replied. "Do you two need any help?"

"You can draw us a bucket of water," Marissa said.

"Pull out a bit of the meat from the firepot to let it cool for the dogs," Maggie added.

†

Smithy was awake and saddling the horses when Nat woke the following morning. "You're up early," she said as she brushed her hair back from her face.

"My aching bladder woke me," Smithy replied.

"I can understand that. I'll be back," Nat said as she climbed from her bedroll and walked toward the bushes.

"I'm going to stroll over the hill, just to check," Smithy called after her.

Nat returned, secured her bedroll behind her saddle, dug out the bag with the biscuits, and took a bite. The fire had long burned out, but she poured water on it as a precaution and then filled their canteens at the creek.

Smithy shook his head when he returned. "No sign of them this morning." He climbed onto Willow and accepted a biscuit from Nat. "Thanks. I think I was dreaming of this during the night."

Nat swung into the saddle and pulled out the last biscuit. "I'm ready for some home cooking."

"Let's go home," Smithy said as he urged Willow forward.

†

Marissa handed Tom two biscuits as he walked through the kitchen. "You need to eat before you fly out of here."

"I will," Tom called back. He stopped long enough to grab his gun.

"I guess I'd better get moving, too," Maggie said. She took the biscuit from Marissa.

"I'll be there shortly," Marissa said. "I'll pack something for a quick lunch and be down."

"I think we'll have a few geese today," Maggie said. "I'll take care of cleaning them if you'll hand the shingles up to Tom.

"That's not a problem," Marissa replied.

Maggie had barely stepped off the back porch when the first of two shots filled the air. "Damn, that was fast," Maggie said with a chuckle.

When Maggie arrived at Tom's cabin, he had two geese lying beside the stack of shingles. "Good job, Tom," Maggie called to him.

"Let them settle back on the lake, and I'll try for a couple more."

Maggie nodded toward the ladder. "I'll hand shingles up to you until Marissa arrives, and then I'll go take care of the birds."

"Sounds good to me," Tom said and scrambled up the ladder and then climbed onto the roof supports.

Maggie carefully climbed the ladder and picked up a shingle to hand up to Tom. "Does it feel like they fit together tightly?"

"Pretty snug," Tom called down.

Maggie picked up the next board to hand up to him. She watched the concentration on Tom's face as he gently maneuvered the shingle to overlap the previous one. He shifted the placement until he got the perfect fit then nailed it to the supports. He had set ten shingles when Marissa arrived.

"Wow, this is looking like a cabin," Marissa said. She climbed into the loft and looked at the progress Tom had made. "I see he has already shot some geese."

"Yep, if you take over here, I'll take care of the birds." Maggie handed her a shingle and climbed down from the loft. "I'll be back."

†

"I lost count after one hundred logs," Smithy said as they passed the small campsite. "There are plenty to ship into town a load at a time. You don't want to send too many, or the mill operator will lower your price. Keep him hungry for good wood."

Nat smiled at Smithy. "I plan on doing just that. We could send Tom into town tomorrow or the next day with a load of cedar for your shingles. Maybe toss a few of the cottonwoods in to pay for the shingles."

"Do you think he'll have enough to finish his roof?"

"With some to spare," Nat replied. "I think we can send enough logs to cover your whole roof. Tom may need to spend the night in town to wait on the shingles, but we've got plenty of other things to do. I want to send a big order back to town with you when you go later this week."

"Do you have some pelts that are ready?" Smithy asked.

"I bet I could round up a few. We will have plenty of seafood to send as well. Remind me to ask Tom to see if there are more pickle barrels. Now that we found new pools, we can fill up even more."

As they neared the end of the trail, two shots from Tom's rifle filled the air. Smithy looked at Nat. "Tom's rifle, so they probably have him hunting something."

Smithy relaxed in his saddle. "Thanks for riding out with me. It was a good break."

"I didn't realize how tired I was."

"When Tom and I come out for good, maybe we can help out. I know there's a lot of things I need you to teach me. Do you think I could run a small trapline?"

"I don't see why you both can't," Nat answered. "I'll make a list of the supplies you'll need."

"I won't need much income, especially if I can eventually sell the store, but would you consider partnering with me to help with the seafood and feeding me from time to time?"

"Feeding you should never be a problem. You will be welcome at our table anytime. We could use an extra set of hands with the seafood, especially with the new pools." She took a drink from her canteen. "I may even consider going a bit further north to explore what else we've been missing."

"You may find more pools no one has ever seen," Smithy said.

"That's true. We may even find a need to build a small shelter depending on how far we travel."

"This is all so exciting," Smithy said.

"We can't wait for y'all to join us." Nat shot him a grin. "Do you plan to talk to Tom about the lumber idea tonight?"

"I thought I might," Smithy said. "I'll wait to see how far he's managed to make it on his cabin."

"We should know that in a few more minutes. We are not far from the lake now."

†

"Two more nice birds, Tom," Maggie said when he brought them to her for processing. "How far have you gotten on the roof?"

"Only about two more rows to go," he answered. "Do you think Nat would be all right with me sleeping down there?"

"Tom, that will be your home soon. You don't need Nat's permission. Go ahead and take your cot when you head back down."

"Yes, ma'am. Thank you for all your help, Maggie. I couldn't have made it this far without y'all's help."

"That's what friends and neighbors do, Tom." Maggie smiled.

Tom noticed Maggie was taking good care of the feathers and had some already boiling in the pot. "What do you plan to do with those feathers?"

"With a few more geese, I could make some pillows or something. I noticed mine was getting thin," Maggie said.

"Should I try to get you a few more then?"

"You can't have too many feathers or smoked geese," Maggie replied.

"Do you think I should start with a small smokehouse or build one the size of your new one?"

211

"I'd say go big," Maggie answered. "There is so much hunting we have yet to do, and so far, we are barely reaching outside a morning's walk."

"If we manage a bison, I could use a smokehouse." Tom smiled.

"We can work on that after you finish your roof. We still have doors and windows to plan out, too. We need to measure for windows before you head into town, so be thinking of where you want them. I'd recommend one in the kitchen for sure."

"I reckon I need to figure out how I'll get water from the spring, too," Tom said.

"Nat's the expert on that. She can figure that out in no time."

"I have so much to learn from you all."

"Plenty of time to learn it, too, so don't feel like you have to rush," Maggie warned.

"Yes, ma'am," he answered, and returned a few minutes later, carrying his sleeping cot and blanket.

"I'll be back down shortly," Maggie called as he passed by on his way to the lake. She began plucking feathers from the geese. "We need to have some smoked geese soon," she called out to Luna.

Luna whimpered and stood from her bed on the porch.

"You are looking good. Do you want to come down with me?" Maggie walked over and moved the bench blocking Luna's path. She watched her take several steps forward and was surprised Luna didn't limp or showed signs of pain. "It must be nice to be young and heal fast," Maggie said. "Let me pick you up, so you don't have to climb steps."

Maggie reached down and cradled the dog in her arms, and set her safely on the ground.

Luna slowly walked toward the processing table and laid down to watch Maggie work. "That's a good girl," Maggie praised her, and she walked into the smokehouse to fetch a bone for Luna to gnaw.

†

When Nat and Smithy crested the last hill, they could see Tom's cabin.

"He has been busy since we left," Nat said. "Should we turn around and wait a few more hours?"

"It looks like he's on his last few shingles," Smithy said.

"Yeah, it does. Let's see if there is anything we can help with."

Marissa turned her head at the sound of their approach and beamed a smile at the riders. "Welcome home," she said.

"Thanks. It was a nice ride, but no signs of bison yet. Is there anything we can do?" Nat asked.

"We are just about done with the roof," Tom called down. "I think we plan on taking a break to prepare a feast for tonight."

"Why don't you two go ahead and care for your horses, and we'll meet you at home soon? Maggie is already there working on a couple of geese Tom shot earlier."

"We heard the shots. I was wondering what you had shot." Nat smiled at Tom.

"Maggie wanted goose feathers for some pillows, so I've gotten four for her today," Tom explained.

"Good job. I reckon we'll see you at the house then." Nat looked at the stack of shingles. "You had quite a few leftovers," she commented.

Tom nodded. "Enough to start Smithy's roof."

Nat looked at Smithy and smiled. "We need to talk about some changes in plans when you finish here. We've got some ideas we want to run by you."

"Sounds good. We won't be much longer," Tom replied and returned to work.

Nat and Smithy rode on to the cabin, with Gyp dancing beside them.

†

Maggie turned when she heard Nat and Smithy approach. She was finishing the last goose and was ready to hang him in the smokehouse when Nat stepped off Hardy.

"Welcome back."

"Thanks. Tom says you are working on feathers for pillows," Nat replied.

Maggie shook her head. "Not entirely true but not false either. Marissa and I thought we would make them a bed for a wedding present."

"That is a great idea," Nat replied. "Will you have enough feathers for the mattress and pillows now?"

"Probably not, but we can add a few more geese to the smokehouse in the coming days. I think six more should do it. Marissa is going to get fabric from the general store for us to use."

Nat's creative wheels were turning. "I may have some heavy rope leftover for supports. I bet we could use some of the cedar boards for rails. I know I can find plenty of saplings for posts and can carve something nice for them."

"I was thinking of ordering a cookstove for them," Smithy said. "One for me too."

"That will set them up the right way," Nat said. "Ours has made a huge difference."

"I hear we are having a feast," Smithy said. "What can we do to help until then? Oh, hey Luna," Smithy said when he saw her curled up in the sun. Gyp had laid down beside her pup.

"I guess someone was tired of the porch," Nat replied.

"I took off her splint, and she's walking well. I carried her down the steps, but she's done some walking." Maggie smiled. "The young ones heal much better than we do." Maggie shrugged at Smithy. "We harvested the pools yesterday, and Tom ran one of your traplines. We skinned two nice beavers and some mink," Maggie said as she pointed out the drying pelts.

"We'll tend to the horses and see what we can get into," Nat teased. She led Hardy to the barn, followed by Smithy and Willow.

Maggie was sitting on the porch steps when Nat and Smithy returned. Nat looked into the barrels. "That will make a nice load into town."

"We've got buttons, smoked fish, and jerky ready for the town delivery as well," Maggie replied.

Nat sat beside her, while Smithy stretched out beside Luna and Gyp. "We plan to send Tom to town tomorrow with a load of logs and an order of shingles to cut for Smithy's house so that he may stay overnight. You did such a fine job on the smokehouse. Would you mind helping us build one for Tom while he's gone?"

"I know where he wants it. He wants a big one like ours. We can start digging as soon as he leaves. We may need more boards cut to finish off the roof. I'll go down and survey the pile and see what we need so you can place that order with him. He'll be none the wiser," Maggie reported.

"Count the shingles, too, so we know how many cedar trees to send, please," Smithy said.

"Go check out the smokehouses and see what you want to send. We've put in more fish since you've been gone," Maggie told Nat.

"Let's go see," Nat said to Smithy. "We need to send that moose hindquarter in, too, for the hog."

†

"Hey Marissa," Tom called down from the roof.

"I bet you need the ladder," Marissa teased.

"Yes, ma'am, I've got no other way down except jumping."

"Hang on, and I'll bring it around." Marissa carried the ladder and leaned it against the edge of the cabin. "It probably wouldn't hurt to make another of these a bit longer in case you have to make repairs. We'll eventually need to cut holes in the roof for a cookstove and fireplace," she reminded him.

"I hadn't thought of that," Tom replied as he scrambled down the ladder and carried it back inside.

"I'd recommend the fireplace close to your bedrooms, once you figure those out," Marissa said.

"I know where I want those." Tom pointed out two areas of the floorplan. "So maybe the fireplace and cookstove here?"

Marissa saw where Tom was indicating and smiled. His ideas were almost identical to their cabin. "That works well." Marissa smiled. "Maggie and I can work on chinking your logs, but you or Smithy will have to do the higher sections."

"What will we need for chinking?"

"Ash from the fireplace and pits, sand, clay, or some mud from the lake. Anything that will mold together nicely to dry and seal any gaps in the logs."

"River rocks. I'll need those too for the fireplace and foundation, right?"

"I like Maggie's suggestion for the clamshells. I think once boiled to rid them of the fishy smell, they will work well, but yes on the fireplace."

"I'll begin bringing some from our watering hole at the creek on my way from town. There are plenty there to choose."

"Flat and a variety of sizes," Marissa suggested.

"What else haven't I planned for?" Tom asked.

"You can bring the bathtub from my cabin here. A hot bath is a luxury you don't want to live without," she smiled. "You can bathe in the lake, but Ruth won't want that."

Tom shrugged. "I'm about ready for a dip in that lake."

"You've been working hard," Marissa reminded him. "You are always welcome to use ours."

"I think the lake will be warm enough to get me clean," Tom replied.

217

†

Tom and Marissa found the others sitting in the front yard at the table when they returned. Luna had joined them as well.

"Look at you, Luna," Marissa crooned and knelt to pet the dog. "Feeling much better, I see."

"I think the bone broth worked wonders on her," Maggie said. "Not ready to run or climb just yet, but it won't be too long."

Nat smiled at Marissa. "So, what's the plan for the rest of the day?"

"Maggie and I have a feast planned for tonight. You, Tom, and Smithy can do whatever as long as it's not in our kitchen," Marissa teased.

"We have some talking to do, and then we may take a trip to the pools," Nat said.

"That's fine as long as you're back in time for supper," Marissa replied.

"Have you ever known us to miss supper?" Smithy teased.

"No, but there's always a first," Maggie said. "I have a quick chore to do, but I'll be back soon."

"Do you need some help?" Tom asked.

"No, but you can hitch Quincy to the wagon if y'all are going to the pools," Maggie suggested.

"I'll be right back then," Tom said, and walked with Maggie toward the barn.

Nat waited until they got out of earshot before looking at Marissa. "I love the idea of making them a bed."

Smithy nodded. "I'm going to get them a cookstove so they can start off right."

"I'm sure between us we can help them get set up. I heard Tom say Marissa said he could bring the bathtub from her place."

"I think we'll all be in good shape," Smithy responded. "This is so exciting."

Tom pulled Quincy around and had already stored empty buckets and the fish trap in the wagon. "Marissa said to give you these." Tom handed Nat the shoes Maggie had made for her.

"Since you got a few more beavers, we'll ask Maggie to make you all a pair of these. They are much more accessible than taking your boots and socks off to wade out to the pools. Just slip your feet in and out. They feel good, too," Nat said as she slipped her feet into them.

"Before we go, there are some things we'd like to discuss with you," Smithy said. "Take a seat. It won't take long."

Tom sat down next to Smithy. "Did I not do something right?"

"No, Tom, you've done everything so perfectly. We wanted to run an idea past you," Nat said.

"I lost count at over a hundred logs along the trail Nat cut that will go to waste if we don't use them. We thought you, Nat, and me on occasion, could move them up to the lake for a stockpile and begin taking a load here and there into the sawmill for sale or more boards if we need them for projects," Smithy said.

"I don't see any problem with that," Tom said.

"I'd like to send you down three days a week to work on that and to begin building my cabin, and keep you on the payroll at the store, so you don't lose income. You could come down on Friday and work through Tuesday when you'd bring a load of logs or goods back to town."

"So, I'd have time to work on my place and yours and still get paid?" Tom asked for clarity.

"That's right, and to help Nat when she needs you. We don't plan on sending big loads of logs to keep the mill owner hungry for wood," Smithy said. "We'd like to load you with some cedar and some cottonwood to take to town tomorrow. You'd have to stay overnight to get my shingles cut, but you could check in with Ruth and take some goods to town for Nat."

Tom looked at Nat with tears in his eyes. "I'd be a fool to turn that opportunity down."

Nat nodded and replied. "Yeah, you would, so don't. We've got work to do around here to build up our three homesteads."

"Deal," Tom said and offered Smithy his hand. "Let's get to work." Tom smiled.

Tom led Quincy down to the beach with Nat and Smithy in tow. "Which way do you want to go?"

"Let's head north, Tom. Those pools seem to be plentiful," Nat answered. "While Tom and I harvest, I want you to do something else," she told Smithy.

"What would that be?" he asked.

"I want you to scout farther north and see if there are more pools or resources we can use. If you think it a worthy spot, see if you can locate a place to add a temporary shelter."

"No problem, Nat," Smithy replied.

When they reached the first pool, Tom climbed onto the wagon bed and removed his boots and socks. Nat looked at Smithy. "You don't need to walk for more than an hour at most. If you don't see positive signs, turn back and come home."

"Will do," Smithy said, then started down the shore. Gyp trotted along with him.

"Let's go see what the pools have to offer today," Nat said to Tom.

Tom and Nat filled every bucket they had with various fish, crab, shrimp, and lobster. Tom dumped the last container of fish into the bed of the wagon and looked north. "Smithy should be heading back by now, shouldn't he?"

"He'll be along directly. Why don't we dig some clams for Maggie while we wait?" Nat suggested.

Tom and Nat filled the bed of the wagon with clams, and they were about to start for home when they heard Gyp barking as she chased a sea bird. Nat could see Smithy walking in the distance. "Here he comes."

They waited for Smithy to arrive with news of his scouting trip. Smithy wore a big smile on his face as he got nearer. "You are going to love what I found," Smithy said. "About a half-mile or so, a small cove acts as a large tidal pool. The tide was out, but there were plenty of creatures to make it worth the trip. Fish I've never seen and huge ones at that." He started walking with them. "The cove would make a good campsite, too, and has freshwater not far away."

"Good job, Smithy," Nat said and patted him on the back. "We can probably blaze a trail wide enough for Rusty and the big wagon with no problem."

"That would be ideal," Smithy agreed.

Nat looked at Tom. "See, the work never ends."

When they pulled up in the yard, Tom and Smithy began dumping the buckets of seafood in the barrels while

Nat started cleaning and filleting the fish for smoking. When there was nothing left but the clams, Tom looked at Nat.

"Will you show me how to shell these?"

"I'd better do that," Maggie said. "Nat will have you massacring the poor things. Put some of them in a bucket of cold water and bring them here."

Tom filled a bucket halfway with water and dumped some clams into it before joining Maggie on the porch steps. Tom and Smithy observed as Maggie showed them how to open the shells and cut the meat from inside. Maggie watched Tom try his hand at shelling and declared, "You've got this. Drop the shells in a bucket, and you can boil them later and take them to your cabin for a drip line. I'll bring a bowl out for you to put the clams into."

"Thanks, Maggie," Tom replied.

"What can I do?" Smithy asked.

"You can scatter the fish remains in the garden for me and start hanging them in the smokehouse," Nat instructed.

†

After finishing their chores, Nat, Tom, and Smithy retired to the table in the front yard. "So the plan is to load up some cedar logs and cottonwood for me to take into town?" Tom said.

"Yes, with some items for the general store. You can also let Randall at the hotel know you'll be bringing a big order in later this week. I do believe the ladies have a list of goods they want you to pick up as well," Nat said.

"I'll get up early and get Rusty ready," Tom said.

"We still have cedar and cottonwood close to the lake, so by mid-morning, we will have the logs loaded. You can add the items from here and be on your way," Nat said.

Marissa arrived and set the table for supper. "Is there anything we can do to help?" Tom asked.

"Draw up a bucket of water. Then you can come inside and begin carrying dishes out," Marissa replied. "You two, just stay out of the way." She winked at Nat and Smithy.

†

After another fantastic meal, Tom bid everyone a good night. Nat loaned him a lantern to find his way and light the cabin for his first night in his home.

"Bundle up, so you don't get cold," Maggie warned and handed him another blanket.

"Thanks, Maggie. I'll see you down at the lake in the morning," Tom said.

"Goodnight, Tom. Sleep well," Nat called after him.

"I bet he's so excited he doesn't sleep," Smithy said with a chuckle.

"I sure know I will," Nat replied. "That bed will feel much better than the cold ground did last night." She stood and stretched. "I think I'll turn in."

"I'll be right there," Marissa said. "I need to finalize our lists for supplies with Maggie and Smithy."

"Goodnight, then," Nat said and walked inside.

CHAPTER NINE

Tom had managed to load several of the cedar logs before Nat and Smithy arrived the following day, and with Nat's help, they cut the cottonwoods to the lengths they needed.

"Stop by the cabin, and Marissa and Maggie will help you load the goods and give you the shopping lists," Nat said as they loaded the last log onto the wagon.

"Have a safe trip, and we'll see you tomorrow," Smithy said.

"Maggie is going to bring Quincy down with the small wagon when Tom leaves. She'll bring shovels down so we can begin setting the posts for his smokehouse."

"If Maggie can load the shingles in Quincy's wagon, I'll go ahead and move them up to my build site," Smithy said. "Should we go ahead and cut some of those pine poles for the smokehouse until she gets here?"

"Yes, that should get us warmed up," Nat replied. They measured out nine-foot sections and had four sawed by the time Maggie arrived with the wagon. "Let's cut the last two, and we can load a few of them on the wagon and start digging the holes."

"What can I do?" Maggie asked.

"Go ahead and measure the spots for the holes and mark them with a shovel, so we know exactly where they will go," Nat answered.

After cutting the last logs, Nat and Smithy loaded two of them onto the small wagon and dropped them at the cabin. Maggie had begun digging the holes, and by the next load, she had one done and was working on a second. Nat and Smithy carried the final logs and put one pole in the hole Maggie had finished.

"If you fill this one in, I'll start digging," Nat told Smithy.

The poles were secured, and Maggie began adding the boards with Smithy's help. Nat dug the center hole for the firepit, placing the dirt next to the cabin to use in the chinking. Marissa arrived with fresh water and an empty bucket.

"Do you feel like playing in the mud?" Marissa asked Nat.

"You want to start the chinking, don't you?"

"I'd like to unless there is something else we need to do," Marissa answered.

"I'll need to collect some buckets of ash from the fire pit and fireplace," Nat stated.

"I've got four filled, but I need Quincy's wagon to bring them down."

"Let's kill two birds with one stone. Help me load the shingles onto the wagon, and we'll drop them at Smithy's build site and pick up the buckets of ash on the way back down." Nat waited on Marissa's answer.

"That's fine with me. You carry, and I'll stack the shingles in the wagon."

"Fine," Nat said, and started carrying out several shingles at a time until they were all safely stored in the wagon. "Do you two need anything from the cabin?"

"Pick up another bag of nails from the barn," Maggie requested.

"The hand saw, too," Smithy added.

"Got it," Nat said and took Quincy's lead. She reached for Marissa's hand as they started around the lake. "We've had such good weather lately," Nat said as they walked.

"I know. I can't believe it hasn't rained in days. Someone must be smiling down on us." Marissa smiled. "At least Tom got his roof on. It will be a good test to see if he has any leaks when it rains."

"That's true. I bet Tom will be surprised when he gets back to see his smokehouse built and part of his cabin chinked. I hope we have enough boards to finish the smokehouse. If not, it will be close."

Marissa shrugged her shoulders. "That way, Tom could add the remaining boards to feel like he had a hand in building it."

"You always think of the little things, don't you?" Nat smiled.

"I try. I know how important this place is to Tom, and well, to all of us. The cove sounds interesting, too. Maggie and I can help out with blazing the trail if needed."

"With all of us working together, it would be a breeze. We could use Rusty to carry the bigger logs to go to town, while Quincy can handle the saplings. We can use the smaller pieces of firewood at the new site or in the smokers."

"I may think of the little things, but you see plans in a much broader scope. You're always looking toward the future. That's one of the many things I love about you," Marissa said.

Nat pulled Quincy to a stop. "I think this will be a good place for his shingles. Give me a minute to walk to the barn for an ax. I want to stack them off the ground a bit to keep them from getting wet or warping."

"That's a good idea. Bring a hatchet, and I'll trim the branches," Marissa offered.

"I'll be right back. Gyp, stay," she told her dog.

†

Smithy and Maggie worked well together. She would nail for a bit while he held the boards in place, and then they would swap positions. They finished one side and were well on the way across the back when Marissa and Nat returned.

"That looks good," Nat told them. "Marissa had an idea while we were gone. I don't think we'll have enough boards to finish it, but if we do, how about leaving the last few for Tom, so he feels like he had a hand in the build?"

"That's a great suggestion. By our calculations, we should be about six boards short on the roof," Smithy said.

"We'll work until we run out and then can help with the chinking."

"That sounds like a good plan," Nat said. She walked to the lake and filled a bucket with water, and mixed water with the ash and soil from the pit she dug. Nat picked up a handful of the mixture and pushed it between the small space between two logs. "Press it in as deep as you can and move on," she told Marissa.

"Kind of like making mud pies when we were little." Marissa laughed.

Nat cocked her head at Marissa. "I guess so."

Maggie shook her head and smiled as she lifted the next board for Smithy. "I doubt Nat ever made mud pies," she whispered to Smithy.

"I'd be surprised if she had. She passed it off well, though," Smithy whispered.

As the afternoon wore on, Marissa looked at Nat. "We haven't given any thought to supper."

Nat slapped another handful of mud on the cabin. "How about some eggs and ham steaks? I can cut a few steaks off the smoked hog, and we can drop them in a pan to warm while you cook some eggs."

"We've got bread for sopping, too," Marissa said. "That won't be hard at all. I don't know about y'all, but I'm ready to head home and get my hands cleaned."

"I agree. We've chinked two sides of the cabin, so we've made good progress," Smithy said. "If you want a break from chinking tomorrow, we can spend the morning working on the new trail. We don't have Rusty, but we can move bigger trees to the side."

Nat nodded. "We could work on that until midday when I expect Tom will return. Then we can finish the smokehouse and maybe the chinking."

"I think that's possible," Maggie agreed. "If you'll cut a few extra ham steaks, I'll put some biscuits on later for breakfast."

Smithy tended to Quincy while Nat washed up and went to the smokehouse for ham steaks. She cut several extra as requested and carried them into the kitchen.

"This ought to be enough," Nat said as she laid them on a platter.

"Go join Smithy on the porch, and we'll call you when supper is ready," Marissa said.

Nat walked out to the porch and took off her boots. She had gotten into the habit of slipping into her shoes whenever possible. "Ah, that's better," she said as she sat next to Smithy.

"They look nice, too. Maybe Maggie will make us all a pair," Smithy said loud enough for Maggie to hear.

"I'll work on it," Maggie hollered back from the kitchen.

Nat smiled at Smithy and pulled out a new block of wood to begin shaving. She wanted to make two wolves as decoration for the head posts on Tom and Ruth's bed. Wolves mated for life, and she hoped Tom and Ruth would have a good life and grow old together.

Smithy watched her hands work the wood. "Do you know what you're making?"

"This time, I do. I want to carve two wolves for Tom and Ruth's bed."

"That's a great idea. I know Tom will be very proud to have a handmade piece from you. He cherishes the knife you made him like a chunk of gold."

†

The smell of ham steaks warming woke Nat, and she climbed out of bed. Smithy was sitting at the table drinking coffee when she entered the kitchen.

"Either Rufus is off schedule, or y'all got up early," Nat said.

"Rufus isn't even awake yet," Maggie said.

"When we finish eating, why don't you and I take the axes and walk down the beach to the cove. We can start cutting a trail, and when Marissa and Maggie bring Quincy down later, we can start loading his wagon and hauling saplings."

Nat nodded. "That's fine with me. We could get a jumpstart, and they can trim and load while we continue to cut."

"Makes sense to us," Maggie said. "There's no need to stand around waiting for you to cut saplings, and I'm sure Marissa doesn't mind a bit of extra sleep." Maggie handed them a plate of food. "Eat up so you can get going."

"I'll go grab the axes and a file and meet you out on the porch. Will you bring the hatchets and a bucket of water when you come?" Smithy asked Maggie.

"Yes. I've already filled your canteens. They are sitting next to your rifle on the porch," Maggie said to Nat. "You'll be in unfamiliar territory, and you don't know the animal population. I'd hate for you to run across a hungry bear."

"I'll keep it close," Nat promised as Smithy left the cabin. "Bring my old rifle on the wagon in case we are separated."

"Will do," Maggie said.

"Don't let her sleep too late. I don't want her to think she can skip out on all the fun," Nat said. "Thanks for breakfast."

"We'll see you soon."

†

Nat looked up at the sky as they walked down the beach. "We may get some rain soon."

"We need some, just not a bunch all at once. A gentle shower for a bit would be good," Smithy said.

"I hope that's what we get. Driving a wagon of any size on muddy roads is no fun. Hopefully, Tom will make it back before it sets in," Nat said.

"Yeah, I didn't think about the wagon being fully loaded."

When they reached the cove, Nat's eyes grew wide with excitement. "This is incredible."

They picked a good spot for a campsite and began the trail back home. As they hugged the coast, they found that there were few large trees in the path.

"I guess the wind and salt from the ocean prevent the trees from growing tall here. Large ones a bit farther in, but this will make our trail much more manageable."

"Yes, it will," Smithy said and resumed cutting saplings. "We should be stocked well for firewood at the new site. Are you planning a small lean-to or something more permanent?"

"I was thinking of a small shelter about the size of a smokehouse to flee the elements, and potentially protect some pelts or other goods if needed," Nat answered. "We have plenty logs to turn into boards, and we can use some of the larger saplings for posts."

"That won't be hard at all to build," Smithy agreed. "We could probably use several more bags of nails. I'll send some out with Tom when he comes next."

"I am excited to have him here more often. I feel like we can complete projects more quickly with the extra set of hands," Nat said as she chopped.

"I hope when he returns at the end of next week, y'all can check on the bison herd," Smithy said.

"I may do that before he comes and send him back for you if they have arrived," Nat said.

"That would work too," Smithy agreed.

†

Maggie picked her way through the forest along the coastline, leading Quincy and Marissa toward the sound of axes digging into the wood.

"It doesn't sound like they are too far ahead," Maggie told Marissa.

"There." Marissa pointed to Nat in the distance.

Nat looked up to see Marissa, Maggie, and Quincy approaching. "Good morning," she said. "Glad y'all made it."

"Good morning," Marissa replied.

"The trail ahead looks like mostly saplings," Maggie stated.

"Yes, that's what we've encountered so far." Nat removed her hat and ran her hand through her hair. "We've decided on a small shelter about the size of the smokehouse at the cove. We can use six of the biggest saplings for poles and the rest for firewood."

"It doesn't look like anything too big for Quincy to handle," Maggie said. "Do you want us to pick out poles and haul them to the cove first? Then we can start working back toward you."

"That's as good a plan as I've heard today. We may have to call it off early if it starts to rain," Nat warned. "I know we won't melt, but no sense risking getting sick either."

"We'll get a move on then," Maggie replied. "You're only about a half hour's walk to the cabin."

Nat nodded and resumed cutting saplings as Maggie and Marissa started trimming branches and placing saplings in the wagon.

Smithy took a break for some water. "We must be over halfway to the cabin by now."

"Maggie said it was only about a half-hour to home."

"Unless it gets much thicker, we should have this knocked out before Tom gets home," Smithy replied as he ran the file across his blade to sharpen the edge.

"Definitely the cutting part. We can always spend a bit of time each day hauling the saplings if needed. I don't see anything that Maggie and Marissa can't lift." Nat took a drink and reached for the file. "This was such a good find, Smithy."

†

"Wow," Marissa said when they reached the end of the trail at the cove. "This is a beautiful spot."

"Look at all the fish in the water," Maggie said. "Maybe more difficult to catch in a larger space, but there are so many."

"I wonder if we can use some burlap or netting to make the catch easier?" Marissa said.

"Or see if the general store can get us some fishnets." Maggie laughed.

"Yeah, I guess those would work well," Marissa replied. "Let's drop these poles and start trimming our way back to Nat and Smithy."

"Let's make a small stack of saplings to use for firewood here since we are already close. Maybe a dozen or so."

"That makes good sense, Maggie."

After piling over a dozen of the closest saplings, Maggie and Marissa started back down the trail. They trimmed the saplings and cut them in half to load onto the wagon.

†

When Nat and Smithy came in sight of the cabin, they were surprised Maggie and Marissa hadn't caught up with them. "Do you want to go check on them, and I'll start trimming?" Smithy asked.

Nat shrugged. "I can hear them chopping, so I think they are good. Let's trim to meet them, and we can load Quincy down."

Marissa smiled and waved when she saw Nat. "We decided to drop the poles and a dozen of the saplings for firewood at the cove."

"That was a good idea." Nat looked at the wagon. "Did Quincy pull this load okay?"

"Yes, I figured we'd go dump these and come back for more," Maggie answered.

"We have the trimming done the rest of the way, so why don't we all head in and have a bit of lunch? Smithy and I can finish loading and hauling the rest."

"How about I cook some eggs to go with the leftover ham?" Marissa asked. "My biscuits are long gone."

"That works for me," Nat replied. She took Quincy's lead and started walking home. She and Smithy unloaded while Maggie fetched eggs and Marissa started warming the ham.

"It will take them a few minutes to cook. Do you want to stay and split the wood for the smokehouse, and I'll bring in more?" Smithy asked.

"I'm good with that," Nat answered. She picked up an ax and began chopping a sapling into smaller sections. "I'll give you a whistle when the food is ready."

†

Maggie brought in a dozen eggs. "Are you up to trying something a bit different?"

"Sure, what do you have in mind?"

"Warm the ham, and we can cut it into cubes, add some cheese and whip up the eggs, then cook them all together."

"Let's give it a try. You whip the eggs and add the cheese while I warm the ham."

"Do you want to add a bit of sausage on the side?" Maggie asked.

"It would be a heartier meal," Marissa said. "If you watch the ham, I'll go get some."

Maggie nodded as she cut small chunks of cheese. She found an onion and decided to add that as well. "Why not?" she asked herself and diced the onion.

Nat stopped chopping as Marissa approached. "Where ya going?"

"We've decided to add some sausage so there will be plenty of meat with the meal."

"That's always good," Nat answered and resumed chopping.

"Where's Smithy?" Marissa asked.

"Went back for more saplings. I told Smithy I'd give him a whistle when the food was ready."

"You two just won't relax, will you?"

"Not when there's work to be done, ma'am," Nat answered.

"Fine, I'll let you know when we're close," Marissa took the sausage and entered the cabin as Nat continued to chuckle.

A few minutes later, Nat heard Rusty's harness. She walked to the back door. "I hope you have more eggs. Tom is on his way."

"We'll add a few," Maggie hollered back. "Go ahead and get Smithy heading this way."

"Yes, ma'am," Nat answered and left the porch. She let out a loud whistle and waited for a return from Smithy. When she heard his whistle, she continued to chop until Tom pulled into the yard. "Welcome back." She looked at the load he was hauling. "Leave this until after we eat."

Tom hopped down and drew a bucket of water for Rusty. "What are you up to."

"Chopping some of the saplings we cut this morning as we blazed a trail to the cove."

"You're already done?" Tom asked.

"Just with the cutting. We still have more saplings to haul here and chop for the smokehouse."

"I can help you with that after we get unloaded. Is it a big enough project for Rusty?"

"No, not really. I think after dumping this load, Smithy will bring in one more which ought to finish."

"Hey Tom," Marissa said, as she wiped her hands on her apron. "You've got good timing."

"Yes, ma'am. I'm rarely late for a meal," Tom grinned. "I got everything on your list and three more barrels. The owner said he hoped for more soon."

"I want you to ask him if he can order a fishnet," Marissa said. "Maggie and I have decided if we had a net, it would make catching the fish at the cove easier. If he can't get one, maybe a big roll, of burlap, and we'll make something that may work."

"I bet he could get one," Tom said. "Especially if it helps to keep him supplied with smoked fish. He says as soon as the town folk see Rusty, they flock to the store to see if he has more fish and sausage."

"That's a good thing," Marissa said. "They aren't hard to make."

"Did you see Ruth?" Nat asked.

"Yes, I took her to dinner last night at the hotel. The owner said he was excited about a seafood delivery and wouldn't let me pay for dinner." Tom smiled.

"I bet she was glad to see you," Marissa said.

"I think so. Ruth's mighty curious as to what we're doing down here," he chuckled.

"She will be impressed with the home you are making. I see you got some river stones for the fireplace," Nat said.

"I thought I'd grab a few while Rusty drank," Tom said.

"After unloading the house goods, we can take the shingles up to Smithy's spot and drop the rest at the lake. Was the mill owner pleased with the logs?"

"He said he'd buy anything you bring in," Tom answered.

Smithy arrived, and Tom drew a bucket of water for Quincy.

Marissa nodded at Nat. "I reckon we'd better go eat before it gets cold. Maggie and I are trying something different for y'all. The food's set up around the front."

"I'll grab some water," Nat said. "Let's eat, boys."

They walked around to the front and took seats at the table.

"Maggie and I thought we'd do a bit of experimenting today to see if you liked this new concoction," Marissa explained.

"It looks and smells good," Nat said as she took a spoonful and a sausage and passed the plate to Tom.

Tom scooped a bite of the eggs and swallowed. "I don't think you'll like this, Smithy, so you can pass them back this way."

"Not on your life," Smithy answered and passed along the plate

"Wow, this is tasty, ladies," Tom said.

Nat took a bite and nodded her head. "I agree with Tom. What is in this dish?"

"Eggs, chopped ham steak, diced cheese, and some sweet onion," Maggie replied.

Marissa smiled. "We did do good, Maggie. This taste is wonderful."

Maggie took a bite. "Something different."

"You can experiment on me anytime," Smithy smiled.

Nat was the first to eat her fill, and she smiled when she saw Tom eyeing the last piece of sausage. "Go ahead, Tom. We'll start unloading Rusty, and then you and I can drop the shingles with Smithy's help."

"I'll carry the dishes inside," Marissa said. "Bring yours when you finish, please, Tom."

Tom picked up the sausage and stuffed it in his mouth, and grabbed his plate. "Right behind you."

They emptied the wagon of everything except for the building supplies, and Tom led Rusty down the trail to Smithy's site. Once they had the shingles stacked, they continued down to the lake. As soon as Tom's cabin came into view, Tom stopped. "You're kidding me, right? You built me a smokehouse?"

"Well, not completely," Nat said. "You have the last boards in the wagon we need, so we thought we'd let you finish the roof."

"Oh, my goodness," Tom said, and his pace sped up as they walked to the cabin. "You've got some of the chinking done, too."

"We made it about halfway on the chinking," Smithy said. "It was nasty but a fun project," he laughed.

Nat looked at Tom. "We need more ash and some mud from the lake before we can continue."

"This is just amazing," Tom said as he surveyed the smokehouse. "You even dug the firepit?"

"Yes, now get your skinny butt on that roof so you can finish it," Smithy instructed.

Tom scrambled onto the roof and nailed the final three boards needed for the smokehouse. "This is fantastic," he said, with tears in his eyes.

"I'm going to pile up more of these boards while you and Smithy stack your river rocks. The rest we'll take back to the cabin. I want to use some of this for the shelter down at the cove."

"I can help with that," Tom said. "Now that I have a roof over my head, I can work on some inside walls at night."

Nat counted the boards on the wagon. "I'll only need the first four piles for the shelter. Let's place the rest of them inside for you to use."

"I want to make sure you have enough for the shelter first," Tom replied.

"Do you doubt my counting ability?" Nat teased.

"Never," Tom shook his head, "but I want to make sure your lumber need is taken care of first."

"There will be plenty more loads of logs and boards in the next few weeks," Smithy interjected.

"Well, let's get unloaded, and we can haul the boards to the cove. Since we'll have Rusty, we might as well collect the rest of the saplings on the way back. Marissa and Maggie can figure out something for supper," Nat said.

"Grab that shovel, too, and I'll start setting the posts. It appears we have this pattern down pat," Smithy said.

"You can set the posts, and I'll leave Tom with you while I pick up the rest of the saplings. With enough daylight, we might be able to get a wall or two up today," Nat suggested.

"You heard the lady, load the hammers and nails, and be sure to grab our measuring ropes." Smithy patted Tom on the shoulder. "I would have never dreamed those would come in so handy."

"They truly have," Nat agreed as she began offloading boards and carrying them inside.

†

Tom and Smithy continued down the path while Nat filled Maggie and Marissa in on their plans. "I can handle supper if you want to go help," Marissa told Maggie.

"Are you sure?" Maggie asked.

"I know you love building, and you and Smithy make a great team. Go, I can handle supper. Just don't make me have to come looking for y'all after dark."

"Gyp, stay," Nat commanded. "Guard the cabin for mama," she cooed to the dog. "We'll do our best to make it back before dark."

"Sooner, if this rain moves in," Marissa said. "I can smell it on the air."

"Yes, ma'am." Nat smiled and kissed her softly.

†

As Nat and Maggie walked toward the cove, Maggie said, "I think she's right about getting some rain tonight." She pointed across the water, and they could see dark clouds beginning to form.

241

"Hopefully, it will hold off for a few more hours yet," Nat said.

Tom was digging holes as Smithy secured the poles. Once they had one side secured, Maggie began building the wall. Nat finished unloading the boards and started down the trail. "I'll be back with fresh water since none of us thought to get some with all the excitement."

"You sure you don't need some help?" Tom asked.

"You are helping," Nat reminded him. "After finishing the poles, you can come help if Maggie and Smithy don't need you. I promised Marissa we'd be home before dark, so don't make me break that promise."

Nat stacked the last board and headed Rusty back down the trail. She was nearly finished with the last of the saplings when she heard faint rumblings of thunder in the distance. Tom caught up with her for the final few logs and then helped Nat unload them by the smokehouse. As the thunder continued to move closer, Nat looked at Tom. "I'll go get Smithy and Maggie if you unhitch Rusty and tend to him and the others. Be sure to give Quincy some molasses. He worked hard today, too."

"I will," Tom said, and walked Rusty to the barn as Nat headed down the trail.

†

Maggie and Smithy had managed to get three walls up on the shelter. Nat pointed across the water at the black clouds, hanging low with the weight of the rain.

"It's time we call it a day," Nat said. "Let's grab the tools and head back home."

Nat saw a bolt of lightning strike the ocean, and the thunder rolled for several long seconds.

"Yep, definitely time to call it a day," Smithy said, and grabbed a handful of tools and started toward the trail. "Let's go before we get wet."

Nat and Maggie took the hammers and nails and quickly caught up to Smithy.

Tom had run down to his cabin for the lantern and was racing back toward Nat's when they emerged from the trail.

"It looks like we are just making it in time," Nat said as the raindrops began pelting the roof.

"I was beginning to wonder about y'all," Marissa said as the group entered through the back door.

"We made it in the nick of time," Smithy said. "You sure have it smelling good in here."

"I thought we were due for a change, so I cooked some goose dumpling soup. I've got cornbread baking, too," Marissa replied as Nat opened the lid on the huge pot on the stove.

"They managed to get three walls up on the new shelter," Nat said. "We are getting good at this building stuff," she added.

"We're getting good practice in," Smithy said. "By the time we get to my place, things will go perfectly."

"That's the plan," Nat said. "Your buildings should go up quickly."

"We need to head back to town in two days. What is your plan for tomorrow?" Smithy asked.

"Marissa does an excellent job of keeping us fed. I think she should stay here and cut the saplings for the smokehouse between meals." Nat looked at Smithy. "You and Maggie can finish the shelter, then join Tom and me to finish up the chinking, weather permitting. Then all he has left for starters is a privy. We can work on the barn and corral once he's here."

"What if the rain doesn't pass through?" Maggie asked.

"We can relax or help Tom build his interior rooms and plan his fireplace," Nat replied.

"That's too many workers inside for me. I think Marissa and I will work on some projects here if it's still raining," Maggie replied. "I'd like to work on some shoes for the rest of us now that we have beaver tails."

"I'd like to sew us some tablecloths now that we have fabric," Marissa replied.

"See, no matter the weather, we always have things to do," Nat said as Maggie and Marissa began serving supper.

The rain continued to fall during the meal.

"It doesn't look like it will be letting up anytime soon, so I think I'll make a run for the cabin," Tom said.

Nat stood and walked over to the door. She pulled her long waterproof coat from a peg. "Take this. It will keep most of you dry."

Tom slipped the coat on and lit his lantern. "Thanks. I'll see you in the morning."

"Watch for leaks tonight," Smithy hollered to him as he walked to the back door.

"Will do," Tom answered.

Nat watched out the back door until the lantern disappeared and then returned to the table to drink some coffee. "That meal was delicious. Thank you for cooking it."

"It was mighty tasty if I do say so myself," Marissa said with a smile.

"I don't believe any of us will have difficulty sleeping tonight, especially with that rain coming down," Nat said and took a sip of coffee.

"Even without the rain," Smithy replied. "I'm whipped."

†

When everyone had retired for the evening, Nat and Marissa snuggled under the covers. "Do you and Maggie plan on starting the mattress cover, or are you going to really make table cloths?"

"I will make tablecloths for our new table, but if Maggie wants to begin the mattress cover, we can," Marissa said. "Do you remember the dimensions for this bed? It's so perfect. I want to make theirs the same."

"Seven feet long and ten feet wide. I had the lumber cut to those dimensions. I'll start working on the frame after they are gone. Smithy will need to send me more rope for supports, too."

"That sounds good. We will probably still need more feathers, though," Marissa said as her hand drifted low on Nat's stomach.

"I can arrange that," Nat said, then gasped as Marissa's fingers slipped between her dampened folds. "I do enjoy your powers of persuasion, though."

"I thought you might need a bit of encouragement," Marissa said as she slowly sank her fingers inside Nat's body.

"How about some mutual encouragement?" Nat requested as she guided Marissa's body on top of hers. "Oh yes, that's much better," Nat replied as her fingers found Marissa's wetness.

Marissa's mouth covered Nat's in a heated kiss as their bodies moved as one, and they came together in a rush of wetness, gasping for air. Nat rolled Marissa onto her back.

"How many beds do you want me to make?" She laughed softly and kissed Marissa sweetly.

"Just one for now, but I'm positive we may need others soon," Marissa teased.

"Not a problem," Nat replied as she tucked Marissa into her body and stared out the window. The raindrops formed small rivers as they flowed down the glass panes. The room would illuminate every few minutes from the lightning, which seemed to be moving closer. Marissa would jump at the rolling thunder that followed, and she snuggled closer to Nat. The wind howled as it circled the cabin, but Nat knew the same current would push the storm farther inland. She closed her eyes and listened to the rain as it pelted the roof, and fell asleep.

†

The following morning the sun was shining. The ground was saturated with the night's rain as Maggie walked around to check the plants in her garden. When she stepped back on the porch, Nat was stretching.

"How did the garden fare?"

"Lots of puddles, but the plants are all in good shape. I was worried that wind would break them in two."

"It did get a bit wild last night," Nat replied. "I'm going to walk down and check on Tom. Will you give us a whistle when breakfast is ready?"

"Sure will," Maggie said.

†

Nat stepped off the porch with Gyp rushing to catch up.

"Wait up, Nat," Maggie called out. "Someone else wants to go."

Nat turned to find Maggie struggling to lift Luna, but she set her gently on the ground. Luna licked her hand and walked toward Nat.

"So, you want a bit of adventure today?" Nat asked as Luna caught up to them. She reached down and stroked the dog's head. "Let's go, girls." Nat took off at a slower pace to allow Luna to keep up. She wasn't limping as bad, but Nat could tell her leg was still tender as she walked.

Tom was outside walking around the buildings when they arrived. "Good morning," he called out. "Is that Luna I see with you?"

"Yes, it is," Nat replied. "She needed to stretch her legs this morning. How did the buildings hold up last night?"

"Everything is good. One small bit of rain blew in, but it was a section that hadn't gotten chinked yet."

"Not bad. Last night's rain was a good test for your roof. If you don't have any leaks, you did a great job. Where do you want to start today?"

Tom smiled up at Nat. "I thought we could work on the bedroom until it dries out a bit out here."

"That sounds like as good a plan as any. Maggie will give us a whistle when breakfast is ready, so let's get to work."

†

The groups worked on their projects until late afternoon. Maggie and Smithy finished the shelter at the cove while Nat and Tom built the first room in the house. They also finished chinking the logs before heading up to check on the rest of the group. They found Maggie chopping the remainder of the saplings and Marissa inside cooking.

"Where's Smithy?" Tom asked.

"I believe he's up dreaming at his build site," Maggie said.

"Let's go check on him," Nat said as she rinsed off her hands. "Then we need to start loading the wagon with seafood for your trip into town."

"I hate to go, but I know the delivery needs to be made, and I'll be able to return in a few days," Tom said as he washed his hands.

"One day soon, this place will be home to you. The trips to town will still be necessary, but you will always be coming back," Nat said.

They walked up the trail to find Smithy rearranging a big log. "What are you doing?" Nat asked.

"Planning out my cabin in my head," Smithy said and looked up at his friends. "I think this will be plenty big for what I need."

"You can always add on if you need more space," Nat told him. Nat smiled when she saw that he had already marked the areas they would notch to lock the logs together. "Are you ready to start notching?"

Smithy smiled. "I thought I might do these four to make my foundation. That way, I think it will feel real and not like a dream."

"That's a good idea. Tom and I will load the wagon and come back to check on you when done. We can help set the first logs," Nat offered.

"It may take me a while," Smithy said.

"As long as we're home by supper, we're good. You know how cranky Marissa gets when it comes time to eat." Nat patted him on the shoulder. "We'll be back."

†

Nat surveyed the full barrels on the back porch. "You know that rainwater just added to the weight. We're going to need to think this through." Nat looked around and came up with an idea. "Let's back the wagon as close as we can, and we can use some of the thicker planks to help roll the barrels into the wagon. We can empty the new barrels and pour some of the water from the full ones in there to make them light enough to move. Then if needed, pour some water back in."

Tom scratched his head. "That sounds doable. I'll position the wagon if you grab the planks."

Working together, they managed to get all six of the filled barrels loaded. Nat loaded several stacks of pelts between the barrels after they secured the lids. "What else will we be sending to town?" Nat asked Maggie.

"I'll box up as many fish as I can in the morning. There will be three heavy bags of jerky and a bunch of sausage going as well. I've got a dozen jars of chowder that can go, too," Maggie answered.

"Do we need to make a list of supplies?" Nat asked.

"I believe Marissa has already started one," Maggie said. "What are you about to do?" she asked Tom.

249

"Go check on Smithy," Tom said. "Do you need something first?"

Maggie nodded. "More geese if you have time to check for them."

"That won't take long at all," Tom replied. "The lake was full of them this morning."

"Get to it then," Maggie said.

"You can take my new rifle and try it out," Nat said as he entered the cabin.

"All right," Tom answered.

Nat smiled. "I'll be up at Smithy's whenever you get back."

†

The clouds were hanging low again the following day, but Nat thought Tom and Smithy might make it to town before the rains hit.

"Be careful, and we'll see you on Friday," she told Tom.

"I'll be here as soon as I can," Tom promised.

They watched the wagon disappear down the drive, and Marissa looked at Nat. "Now what?"

"It looks like we've got rain coming in again. Why don't you and Maggie continue on the inside projects, and I'll run my traplines?" Nat reached for her backpack basket and her gun. "If I scare an elk or deer up, do you need it for sausage?"

"We can always use more meat for sausage and jerky. That was a big load we sent to town just now, but it will sell in no time according to Tom's report," Marissa answered.

250

"Very well. If you hear a shot, hitch up Quincy and come find me," Nat said.

By mid-morning, Nat had filled her basket full of mink and carried a large beaver as she started for home. The wind had picked up, and Nat wondered if it was blowing in or away. The sky was still dark, but there were no rumbles of thunder. As she circled the lake, a nice buck was heading toward the woods. Nat lowered the beaver to the ground and brought her rifle to her shoulder. She dropped the deer cleanly and managed to drag him near a tree to begin processing. By the time Maggie reached her with the wagon, Nat had skinned the deer and cut it into quarters. With Maggie's help, she loaded him into the wagon.

"He will make some fine sausage and some meals, too," Maggie said. "After we hang him, I'll work on the hide if you want to process the pelts from your line."

"That's too good a deal to pass on," Nat answered.

"I had an idea while I was chopping wood," Maggie said.

"Should I be worried?" Nat teased.

Maggie smacked Nat's shoulder. "Probably," Maggie teased back. "I can handle things around here for a day or two if you want to invite Marissa to ride down to check for bison. I know she's not keen on sleeping on the ground, but it's worth asking."

Nat picked up her rifle and stored the beaver and basket in the wagon. "I can ask," she said.

"Maybe Marissa can handle one night on the ground," Maggie suggested.

"If not, I'll ride quickly and be back early the next day. We need to hit the pools hard to refill our barrels. That was an excellent first order, and I'd enjoy seeing more head that way. Or maybe smaller orders with some logs on the wagon as well. We've got plenty to send a load each week."

"If the weather holds, do you want to hit some of the pools today? I'm sure Quincy wouldn't mind a workout."

"That's good with me," Nat said. "Maybe we should take some of the intestines down to bait the pools. No telling what that might bring into the area."

When they reached the cabin, Maggie said, "I'm going for the salt. Do you need anything?"

"Some cold water," Nat said.

†

As Nat suspected, Marissa declined the offer to ride with her to check for the herd. She was disappointed but not surprised at her decision. Nat left early the following morning. She had to admit she still loved the solitude of the woods with no one but Gyp and Hardy. It reminded her of the years she had spent trapping along the border, and those memories brought back fond times with her father. The rain had washed the earth clean, and the smell of spruce and aspen filled the air along with late spring wildflowers in bloom.

In the distance, Nat saw a large lake that had remained hidden in her hasty travels. She looked down at Gyp. "That lake is worth checking out one day. Not today, though."

Gyp trotted ahead of them and frequently left the trail to chase a scent. Minutes later, she would emerge in front of Nat and wait for her to catch up before trotting along. As they passed the first campsite, Nat pulled out a jerky strip and tossed one down to Gyp. The music of birds and small creatures calling to their mates or offspring filled the air. A moose bellowed in the distance catching Gyp's attention. She let out a short huff.

"He's way too far off for us," Nat said with a soft laugh.

Nat reached the larger campsite and was pleased to find it in good condition. Instead of dismounting and walking to the top of the ridge, Nat decided to ride. The meadow was deep green with sweet grasses and small bushes, but there was no sign of the bison. Nat cringed at the thought that the stories were true. It would be a shame on humankind if the bison became slaughtered out of existence. She checked the sun's position and decided to ride a bit farther south before turning for home.

Nat topped a ridge where she could see for miles in every direction. Looking farther south, she saw a large dark area against the horizon and was about to discount it as burned trees when she realized the mass was moving slowly. She strained her eyes to see across the miles, and her heart raced when Nat recognized a large herd of bison moving north. They would migrate slowly north as they grazed, but they were coming. Maybe three to four days before they reached the meadow, but they still looked plentiful.

"Here they come, Gyp," Nat told her companion, but Gyp was unable to see the herd as it wavered against the horizon like a dark wave of heat across the land.

Excited about the prospect of a hunt, Nat started back toward home. She knew it would be too dark to travel soon, but she would ride back to the first camp and leave whenever the sun rose the next day. Nat would ask Maggie to ride to town to relay the message to Tom and Smithy while she worked hard to get ahead of their chores.

She made a small campfire and stretched out on her bedroll with Gyp tucked in close, and fell into a peaceful sleep.

Nat rode hard the next day to arrive home and get Maggie on her way to town. When she arrived, she told Maggie and Marissa the plan and saddled Willow for Maggie.

"I will stay behind if you would rather ride to town," Maggie said.

"I've got to run traps and do some things you can't do," Nat explained. "If you don't want to go, I understand. I can ride in myself."

"No, not at all," Maggie said. "I don't mind at all. I'll stay with Tom and ride home tomorrow. Do you think they will come then?"

"There was not much on the list for Tom, so if he has already gotten it, fine, or if he can get it early, you could ride back with them." Nat walked to the barn and saddled Willow.

Nat helped Maggie into the saddle. "You should have plenty of time to make it before dark. Ride faster, and you get there sooner. Just break at the creek for a drink."

"I will," Maggie replied. "If you can run your lines, I'll keep a check on the pools until y'all come back from hunting."

"No, ma'am, you aren't getting off that easy. We need you and Quincy to haul the hides," Nat instructed. "Maybe a quarter or two, depending on how big they are."

Maggie beamed at being included in the hunt. "Should we ask if Ruth can come to help Marissa and keep her company?"

"That's not a bad idea. Ask Tom what he thinks."

"I will." Maggie waved at Marissa as she rode Willow down the trail.

Nat walked up on the porch and took Marissa in her arms for a kiss. "I've got lines to run. Do you think we could have more of those eggs you cooked the other day?"

"That will be easy. You want sausage, too?"

Nat nodded. "Yes, please. I will be hungry when I finish running my lines."

"What can I help with?" Marissa asked.

"You can add more wood to the smokehouses, and if I get back in time, you can keep me company while I skin my catch." Nat saw the grimace on Marissa's face and knew she didn't enjoy watching anything processed. "Or if you prefer, you can keep working on your sewing projects."

"I think I'll do that instead. Or, I can go dig clams."

"I can skin later tonight while you cook. When I get back, I'll hitch Quincy, and we can check out some pools. You can dig clams while I fill buckets."

Marissa kissed her softly. "Hurry back. Maybe we can enjoy a night alone together. It's been a while since we had one."

"Maybe a nice bath together?" Nat asked.

"I'll carry in some water, and we can get some heating while you do your skinning," Marissa replied. "A bath together would be nice."

Nat reached down for her basket and rifle. "I'll be back soon. Gyp, stay."

"Oh, let her go with you. I've got my pistol and Luna for protection," Marissa said.

"Come on then, Gyp," Nat called, and Gyp flew off the porch.

255

†

Maggie rode quickly, and when she reached the creek, she dismounted Willow and led her to the water to drink. She smiled when she remembered using a stump to climb onto a horse before and used the same method to get back onto Willow. Another hour and she would reach the town.

†

Nat walked her lines and placed several marten and mink in her basket. She hadn't caught any beavers, but as she turned for home, her last set held a wolverine. They were vicious fighters, and Nat felt like this one was playing dead. "Stay back, Gyp," she said as she began walking toward the animal. Nat's keen eyesight saw the animal breathing, and before she moved any closer, she shot the wolverine. Nat released the trap and reset the mechanism. The wolverine was massive, and his pelt would bring in top dollar. Satisfied with her haul, Nat and Gyp started for home.

Quincy was eager to leave his stall and danced toward the wagon, ready to work. Nat filled the wagon with buckets, a rake, and the fish trap while Marissa filled a water canteen.

"Let's go," she said after brushing a strand of hair from her face.

Nat had changed out of her boots and socks, preferring the more comfortable shoes Maggie had made. She took Quincy's lead, and they walked to the shore.

"Let's stay close. I can do the cove pools in the morning while we wait for the others to arrive."

"What kind of supplies do I need to pack for your hunting trip?" Marissa asked as they walked.

"My bedroll for sure. I think flour, some meal, jerky, and some ham steaks. A few smoked fish, too. Would it be too much trouble for a couple of pans of biscuits?"

"Not at all. I imagine y'all will be busy once the hunt begins and won't be up to cooking much. I'll pack simple things Maggie can use to keep you fed well. I can cook a roast from your latest buck to send. You could eat that with biscuits or a couple of loaves of bread."

"That all sounds perfect. Toss in a couple of jars of chowder and our cooking gear, and we'll be good," Nat said. "We'll both have busy days after tomorrow."

"If we catch some shrimp and lobster today, do you want to have some seafood tomorrow night?" Marissa asked.

"I would never turn that offer down," Nat replied. "I may find more crab at the cove, too."

†

When Maggie entered the town, Smithy was on the front porch of the store. He looked up to see her and came rushing forward.

"Is everything okay?"

"More than okay. The bison are on the way," Maggie said. "Nat asked me to come to tell you and Tom. Is he around? I need to see if he's gotten the supplies from the store yet and to ask if Ruth could stay with Marissa while we're away."

"That's a good idea. I think Ruth's parents would be okay with that. Let's go ask Tom and Ruth." Smithy helped Maggie off the horse.

She groaned when her feet touched the ground. "It's been a while since I've ridden this far."

"You can ride in the wagon with me, and we'll tie Willow to the wagon," Smithy said. "I'm sure Tom will ride Buck."

†

Tom and Ruth were excited about the hunt and liked the idea of Ruth staying with Marissa. It would give her a small taste of what life in the wilderness would entail. Her father gave his consent, and Tom would pick her up early the following morning.

"Have you picked up the supplies from the store yet?" Maggie asked.

"I have them ready for the delivery tonight a soon as I finish here," Tom answered.

"Go and get Rusty hooked up and get the supplies," Smithy told him.

Tom nodded and looked at Maggie. "You're staying with me, right?"

"Yes, I am."

"Let me take Willow then, and I'll get her settled in at home."

"She's tied up out front," Smithy said. "Dinner at the hotel when you get done?"

"Fine by me," Tom replied.

"I'll meet you at the store. I want to do some browsing," Maggie said.

"Come back here when you finish shopping, and we can meet Tom for dinner," Smithy said.

Maggie walked across to the general store while Tom rode Willow out to get Rusty.

†

Nat stepped out of the tub and wrapped a towel around her body before extending her hand to Marissa. "That bath felt good," Nat said as she wrapped Marissa in a towel.

"Yes, it did, but it won't compare to how I'm about to make you feel," Marissa teased. She grabbed Nat by the hand and dragged her into the bedroom. "It's been so long since we could run around naked and sleep skin to skin," she said as she pulled Nat down on top of her.

"This is very nice," Nat said as she wiped Marissa's damp hair from her face.

Marissa surprised Nat when she rolled her body and climbed on top of her. "Very nice," Marissa said as she buried her face in Nat's neck, nibbling at the tender skin beneath her ear. Marissa's hips began to grind, and Nat guided her until they were mound on mound.

Nat let out a low moan as her desire soared. Marissa's mouth moved down to cover Nat's breast, and Nat groaned when their bodies separated.

"It will feel even better soon, I promise," Marissa whispered as she kissed her way down Nat and buried her face between Nat's legs. Marissa's tongue slipped into Nat's entrance, and Nat's body arched. Marissa's fingers toyed with Nat's nipples as her tongue lapped hungrily, feasting on the juices flowing from her center. Nat's fingers entangled in Marissa's hair, pulling her face deeper as her body began quivering.

"Oh, yes," Nat purred as her body released her pent-up desire.

Marissa looked into Nat's desire-darkened eyes and smiled, quite pleased with herself. "That was delicious."

"It felt divine," Nat replied. "Now it's my turn," she said and rolled Marissa onto her back. Nat decided to tease Marissa and took a leisurely route down her body, sucking her breasts deeply into her mouth as her fingers swirled atop Marissa's skin.

Marissa arched her back, her body begging for more as Nat's tongue licked a circle around her belly button and her fingers dragged through Marissa's wetness. Nat locked eyes with Marissa as she licked the juices from her fingertips.

"So, delicious," Nat purred in a husky voice. "I think I will have a better taste."

"Yes, please," Marissa said as Nat kissed down her body and her tongue glided across her opening.

Nat's fingertips gently parted Marissa's lips as her tongue pressed past them to begin a deep sensual kiss. Marissa's moans filled the room as Nat teased her to the edge of release, then slowed her motion.

Frustrated, Marissa buried her hands in Nat's hair and raised her hips. Sensing Marissa's need for release, Nat slipped a finger inside Marissa as her tongue swirled. Marissa let out a scream of pleasure when Nat's finger touched her special spot, and she began convulsing with her climax.

"My, my, that must have felt good," Nat teased as she climbed up to lay beside Marissa.

"That was beyond anything I've ever felt good," Marissa said as she tried to calm her breathing.

Nat's fingertips circled the darkened area surrounding Marissa's swollen nipples. "I adore the way your body reacts," Nat said.

"You make me feel things I've never felt before," Marissa answered. Her fingers played in Nat's hair as her eyes grew heavy.

Nat smiled and leaned down to kiss her lover. "We have a busy day ahead of us. Sleep well, my love."

"I've no doubt I will," Marissa answered with a groggy voice. "Goodnight, Nat."

Nat blew out the candle and, after pulling the covers over them, cradled Marissa's body.

†

Nat led Quincy down the new trail and began harvesting at the cove. Catching the fish in an immense pool was much more complex, so she didn't spend a lot of effort chasing them. Nat focused on the crab and lobster, then led Quincy to the beach. Nat found the small tidal pools loaded with the salmon, and she filled up the bed of the wagon quickly. Lobsters filled four more of the buckets before she began digging clams. With two buckets of clams, Nat and Quincy continued down the shore toward home. Nat hoped to have all the pools harvested before Maggie and the men arrived from town. She knew Maggie would be up and ready to hit the trail with the first crack of dawn. She was finishing the last of the pools when Tom and Ruth came running down the beach.

"Welcome back," Nat said. "It's good to see you again, Ruth."

"Thanks for inviting me out here. I couldn't wait to see all the fantastic things Tom tells me about this place." Ruth smiled and reached for Tom's hand.

"Wait until you see what we brought you," Tom offered. "Jacob, the general store owner calls it a gill net and said it should work perfectly in the cove."

"That's a good thing. I finally got tired of chasing those damn fish this morning, so I went to the smaller pools where I could catch them."

Tom lifted the last bucket into the wagon. "If you want, we can go try it out after we dump these off."

"Fine with me. I can't stand the thought of those fish getting one over on me this morning." Nat walked to Quincy and picked up his lead. "We can leave the net in the shelter when finished, so we don't have to transport it every time." She looked at Tom. "Are y'all hungry?"

Tom laughed. "You know me. I can always eat."

"Let's go see what Marissa has planned. I'll start processing these fish if you dump the crab and lobster in the barrels. I think we can have some fried clams and shrimp tonight if that sounds good to you."

Maggie was looking over the gill net with Smithy when Nat pulled Quincy to a halt. "You want to try it out this afternoon?" Nat asked.

"I sure do," Maggie replied. "I bet this will work perfectly."

"Will you ask Marissa if she has any plans for lunch? I'm starving, but we need to handle this load before we can head to the cove."

"I can help you with the fish while the young'uns empty the buckets," Smithy volunteered.

"I'll help, too, unless Marissa needs my help," Maggie replied.

"Ask her if we can fry some shrimp and clams for dinner? I know she's been busy baking all day for our trip, so I'll cook," Nat said.

"I've been sitting on my butt all morning while you've been working hard. I'll cook supper," Maggie insisted.

"I won't argue with you," Nat said as she led Quincy to the processing table.

Tom reached into the wagon for the first buckets. "Bring those back when you've emptied them. We have fish to catch," Nat teased.

"Yes, ma'am," Tom answered, then he and Ruth began storing the seafood in the barrels.

Smithy grabbed several fish and carried them to the table. Nat had caught more fish than she thought, but Maggie brought out a knife and helped. Tom emptied the buckets of fish remains in the garden. When he brought an empty bucket back, he looked at Nat. "I think we should take some of these down to the cove. I bet the scent would bring in more of the crabs."

"That's a good idea. The garden is getting a bit fragrant. We could use the remains to bait the smaller pools as well." Nat nodded to two full buckets. "Are you up to starting with those?"

"Yes, ma'am," he said. He grabbed the buckets, and Ruth followed him to the shore.

"Did anyone think to remind Marissa about not mentioning the cabin? I wasn't sure if Ruth was coming, so I didn't mention it to her," Nat asked Maggie and Smithy.

"I told her. I think she was surprised that Ruth would be staying with her," Maggie said.

263

"Yeah, I probably should have talked with her about it, but it will give them some time to get to know each other," Nat said.

Marissa stepped out on the back porch. "How much longer do you think you'll be?"

"Not more than five minutes. Do you need something?" Nat asked.

"I've warmed up some chowder. Why don't you bring some smoked fish as well?" Marissa suggested.

"We'll finish here if you want to carry some inside," Nat told Maggie. "Are we eating outside?" she asked Marissa.

"Yes. It's such a beautiful day. More comfortable than the cabin, too. I've had the stove going all day."

"I can smell the fresh bread every time the door opens," Nat said.

Marissa smiled. "I've got the bread and biscuits ready for your trip. We can pack up the rest of the food later."

"Thank you," Nat said. "We'll be in shortly."

†

Tom laughed when they stretched the net to full length and began walking toward a school of fish. "These fish don't stand a chance. It's so simple I almost feel guilty."

"I can always give you the fish trap, and you can run after them if it gives you a cleaner conscience," Nat warned.

"No, ma'am, I'd much rather take twenty fish at a time," he tossed back at her.

When they dragged the net out of the water, Smithy and Ruth helped them dump the fish into the wagon. "I say we get one more load and call it a day," Nat suggested. "We need to clean the shrimp and clams for supper."

Ruth and Tom folded the net, and Tom hung it in the shelter to dry. "That was a great purchase," Nat said.

"It works like a charm," Maggie said. "If you two want to start back, I'd like to dig a few more clams for tonight," Maggie said. "Tom and Ruth can help me, then Tom and I can shell while you and Smithy filet the fish."

Tom grabbed two empty buckets and the rake. Gyp and Luna had been dozing in the sun. When Maggie started toward the beach with the rake, Gyp ran along with her.

"Slow down a bit for your assistants," Nat hollered to Maggie.

Maggie saw the dogs trotting in her direction and smiled.

"Let's get these fish in the smoker," Nat told Smithy as she grabbed Quincy's lead.

"Ruth was so excited to be invited," Smithy said as they walked. "It will give her a good taste of the hard work it takes to live out here. I hope Marissa will have her help with chores."

"I know she'll have her collect eggs. Marissa hates the hens pecking at her. I've done the more strenuous chores, but she can keep the smokehouse fires fed and help Marissa with the indoor tasks. I'm sure Marissa will spend some time in the garden, and they have antlers to make more buttons. I seriously doubt they will run out of tasks to do."

CHAPTER TEN

Maggie walked beside Quincy as the caravan started for the bison hunt. Smithy and Tom chatted excitedly with Nat, who informed them that they would only take six bison on this trip.

"I think that's about all we can hold with the two wagons," Nat said. "Maggie and Quincy will haul the pelts and heads while Smithy, you, and Rusty haul the meat."

"What do you plan on doing with the heads?" Tom asked Nat.

"I'll remove the brains to cook down to help process the hides, and if you and Smithy want to process them for mounting, they are all yours."

"I'd like to have one to hang on my smokehouse," Tom said. "The rest we can sell if that's what Smithy wants."

Smithy nodded. "I do think they'd bring a handsome price, especially since they are in limited supply."

Nat looked at Tom. "We need to fire up your smokehouse and get the meat hung as quickly as possible. Not only will all that fresh blood attract unwanted guests, but the meat will only be good for a short period in the heat, even after we salt it. That's why I brought along lanterns. We may end up driving through the night."

"That's fine with me," Tom said. "It disgusts me to think of the bison that were slaughtered for their hides and then left to rot."

Smithy agreed. "It was a terrible waste."

They stopped at the small camp to water the animals and eat a quick meal. Maggie served some of the smoked fish as Nat and the others refilled canteens.

Gyp looked at Nat, who tossed her a strip of jerky to gnaw on while they ate. "So much for your staying behind," Nat laughed. They had only been gone for twenty minutes before Gyp caught up to the wagons.

"She loves you too much to be away from you for long. She knew with all the supplies and commotion, it wasn't just an afternoon adventure you were having," Maggie replied.

"She's been beside me every step of my journey for years now. I don't reckon that's going to change." Nat reached down to scratch Gyp behind the ears.

"Nope," Smithy said. "She'd run through fire for you."

"That makes me think of something we haven't discussed." Nat looked at Maggie. "We need you to watch over us after we've taken down the bison. I need you to make sure none of the herd comes back for revenge or a hungry bear comes for an easy meal."

"That's a bright idea. None of us has experience with these animals, so we don't know how they will react," Smithy replied.

"I will keep a sharp eye out on you, and Gyp will help me," Maggie replied. "I'll need a short rope to hold her back once you begin hunting."

"I'll make sure she's safely tethered beside you on the wagon. We can move to the top of the ridge to give you a clear view of the meadow." Nat stood and took a final drink before swinging up on Hardy. "Let's get going. I want to get settled in and a hot meal in our bellies before dark."

"We should reach camp in plenty of time, shouldn't we?" Tom asked.

"With time to spare," Maggie said.

†

Marissa and Ruth spent time splitting wood and feeding the fires in the smokehouses. "Tom says you enjoy hunting and fishing," Marissa said.

Ruth nodded. "I've hunted with my father since I was little. I enjoy adding food to my family's table. There was a period when he was sick that he depended on me to bring in fresh meat."

"Those are good skills for a woman in the wild to have. If nothing else, you will never go hungry." Marissa smiled.

Ruth tossed some branches into the fire. "Do you worry about being safe when you're alone out here?"

"Until those two men attacked us, I felt very safe. Probably too safe and let my guard down. Before then, we didn't have as much as a stray cat show up, except Tom. He turned out to be a blessing."

Ruth's face turned pink. "He is a good man. I've grown very fond of him, too."

"He thinks the world of you. Do you see Tom as someone you can spend your life with?" Marissa asked.

Ruth nodded. "I would like that. I know he and my father have been talking, so maybe he will propose soon."

"I think he's just making sure the two of you will start on the right foot."

"I will work right next to Tom to make our future together," Ruth replied.

"It indeed takes working together as a team. You have to understand both your strengths and weaknesses and learn to complement each other." Marissa sighed, thinking of Nat. "What would you like to eat tonight?"

"I enjoy the smoked fish, and it doesn't appear we will run low anytime soon," Ruth answered.

"The newest pools have been a godsend. The fish we have been able to harvest are much more plentiful than the smaller tidal pools. Would you like to help me catch more tomorrow?"

"It looks pretty easy with the net," Ruth said, "but I bet it is still heavy work."

"Especially now. I just remembered Nat and the others are using both wagons," Marissa said. "Scratch that idea. We can work on some sewing projects, or I can teach you to make buttons."

"I'm not the greatest with a needle and thread. Mama has tried to teach me, but I'd be willing to learn how to make buttons," Ruth answered.

"Tomorrow we can work on making more sausage. I have a feeling we will need space in the smokehouses once our group returns."

"I sure hope so. This hunt has been a source of excitement for Tom and Smithy ever since Nat mentioned it. Tom's eyes grow wide with excitement every time he talks of them."

"I'm sure they will all have stories to tell when they return," Marissa said.

"I'm sure they will." Ruth smiled.

†

When they reached camp, they tied off the animals and walked toward the ridge. Nat didn't have to see the herd to know they had arrived. She could smell the musky scent of the large animals and could hear mothers calling to their calves. The hunters crept to the edge of the ridge and laid on the soft ground to look in amazement at the large herd of bison grazing peacefully in the meadow.

"They are amazing," Tom said with wonder in his voice. "I've never seen anything so massive."

"I'm not sure we'll be able to fit six of them in a wagon," Smithy said.

"It will be a heavy load," Nat agreed. "Should we drop to five instead?"

"That's probably a wise move," Maggie said. "We can always come back later if you think they will stay in the area for long."

"I would think a few weeks before they are finished grazing on the sweet grasses," Nat said. "The herd is more extensive than I remember."

"This herd must have escaped the massive slaughter," Smithy said.

"I think we should take our five and be satisfied with that," Nat said. "We want there to be a future herd to hunt."

"I agree. We won't go hungry," Maggie said. "We can keep half the meat for ourselves and take the rest to town once it finishes smoking."

"I owe one hindquarter in exchange for a lifetime supply of ammunition," Nat replied. "The rest will go to the general store and hotel."

"A solid plan," Smithy said. "Come along, Maggie. We can start a fire and tend to the animals while these two devise our plan of attack."

Tom looked at Nat. "So, what is our plan? I know you have one."

"We will spread out, and when you, Smithy, and I are in place, we can fire simultaneously. You and Smithy can take two, and I'll take one. Hopefully, they will go down with one shot."

"You and Smithy have the repeaters. I think you both should take two. It will take me too long to reload," Tom said.

"That's why you are swapping rifles with me tomorrow. I'm comfortable with my father's rifle, so I will use it while you use mine," Nat replied.

"I can't do that," Tom said.

"Sure, you can. I think we may be able to do some bartering and maybe trade one of the heads for a repeater for you," Nat said.

"You think so?" Tom asked, so excited his voice nearly squeaked.

"I think it will be too irresistible for him to turn down once he sees the massive heads," Nat said. "Make a big commotion when you head back into town with them, and Bill will be knocking your door down."

"You are shrewd," Tom praised.

Nat shrugged. "It's all about supply and demand. You'll have four bison heads, and people will be drooling over them. What better trophy to have hanging on the wall of a gunsmith's shop?"

"I would love to have one of those."

"Make him want to trade you then," Nat replied. "Let's go set up camp and get a hot meal in our bellies."

"I'm good with that," Tom said, and they walked back to camp.

Maggie had some chowder warming over the fire and a pan of cornbread heating on a rock. "Do you want to eat the rest of the fish tonight?"

"Sure, we can start on the roast tomorrow. It's going to be a long day," Nat said.

"I will place some ham in the biscuits for a quick meal in the morning, and we can eat slices of the roast with fresh bread and cheese. I'll make enough so we can eat those on the way back, too," Maggie stated. "Do you still plan to make it home tomorrow night?"

"I'd like to, but it depends on how things go tomorrow. We may only make it as far as the small camp, but that will put us closer to home," Nat said.

"We'd have to guard the wagon full of meat," Smithy said. "I'd hate to do all that work for a bear to claim a free meal."

"We can take turns sitting watch," Nat said. "Remember, there's no meat worth losing your life over."

"I agree with that. A bear can only carry one quarter at a time. We'll put the smallest on the end of the wagon, just in case," Smithy said.

"Hopefully, the entrails and organs we leave behind will be enough to occupy them until we get out of the area. I haven't seen a bear, but I guarantee they are here." Nat looked at Tom. "We all need to keep our eyes and ears open and keep a gun with you at all times."

Tom nodded. "I will."

"Tom and I have discussed tomorrow's strategy," Nat said. "We will be exchanging rifles, and I want you and Tom to take two, and I'll get one. We need to spread out a hundred paces apart. I'll take the farthest south so I can get Rusty, and Maggie can bring Quincy. Tom will give Maggie the repeater so she can stand watch while we start skinning and harvesting."

"Yes, ma'am," Tom said.

Nat held their full attention. "We all need to start skinning once we have all five bleeding out. The hides and heads we'll put on Quincy's wagon, and the quarters will go in Rusty's wagon. After we eat a quick breakfast, we need to pack up camp and get the animals ready."

She looked at Maggie. "I need you to keep Gyp close. We can't have her barking or chasing the herd."

"I will tie her to the bench on Quincy's wagon. She can help me keep watch." Maggie reached over to stroke Gyp's head.

"One more thing." Nat looked at Tom. "You're probably the fastest with a saw. When you get one skinned, use the bone saw to remove the head, and you can start cutting quarters."

Tom beamed at Nat. "I sure will," he said.

"Be sure to sharpen your knife blades tonight. I would guess the bison hides will be thick. Don't worry about removing the fat. We can focus on that when we get home." Nat pulled out her favorite skinning knife and honed the blade while they waited on supper to warm.

A blanket of stars was overhead as Nat looked up from the fire. The moon was on the rise and the glow filled the night. Maggie saw her looking at the sky.

"A full moon is an omen for a good hunt."

"I hope everything goes as planned tomorrow," Nat said. "Thank you for coming with us to help."

"I wouldn't miss it for anything," Maggie said. "Do you want to walk out and take a peek?"

They found Tom lying at the top of the ridge. Nat and Maggie stretched out beside him. "They are magnificent," Tom said.

"Yes, they are. I have waited all my life to see a large herd like this," Maggie said. "I heard many stories as a young girl, but not until today have I seen them in such a beautiful way. I was afraid they were all gone."

"Hopefully, that will never happen," Nat said. "We will only take what we can manage, and maybe we can hunt again this year, or next year when they migrate through."

"That would be great," Tom said. "I can't wait to try the meat."

"I found onions down by the creek. If you separate several of the livers, I will fry some when we set up camp. The iron-rich protein will replenish our energy after a long day of physical labor," Maggie told them.

"That sounds good," Nat said. She nodded and pointed to the shelter. Smithy was already sleeping soundly. "I guess he was tired."

"We should all get a good night's rest. The morning will be on us before we can blink," Maggie joked.

They all stretched out in their bedrolls, and Gyp snuggled up next to Nat.

CHAPTER ELEVEN

Maggie was warming the ham when Nat awoke. Maggie was trying to be as quiet as possible as she packed up camp to allow the others to sleep a few more minutes. Nat rolled up her bedroll and stored it under the wagon bench.

"What else can I do?" she whispered to Maggie.

"You can feed the horses and Quincy. He and Rusty will have a busy day." Maggie handed Nat a jar of molasses. "Treat them good."

Nat took the jar. "Thanks for remembering."

"Don't thank me. Thank Marissa. She remembered to pack it," Maggie said with a shrug.

When Nat finished feeding the animals, Tom and Smithy were awake and storing their bedrolls.

"The ham is warm whenever you're ready," Maggie said.

The three hunters ate a quick meal, eager to start the day. Nat tethered Gyp to the wagon bench after she hitched up Quincy. They stored the rest of the camp supplies and were ready to hunt.

"You stay with Maggie," Nat told Gyp. "Whenever you hear the first shot, drive Quincy to the top of the ridge. When things settle down after the herd stampedes, you can bring Quincy down, and I'll return for Rusty. Keep a sharp eye out."

"I will," Maggie promised.

Nat looked at Tom and Smithy. "Are we ready?"

"Yes, I think we are," Smithy said.

She handed Tom her rifle. "Remember to aim for older bulls. We must ensure we do not take a female that may have a calf. The only exception would be an older animal that is having difficulty running."

"Got it," Tom said.

"I'll give you several minutes to get into position and pick out your targets. Once the first shot sounds, the herd will scatter, so you may not see your second target any longer. Take another target if you can, but if not, no worries." Nat looked at Tom and Smithy. "Raise your rifles once you are ready. Count to five after I've raised mine, and the hunt begins."

Tom and Smithy walked ahead of Nat as they headed down the ridge using the tree line to camouflage their approach. Nat reached her location first and gazed across the meadow at the large herd. She selected a large bull and then turned her attention to Tom and Smithy. Tom was surveying the animals while Smithy continued to walk. When Smithy finally stopped, Nat waited for several minutes until he had picked out his targets. One by one, they raised their rifles. Nat's heart pounded as she slowly counted to five and pulled the trigger. The bull she targeted took two steps forward before falling to his knees and toppling to the ground.

Tom's shot rang out, and Nat watched with pride as the first animal fell, and then his second target required two attempts to bring the big animal down. Smithy's gun fired seconds after Tom's, and he was successful in bringing down two bulls. The bison stampeded, filling the air with dust and panicked cries as Nat climbed the ridge to find Maggie on her way with Quincy.

"I'll be right behind you," Nat said, and handed Maggie the rifle. "Tom will bring you the repeater as well." She walked over to Rusty and grabbed his reins as she started for the ridge. Nat quickly caught up with Maggie. "Be careful with any animal that comes back this way."

Nat watched the herd as they settled in a thousand yards from where they had been grazing. Nat hoped the bison would remain close, and since there were no additional shots, would recognize the hunt was over. Nat stopped Rusty several feet from the bison she had killed. His nostrils flared with the smell of blood in the air, and he stomped his feet. Nat set the brake on the wagon before tending to her kill.

Nat walked cautiously toward the large animal and saw no sign of life. She withdrew her knife and began the hard work of processing such a large animal. Tom and Smithy were busy with their kills as Maggie and Gyp watched over them.

It was still early morning, but the physical labor brought beads of sweat rolling down Nat's face. Her knife sliced through the thick hide, but she was thankful for sharpening the blade the previous night.

Tom looked up to see Nat was nearly finished, picked the saw from the wagon, and rushed over to remove the head.

Nat looked up when Tom arrived. "Help me roll him so I can remove the hide. Then you can begin quartering him while I work on your kills."

"Yes, ma'am. Which organs do you want to keep?" Tom asked.

"Definitely the hearts and liver," Nat answered. "The rest we will leave for scavengers, so hopefully, they won't follow the blood trail."

Nat rolled and carried the heavy hide to Quincy's wagon before walking on to the next kill.

Maggie felt the weight of the hide as it dropped onto the wagon bed. "That must have been heavy. I'll pull the wagon up to the next bull," Maggie told Nat.

She felt confident Tom could lift the quarters into the wagon but would return if he needed her. "Call me if you need help. Bring Rusty after you've loaded the meat."

Tom nodded. "I will."

Bison blood covered Tom's arms. Nat looked down to find droplets of blood falling from her fingertips, staining the bright green grass as she walked across the meadow. Nat knelt to begin the process of skinning Tom's first kill as the flies started swarming to the blood.

Tom worked quickly to dissect the animal and began carrying the heavy quarters to the wagon. Nat was right. There was no way they would have been able to haul more than six animals. The load would be heavy enough with five.

With Tom's help, Nat removed the hide and rolled it before storing it in the wagon, then moved farther down the meadow. Smithy had finished skinning his first kill, and Nat walked down to help him roll the animal to finish removing the hide.

Smithy was huffing and puffing when he rolled the hide and lifted it to his shoulder. "Even the hides weigh a ton." He groaned under the weight.

"Do you need me to carry it for you?" Nat teased.

"No, smart alec, I was just commenting," Smithy shot back at her.

It was well into the afternoon by the time they finished processing and loading the meat. Nat climbed onto the wagon bench beside Gyp.

"That was hard work." She let out a deep sigh when she sat down. "I think I'll brave the cold water of the creek to wash this blood from me."

"Good thing Marissa packed you clean clothes," Maggie said.

"Yes, it is. Between the blood and sweat, I'm sure I smell pretty rank."

"You go first when we get back to camp. Tom and Smithy can help me salt the meat and hides while you bathe, then if they are brave enough, they can hit the water."

Maggie drove to Rusty's wagon, and they surveyed the pile of meat. "Leave the organs near the back," Nat said.

Tom gave her a questioning look.

"Maggie will cook the liver for dinner and the hearts we will use as an offering if we get company tonight. I'd rather toss a bear a heart than try to get a quarter off the wagon."

"That makes perfect sense," Smithy said.

"Let's head back to camp, and I'm going to bathe while you two help Maggie salt down the meat and hides. Then if you're daring, you can bathe while we stand guard."

"You're just full of yourself today," Smithy joked. "We did good, didn't we?"

Nat returned his smile. "Yes, we did. Even the bison stayed in the area. I don't know for how much longer, but they didn't stampede. This grass must be tasty and sweet."

Nat turned once they reached the ridge and saw the five blood-stained areas of grass. "Thank you for your sacrifice," she spoke aloud.

"We will make sure every part of them go to a good use," Maggie said.

When they reached camp, Maggie took charge. "Tom, I want you to remove the hides and unroll them on the grass in the sun, and Smithy, you can pull out the bags of salt. As soon as I get Nat set with clean clothes, I'll return to help."

Maggie then took clean clothes and followed Nat to the water. "I'm leaving your rifle, too, just in case you get a visitor."

"Thanks, Maggie. I'm sure this won't take long. This water is cold," Nat said when she dipped her foot into the water.

"I'll see you soon then," Maggie replied, and headed back to camp.

Tom had finished rolling the hides out, and Maggie began sprinkling them with salt while Tom and Smithy coated the meat. Maggie completed salting the hides and went over to inspect their job. "Don't be shy with the salt," she told them. "The meat will soak it in quickly."

Tom nodded toward the hides. "What do you want to be done with them?"

"They can soak up the sun until we are ready to break camp. Then you can roll them back up and load them into the wagon." Maggie fed and watered Quincy and Rusty.

When Nat returned, she stuffed her dirty clothes into the back of the small wagon. "That was cold, but it felt good to get the blood off my skin." Tom had jumped down from the wagon, and Smithy was climbing out.

"We've got the salting done," Tom said. "I don't think I'm going to bathe, but I'll wash off for sure."

"I'll get the horses saddled while you clean up," Nat told Smithy and Tom.

Nat and Maggie walked to the ridge while they waited on the men to check the herd. "I've waited all my life to see this," Maggie said as she looked out over the grazing animals. "It was well worth the wait."

"I hope we will continue to see them together for years to come," Nat said and slipped an arm around Maggie's shoulder.

"Me too, my friend. Me too," Maggie replied and leaned into Nat. "I would have never dreamed making some breeches for a wild young woman would have turned into such a grand adventure, but I'm so glad it has."

"We have had some good times, and lord knows we've worked hard to build what we have," Nat replied.

"Our family continues to grow, too," Maggie said with tears in her eyes.

"Yes, it does." When they heard Tom and Smithy return, Nat turned to Maggie. "Let's make it to the small camp. I'm ready for some liver and onions. I haven't had that in ages."

"You will have all you can eat tonight," Maggie promised.

"A hot meal in our bellies, and I don't think any of us will have trouble falling asleep tonight," Nat said as they walked to camp. "I don't know about y'all, but I'm too exhausted to drive home tonight. We can get up at first light and be home by midday."

"I haven't done near the physical labor you three have today, so I'll take first watch tonight," Maggie offered.

Nat nodded. "I don't think anyone will argue with you over that."

†

An hour into their progress, Nat looked at Tom. "Will you ride ahead and get a fire started?"

"I'll get our water buckets filled, too," Tom nodded. "Anything else?"

"If you see more wild onions down by the water, pull and rinse them. We can never have too many onions with liver," Maggie said to Tom.

"That sounds so good," Smithy said. "I'm starving."

"We can stop for a quick bite if you want?" She looked at Maggie. "Maggie sliced bread, meat, and cheese. We can eat that while we travel."

"I wouldn't mind a bite," Tom said.

Nat stopped the caravan long enough for everyone to get food. Tom took the food and began riding ahead of them.

"I never tasted anything as good as this does today," Smithy said.

"You must be hungry," Nat teased.

"I haven't worked this hard in years," Smithy admitted. "It was incredible, but I'm sure these old bones will be aching tomorrow."

"When we get home, we have plenty of work ahead of us that will ease that ache," Nat told him. "Hanging the meat in the smokehouses and starting on those hides will take close to a full day."

Nat swung up in the saddle when she finished her meal. "Are you two fine with driving while you finish?"

Maggie smiled. "Quincy and Rusty do all the hard work. We just sit here."

"Let's move on then. I'd love to be settled and close to eating by nightfall. Come on, Gyp," Nat called to her companion, who trotted along beside her.

Tom was sitting on a log, watching the fire when they arrived at camp. "I was starting to get worried," he told Smithy.

"No need to worry," Maggie said. "Is your blade still sharp?"

"Yes, ma'am, I cleaned my knife and honed it while I was waiting," Tom answered.

"Good. I need you to slice the liver for me while I get a pan of grease heating," Maggie told him. She looked at Smithy. "You can help him too."

"Let me unhitch the wagons, and I'll be right there," Smithy replied.

"What can I do?" Nat asked.

"Feed the animals and then take a seat by the fire." Maggie showed Tom the thickness of the meat she wanted the slices. "Lots of it," she said. "I think everyone has worked up an appetite." Maggie tossed a piece of liver to Gyp.

†

After a sumptuous meal, they sat around the fire sipping coffee and relaxing.

"Maggie has volunteered for the first watch, and I'll take second while you two get some rest. Tom, I'll wake you when it's your turn."

"Thanks for a great meal, Maggie. Thanks for a fantastic experience today, Nat. It was far better than I'd dreamed," Tom said as he stood. "I am whipped. Wake me when you're ready."

"I will. Get some sleep. You did most of the heavy work today, so you should be exhausted. You hauled several thousand pounds of meat," Nat reminded him.

"I feel every pound of it."

"Let's hit the bedrolls and get some sleep," Smithy said as he stood and stretched.

Nat poured her and Maggie fresh coffee as they started the first watch for predators. "Here you go," Nat said as she handed the coffee to Maggie.

"Thanks, Nat."

Nat sat beside Maggie and gazed into the darkness. "It's beautiful out here, isn't it?"

"Very peaceful, and I hope it stays that way tonight," Maggie said as she stroked Gyp's fur. "You'll let us know if anything comes close, won't you, pretty girl?"

"I'm sure she's on full alert," Nat said. "She's helped me stand guard many times in the woods."

As the moon rose, the nocturnal creatures began to awaken. Crickets and other insects chirped. An owl called out to its mate, and a pack of wolves was hunting in the distance.

When a howl broke the air, Maggie looked at Nat. "It's okay. The wolves are moving south, probably following the scent of the kill site."

Maggie smiled at Nat. "Putting spruce boughs across the wagons was a great idea to hide the scent of blood."

"My father taught me that years ago," Nat replied. She fell silent for several minutes as she drifted back to the memories of her father. She was tired, but she didn't think sleep would come anytime soon. Nat looked at Maggie. "I probably won't sleep for a while. Why don't you go ahead and lie down?"

"I won't be able to sleep either, so if you don't mind the company, I'll sit with you and do some sewing," Maggie answered.

"Fine with me." Nat pulled out her knife and began honing the edge. "Once we get everyone settled, I do want us to try our hand at making knives."

"I know we can do it, and the wheel grinder Smithy sent will be great for that project. We can do that on cold winter days," Maggie added. "I meant to ask earlier, but what do you want me to do when we get home?"

"I trust you to remove the brains without destroying the skulls," Nat laughed. "We'll boil them and use them in preparing the hides once we scrape the rest of the fat from them. I think it's time to start teaching Tom and Smithy how to tan."

"The bison hides are much thicker than I thought they would be," Maggie stated. "They would make a warm blanket for cold winter nights. As large as they are, we could probably make two from each hide."

"I agree. We need to boil the hides after we scrape them to get rid of the musky odor. Toss in some lye flakes to help. Then after they dry, we can use the brain paste to start tanning."

"Are you pleased with how the hunt went today?"

"I am," Nat smiled. "We took only what we needed, and we'll use every bit of the animals, so nothing goes to waste. I think we all had a fun experience."

"I would say so by the smile that was plastered over Tom's face today. Smithy enjoyed himself, too. I wish I could have done more to help," Maggie said.

"Protecting us was extremely important. You and I will have our work to do once we get home," Nat promised her.

Maggie nodded, and a smile played across her face as she resumed sewing.

"I sure hope you'll make me another pair of those," Nat said. "They are so warm and comfortable."

"You keep bringing in the beavers, and I'll keep making them. We should have some scraps from the bison hides we can use. too."

"I bet those would be warm and thicker than the buckskin, too."

Nat finished sharpening her knife and slipped it back into the sheath. They sat in silence for a while as Maggie sewed and Nat stared up at the night sky. "Sometimes I miss this, and then I think of the warm bed and family I have waiting for me at home."

"It doesn't hurt you to take a few short adventures now and then to give you some time under the stars. I think it makes us appreciate what we have at home even more." Maggie looked up to find Nat yawning. "Why don't you lay down and get some rest? I'll wake Tom in a bit and lay down myself."

"I think I will," Nat replied. She stood and stretched. "Do you want more coffee?"

"No, I think my bladder is full enough. Goodnight, Nat."

"Goodnight, Maggie. Thanks again for a wonderful day."

Nat stretched out on her bedroll and slipped into a deep sleep while Maggie watched over them.

†

Deep into the morning, Maggie woke Tom to take over the watch, and she burrowed down into her bedroll. Smithy woke early and built up the fire before joining Tom.

"I've got this if you want a few more hours sleep," Tom said.

"No, I'm good. Everyone will be up in a few hours anyway," Smithy said as he sat beside Tom. "Yesterday was quite the day, wasn't it?"

"That was the most exciting hunt I've ever been on," Tom said.

"Me, too," Smithy agreed. "I hope the bison will return every year." Smithy looked at Tom. "When do you plan to propose to Ruth?"

"If we can spend a few more days out here when we get back, I'd like to do it here. Maybe tomorrow night so she can see and help with the planning of the cabin."

"I think that would be perfect. I bet Ruth and Marissa have a feast planned for our return. After the meal would be a great time, especially if it's light enough for you to show her the cabin."

"Maybe we should ask Marissa if we can have an early meal to have plenty of daylight left," Tom suggested.

"I'm sure Marissa wouldn't have any problem with that," Smithy replied.

Gyp had been lying down between them as they talked, and she suddenly jumped to her feet, a low growl coming from deep within her.

"What is it, girl?" Smithy asked as he stared into the darkness.

The hackles on her back rose as did the volume of her growl, which woke Nat. Nat jumped to her feet and rushed over to the fire. Gyp had taken a few steps forward away from the group.

"Stay close, Gyp," Nat commanded. Nat picked up her rifle and took a few steps ahead. Her eyes adjusted to the darkness, and she could see a massive dark figure just outside the glow of the fire. The animal reared up on his hind legs, and Nat immediately recognized the bear. He dropped down on all fours and began shifting from side to side as he weighed the options for his next move. His muzzle sniffed the blood in the air as his tongue lapped at his lips.

"Tom, slowly walk over to me, and Smithy, bring your rifle, but don't make any quick movements." Nat kept a careful eye on the bear as Tom arrived. "Walk to the back of the big wagon and bring out two of the bison hearts."

Tom carefully edged toward the wagon. Smithy arrived with his rifle and stood to the right of Nat.

"We have a hungry bear who wants an easy meal," Nat spoke softly. "Tom, I want you to throw a heart as far as you can toward the bear. Past him, if you can."

Tom reared back and hurled the bloody heart as far as he could. It rolled past the bear when it struck the ground, and he began chasing after the free meal. Nat was relieved when he caught up to the meat and started eating. "Good job. Smithy, I need you to wake Maggie and begin breaking camp while Tom and I keep an eye on our friendly bear. We have four more hearts to keep him occupied. If all goes well, we will keep him fed until we are out of sight. Saddle the horses, and Tom and I will stay behind a few minutes to make sure he doesn't plan to follow us."

"I'm on it," Smithy said as he set his rifle close to Tom and went to wake Maggie.

Nat could hear them working quickly in the background while she and Tom monitored the bear. It took several minutes for him to finish the first heart, and he turned back to them. "Get a running start this time and see if you can drive him farther away."

Tom ran five steps before hurling the heart. It sailed beyond the bear, and Tom managed to move the bear another twenty feet away. "Get another?" he asked.

Nat turned quickly to see Maggie hitching Quincy and Smithy saddling the two horses. "Yes, bring two more," she answered.

Maggie and Smithy worked together to get Rusty hitched to the wagon and the rest of the camp supplies stored under the bench.

"We're good," Smithy called to Nat.

"You and Maggie go ahead and start up the trail. Tom and I will make sure the bear does not follow, and we'll catch up to you. Don't stop unless you have to and keep a rifle close." She looked down at Gyp. "Go with Maggie." Gyp rushed and jumped into the seat beside Maggie.

"We will, Nat," Smithy said. "Let's go, Maggie," he called out, and she urged Quincy ahead as Smithy climbed onto the large wagon bench. "Stay safe," he called back to Nat.

The bear heard the wagons start to pull away and turned toward Nat. "Toss him another, Tom. If he starts to charge, I've got him in my sights. Hopefully, he will be smart and take the free food."

Tom hurled the next heart with all his might, and it rolled twenty paces past the bear. The bear took a final look at the wagons disappearing and ran after the meat.

"He has one more chance to eat his fill, and if he chooses to charge us, I'll have no choice but to fire," Nat said. "If I have to shoot, grab Smithy's gun and start shooting. It will take several shots to bring him down, and I don't want him close."

Nat chanced a quick look up the trail and saw no sign of either wagon. "Hopefully, they will be half a mile or so ahead before the bear finishes off the last of the hearts." When she returned her attention to the bear, she could see he was slowing down his eating rate. "That's a good sign," she whispered. "Let's wait to see what he does after he finishes. If he turns to the woods, that would be great, but if he turns toward us, hurl that heart as far as you can and get the horses.

Nat's memories of her two encounters with a bear flooded her thoughts. Neither of them had turned out well. The first attack had killed her father and the second bear tried to rip her face off. She sent up a prayer that the bear would get his fill and not follow them. Nat watched as the bear finished the meat and sat staring at them. Nat locked eyes with the bear for several long seconds, and then he turned away and slipped into the woods.

"Thank goodness," she said after letting out a sigh of relief. "Get the horses."

"What do I need to do with this?" he asked, holding out the last heart.

"Toss it a few feet ahead of us. I'll keep an eye out until you bring the horses," Nat replied.

Tom raced for the horses, and Nat swung up in the saddle. "Let's get out of here," Nat called. She looked over her shoulder and saw no sign of the bear and then urged Hardy into a canter. Tom caught up with her, and when the wagons came into view after a nice run, Nat breathed a sigh of relief.

Maggie heard them approach and pulled Quincy to a stop. She had been assembling meat biscuits while Quincy trotted down the path. She motioned to Tom. "Take two of these to Smithy and come back for yours."

Tom took the biscuits, and when he returned, Nat looked at him. "I want you to tether your horse and ride with Smithy. Keep an eye on our backside. "I'll ride beside Maggie. We will be home before lunchtime with this early start."

"Do I need to take the spruce boughs off?" Tom asked.

"No, just leave them on for now. Maybe it will continue to mask the scent from any other predators in the area." Nat took the biscuit from Maggie, and they started back on their journey.

"Good morning," she told Maggie.

"That was a heck of a way to start the day. I don't think Smithy even realized how sore he was until we climbed onto the wagons." Maggie laughed.

"He was moving pretty quickly." Nat shot Maggie a wink.

†

When they reached the last hill before the lake, Nat called them to a stop. They all dismounted and stretched. "It's good to be home," Nat said.

"I'd like to hang all but four hindquarters in your smokehouse," Nat told Tom. "The rest can fit in ours. When we arrive at our cabin, I need you and Smithy to hang the quarters and help me with the hides. I'll get the washpot going, and we can work on scraping off some of the remaining fat. As soon as we get one cleaned, we will get it to the pot, add some lye chips to reduce the musky smell. Maggie will remove the brains and prepare them for the tanning solution we will use in a day or so, after the hides have dried a bit."

"May I ask a favor?" Tom blushed. "I would like to propose to Ruth tonight after dinner and take her to see the cabin. Would you ask Marissa if we can eat early enough to allow me to bring her to our new home while it's still daylight?"

"I'm sure we can arrange that," Nat said. "I'll speak to Marissa as soon as we arrive."

"Thanks. It would mean a lot for her to agree to marry me in front of my family," Tom said.

"We will be honored to be your witnesses," Smithy said and slapped Tom on the back. "Let's get this meat hung and a fire started."

Maggie filled the pit with wood and started the fire while Tom and Smithy hung the quarters. Nat watched to make sure they had everything settled. "I'm going to ride to the cabin and let the ladies know we are home."

"We won't be far behind you," Maggie called back.

CHAPTER TWELVE

Nat and Gyp walked beside Hardy the rest of the way home. She tethered Hardy outside the barn and pulled the saddle off his back. There was no sign of Marissa or Ruth in the yard, so Nat walked inside searching for the two women. The aroma of fresh bread and a pie filled her nostrils as soon as she stepped inside, but the cabin was empty. Nat walked out onto the front porch and to the edge of the yard. She smiled when she heard laughter and saw Ruth and Marissa squealing as they waded to the pool in the cold water. Nat saw several buckets on the beach filled with seafood.

"Let's go see if they need help," Nat told Gyp, who ran ahead of her.

Marissa and Ruth were carrying two full buckets to the shore when Nat came into view. Marissa's face beamed with a smile. "Welcome home. I didn't expect you this early."

"We had an early morning intruder who wanted a free meal. He got us on our way much sooner than we planned," Nat replied.

"An intruder?" Marissa asked.

"A large bear thought he could steal our bison," Nat replied. "We taught him differently, though."

"That must have been a scare," Ruth said.

"It was, but it all worked out, and we made it home sooner than we planned, which is good. But we're all starving," Nat replied. "Can we get an early supper?"

"We will get started on it right after we get some food into you. How about eggs and sausage? We can toast up some fresh bread, too, for some jelly," Marissa offered.

"That sounds good. The others shouldn't be too far behind me. We've got a lot of work to get done today with the hides, but a hot meal before we start would be great."

"We've got plenty eggs and sausage. It won't take us long," Marissa said. "Will you help us with these buckets?"

"It would be my pleasure," Nat said. "Ruth, can you take those two, and we'll get the rest?"

"Yes, I can." Ruth picked up two buckets and started up the trail.

Nat waited for her to get out of earshot before she turned to Marissa. "Tom is going to ask her to marry him tonight after supper, and he wants to show her the cabin before dark," she explained.

"That's excellent news. We'll have a feast for supper to celebrate then," Marissa said.

Nat picked up two buckets. "We are hungry, though. We ate the last of your biscuits while we traveled, and mine are long gone."

"We'll get a hot meal in your bellies so you can finish your work while we cook up a feast. I'm so glad you're home. I missed you."

"I missed you, too," Nat said and leaned down to kiss Marissa.

As they returned to the cabin, Smithy, Maggie, and Tom were busy at work. Tom was carrying in the last of the hindquarters, and when he stepped out of the smokehouse and saw Ruth approaching, his face lit with a smile.

Maggie added wood to the wash pot fire and then checked the wood in the smokehouses.

Nat set her buckets on the porch and returned to the wagon. "Marissa and Ruth are going to fix us a hot meal before we start into the hides. Let's finish unloading and tend to the animals while they cook."

Marissa and Ruth emptied their buckets and walked into the cabin to begin cooking. Tom laid the rolled-up hides on the skinning table and then helped Smithy tend to the animals. Nat walked into the barn for several scrapers they would use on the bison pelts and put them on the table. Maggie carried empty buckets over to the bison heads.

"Let's get washed up and go eat," Nat said. "We're all set for an early supper," she told Tom.

"Thanks," he said, and rushed ahead to wash his hands.

"Carry these plates outside," Marissa said to Nat as she entered the kitchen.

"Yes, ma'am, what else can we help with?" Nat asked.

"I think we're just about ready to start serving," Marissa said. "Oh, you can take this plate of toast and the utensils."

"I'll grab some jelly," Maggie said as she walked to the pantry.

"Can I carry out that plate of sausage?" Smithy asked.

"Only if you can keep Nat and Tom out of it until the rest of us get there," Marissa teased as she handed him the plate.

"Why do you give me the hard jobs?" Smithy groaned.

"Because you can handle them," Maggie replied and shooed him out the door.

"Ruth and I will bring the rest in a minute," Marissa said to Maggie. "Will you carry cups and send Tom for a bucket of water?" she asked Ruth.

"Yes, ma'am," Ruth answered and picked up a stack of cups.

Marissa filled a large dish with the scrambled eggs and carried them outside. "Now, you all can eat," she declared as she passed the bowl to Nat.

"Thanks for cooking for us. My breakfast is long gone," Tom said.

"Well, I hear you have a lot of work left to do, so eat up and get to it so we can have a big supper before it gets late," Marissa said with a wink to Tom.

†

The aromas from the cabin were tantalizing and kept the group motivated to get the work done. Tom hung the last of the bison hides along the porch railing, and Maggie's brain paste was made and stored in a sealed bucket.

Nat turned to them. "That's enough today. Let's wash up and relax until supper is ready."

Nat sat in her favorite chair on the porch and pulled out her knife to do some whittling while they waited on supper to arrive. Maggie stayed in the kitchen to help. Tom and Smithy were sitting at the outdoor table having a serious conversation. Nat smiled as she looked at Tom, who was intently listening to Smithy. He had been fidgety all afternoon, and Smithy was probably trying to calm him down and reassure him everything would turn out fine.

When the food arrived and everyone was seated around the table, Nat thanked everyone for making the first bison hunt a success, and Marissa and Ruth for providing delicious meals.

It was delicious, and even Smithy ate his fill of the plentiful seafood. "I can't wait to live here and be able to eat like this all the time," he said. "I'll have to work hard to keep all the extra pounds off."

Nat smirked. "That won't be a problem. I've got big plans for you," she teased.

Tom looked at Nat, who nodded at him. "I do believe Tom needs our attention."

Tom stood up from the table and knelt in front of Ruth. "Ruth, since we met, my world revolves around you, and you bring the sunshine to my life. Would you do me the pleasure of becoming my wife?"

Ruth had a tear running down her cheek when she nodded and said, "Yes, I would love nothing more."

The group broke out in applause.

"Good job, well done," Smithy said.

"Congratulations," Nat said. "We all think you make a fantastic couple." She looked at Tom. "I do believe Tom has something to show you."

He stood and reached for Ruth's hand. "Will you join us?"

"Yes, we will," Marissa said. "Let's go."

Nat stood and reached for Marissa's hand as they followed Ruth and Tom to the lake. As they topped the small hill, Ruth saw the cabin near the lake, and she gasped and covered her face with her hands. Tom waited several seconds for the shock to wear off. "This will be our new home."

"It's beautiful," Ruth cried out.

"The inside isn't complete yet, but I didn't think I could keep it a surprise any longer. Come and let me show you around."

"I think we'll let the two of you take it from here. Check the wood in the smokehouse before you come back to the cabin," Nat said.

"Yes, ma'am. We'll see you in a bit." Tom smiled.

"Don't be too long. There's apple pie for dessert," Smithy called out.

"Stop it," Maggie said and punched Smithy's shoulder. "Don't rush, young love."

"Ouch, Maggie. Who taught you to punch like that?" Smithy teased.

"Come on, you two," Nat said.

"I'm glad that's over with," Marissa said. "I was having such a hard time not talking about the cabin."

"Speaking of cabins," Smithy said, "I'm going to suggest Tom, and I stay down at his place at night to keep the smokehouse fire fed and give you ladies more room."

"It does get a bit crowded with six of us," Marissa replied.

"I have room to share with Ruth," Maggie offered.

"She can use one of the cots," Smithy said. "I don't mind sleeping in a bedroll. It's strangely been fun."

Marissa cocked an eyebrow at Smithy. "You've got a strange sense of fun."

"What can I say? The hunt made me feel like a young man again," Smithy replied.

"It was fun," Nat agreed.

"What's the plan for tomorrow?" Maggie asked.

"We need to start tanning the hides. Smithy and Tom can work on his fireplace and interior walls. I'd like to hook up Quincy and take a trip to the cove."

"I'm sure it's filled with all kinds of goodies," Marissa said. "Ruth and I were going to make a trip until I remembered you had Quincy."

"I'd like to send a load of seafood back with you when you go," Nat told Smithy. "It will be a while before the bison finishes smoking."

"Maybe by the end of next week?" Smithy asked. "Tom and I could come out then for bison and logs."

"That should give it plenty of time. If you can spare Tom a few days, we can start pulling logs for your cabin. Then when you both return, we can start your build. Maggie, Marissa, and I can notch the logs in between projects."

"I can take the load back myself and get Ruth home," Smithy said. "If Tom is good with staying, he can stay out all week and go back with me the following week." Smithy looked at Nat.

"I'm sure he'd love that," Nat said.

301

"Would it be all right if I start bringing Blue out, too?"

"You should know by now, Blue is always welcome," Nat replied.

†

When Tom and Ruth returned, they joined the others on the front porch.

Ruth sat beside Tom on the steps. "I want to thank you all for helping Tom build such a beautiful cabin. It will make a lovely home for us after we marry."

"I'm not rushing you, but have you arrived on a wedding day?" Marissa asked.

"The sooner, the better, but I need to discuss this with my parents," Ruth said.

"Give us enough time to clean up and look presentable," Nat said.

"You will be the first, or maybe second to know," Tom said.

"Would you be okay staying out here this week and letting Smithy take the order in and take Ruth home?" Nat asked.

Tom looked at Smithy. "Heck yeah."

"I told him we'd pull the logs for his cabin, and you can continue working on yours. He'll come back out next weekend, and we'll begin his build," Nat explained. "You can take a load of seafood and some logs back to town when y'all go back."

"That sounds perfect," Tom agreed.

"Would you mind if I came back out with Smithy?" Ruth asked. "I'm sure there are chores I can help with."

"We never turn down help," Maggie replied.

Smithy stood and stretched. "I'm bunking down at the cabin with you so that the ladies can have a bit more room. Ruth can use my cot."

"You can sleep in mine," Tom offered.

"I'm good with my bedroll," Smithy answered. "I think I'm going to head to the lake before it gets too dark."

"Hang on a minute, and I'll go with you. We need a good night's rest." Tom turned to Marissa. "Thanks again for the great meal. We'll see you for breakfast."

"We'll cook up a good meal," Marissa promised. "We have a long day." She turned to look at Ruth. "Are you up to an adventure to the cove while everyone else works here?"

"I'd like that," Ruth replied. "I had fun with you today."

"I did, too," Marissa smiled warmly.

Maggie smiled. "I guess we have tomorrow planned, except for meals. I'll take care of breakfast, and we can have smoked fish at lunch with some chowder. Could we try some bison for supper?"

"Why don't we cut some steaks and see how they do?" Nat asked.

"Fine with me," Marissa replied. "I'll bring out some canned vegetables to go along with some fresh bread. I'll put a few loaves on in the morning if you watch them while we go to the cove, Maggie."

"Deal," Maggie said.

"Let's call it a night," Nat suggested. "Lots to get done tomorrow."

Nat and Marissa snuggled under the covers. "It's good to have you home," Marissa said. "It was lonesome without you."

"This bed sure is more comfortable than my bedroll, too. Gyp's not as much fun to snuggle up to either." Gyp heard Nat say her name and trotted in to settle down at the end of the bed.

"Now we're all set," Marissa said as she nuzzled Nat's cheek.

†

The smell of bacon and sausage pulled Nat from her slumber, and she walked into the kitchen to find Maggie, Marissa, and Ruth hard at work. "You have it smelling good in here."

"We thought we'd cook up some flapjacks to go with the eggs and meat," Marissa replied.

Nat pulled up her suspenders. "I'll go hook Quincy up to the wagon and fill it with empty buckets while y'all cook."

"I've already checked the smokehouse fires," Maggie said as Nat headed for the door.

"Thanks," Nat answered and stepped out into a beautiful morning. Tom and Smithy arrived as she walked into the barn. "Good morning."

"Morning. What you up to?" Tom asked.

"I'm going to hitch Quincy up to the wagon for Marissa and Ruth. They are going to harvest the cove while we work here."

"I'll take care of that if you want to feed everyone else. I'll put a feedbag on Quincy," Tom offered.

"That works for me," Nat said as she started filling feed buckets for the horses.

Maggie and Ruth were carrying plates of food to the table when Nat and the men walked inside. "What can we help with?" Nat asked.

"We've got it. Go have a seat, and we'll be right there," Marissa said.

†

After breakfast, the groups split to do their work for the day. Tom and Smithy built a large portion of the fireplace and finished off a second bedroom. Nat and Maggie started tanning the hides and hung them on the barn wall. When they finished, Marissa and Ruth had not returned. "Are you up to a walk to the cove?" Nat asked.

"Why not? Let me pull the bread out to start cooling," Maggie replied.

Nat walked inside and picked up her rifle and her soft shoes. She waited for Maggie outside, and Gyp and Luna danced around her, wanting to go. "Fine with me," she told them, and when Maggie arrived, they started down the trail.

"I think we can harvest the pools near the cabin tomorrow, and that should give Smithy plenty to take back with him. He and Tom can start hauling some logs for his place, and we can notch logs."

"With all four of us working on them, it shouldn't take long," Maggie replied.

"That's what I think, too," Nat replied.

They could hear Marissa and Ruth's laughter as they approached the cove. Nat looked at the filled buckets in the back of the wagon. "They've done well this morning."

Marissa laughed as they pulled the net, and the flailing fish were soaking them with the chilly water.

"You two look like you're having fun," Nat called out. "Do you have much left?"

"No, I think this is the last of the fish," Marissa called back.

"Bring Quincy down to the beach when you get done, and I'll clear out the pools there."

"All right, Nat, we'll be there soon."

Nat shook her head and picked up the fish trap and two buckets. "Will you empty two and bring them?"

"Yes, I will," Maggie replied.

Nat looked up from a pool and saw Quincy coming down the beach. "Good timing," she told Maggie as she filled the last empty bucket.

Maggie had been digging clams and had a large pile next to the filled buckets. "I'll make a large batch of chowder to jar up and send to town."

"That will be good. I wouldn't mind having some of the fried clams again soon."

"They are good that way," Maggie replied.

"Two down and one pool to go," Nat told Marissa. "If you start loading, I'll harvest." Nat emptied a bucket and walked into the water.

Nat filled three more buckets before they started for home. Maggie and Nat prepared the fish for smoking while Marissa and Ruth dumped the buckets into the barrels.

"That was fun," Ruth said. "I'll look forward to helping on this project."

"We will need to get a garden spot ready for you and Tom to plant," Nat replied. "I'll ask Tom where he wants a plot, and we can start turning the soil."

Marissa smiled at her. "Don't forget we'll have Tom here all week. He and Quincy can plow while we notch Smithy's logs."

"Better yet, Tom can use Rusty tomorrow. His size and strength will make it a much faster job," Nat said. "If he gets up early, he can have it done with plenty of time to load some logs and the barrels and supplies for town. You two will need to make a list of what Smithy needs to bring back. Just make sure to add several bags of salt for me."

"I was thinking of something yesterday while we were coming home," Maggie said. "Why don't we start making our salt? We have a never-ending supply of salt water to boil down."

"That's a good idea, but it will take much longer. We can try our hand at it, and if it works well, we can make it as often as we can. We've got a big washpot to use and plenty of firewood," Nat stated.

"I'll use Quincy and go down to fill the buckets," Ruth volunteered.

Maggie smiled at Ruth. "I'll come along to help."

†

For the next two days, they continued to work on projects. Tom and Smithy had finished the fireplace and had cut a hole for the woodstove chimney. "I'll bring the stove out as an early wedding present next weekend," Smithy told them. "Until then, keep a shingle over it to prevent any water from coming in."

Smithy and Tom began bringing loads of logs for Smithy's cabin while Nat and Marissa made the railing and steps for Tom's cabin porch. Maggie and Ruth collected water and began the slow process of making salt. They packed boxes of smoked fish and clam chowder for Smithy's return to town the next day while waiting on the water for the salt to cook down.

Tom and Smithy dropped two more loads of logs for the cabin and loaded the wagon halfway with logs to send to the mill. Smithy would have them cut into boards for his home.

†

After loading the barrels and items for the town on the wagon, Tom kissed Ruth. "I'll see you this weekend."

"I'm so excited to be coming back. I had a wonderful time this trip," Ruth told him.

"Bring some seeds and any starter plants you can, and we'll plant your garden to get it growing," Maggie told her as she climbed into the wagon.

Ruth looked at Smithy. "Will you help me with that?"

"I'd be delighted," Smithy replied. "I've got your list, and we'll be back out as soon as possible. I'll pick up your windows, too," he told Tom.

Ruth waved as they drove away. Nat turned to the others. "If you and Maggie can start notching, I think Tom and I will hunt down a spring and set up his water supply," Nat said.

Maggie and Marissa were making progress on the logs when Nat and Tom finished the waterline. "Do you want our help here?"

"No, we can finish this," Marissa replied.

Nat looked at Tom. "Let's hitch up Quincy, and I'll saddle Hardy, so we can cut and haul some logs for the mill

308

and start a pile near the lake. The short ends we can use to begin your firewood stack and feed the smokehouses."

"I'll get the animals ready if you fill several canteens," Tom offered.

"Once we finish, Maggie and I will work on some sausage, and later start on supper. I do remember someone mentioning fried clams and shrimp," Marissa replied.

"That will taste good," Nat agreed. "We'll see you later." Nat kissed Marissa and jogged to catch up with Tom.

†

By the end of the week, Smithy's logs were ready for the build, and Tom's cabin had holes for the windows cut. A large pile of logs waited to go into the mill, and they harvested a load of seafood.

Tom and Nat were chopping firewood at the lake when Smithy pulled Rusty in front of Tom's cabin to unload his windows, stove, and other supplies. Tom reached up to help Ruth down from the wagon and kissed her.

"Welcome back."

"I couldn't wait to get here," Ruth answered. "I got all types of seeds and vegetable plants for us to grow. Maggie said she would help me plant them while you all work on Smithy's cabin."

"That is a good plan," Tom replied. "Let's get the wagon unloaded, and we can all get started."

Smithy nodded at the pile of logs. "You have been busy this week."

"We've barely put a dent in the trees we cut along the trail," Nat told him. "None of us will have to down trees for firewood for a while."

When they unloaded the windows and stove, Smithy looked at Tom. "You and I can put these in tonight."

Tom nodded. "We certainly can. Thank you for the stove."

"We also brought a large barrel for a water barrel," Ruth said.

"We will hook that up too." Tom smiled at her.

†

After a fast meal of bread, sausage, and cheese, the teams began their projects. Marissa ground the meat Nat had cut for her to stuff into the link casings. Ruth and Maggie planted the garden, while Tom, Smithy, and Nat built the foundation to Smithy's cabin. When the flooring was complete, they began building walls. By the end of the day, they had made half of the walls.

"It'll take Rusty's help to finish the walls, but I think we can have the shell finished tomorrow," Nat said as she wiped the sweat from her face and took a long drink.

Smithy's eyes sparkled with excitement. "It's coming up quickly. Thanks for all your help."

"I think Tom and I can finish the logs if you want to begin your interior rooms," Nat said. "It will look like home when you get those in."

"We can stop at the creek coming back next weekend to get river rocks for your fireplace, too," Tom said.

They stored the tools inside the walls and walked to the cabin to see how supper was coming. Ruth was sitting on the back porch, stuffing the ground meat into the sausage casings while Marissa and Maggie cooked.

"Do you want some help?" Tom asked.

"Sure, get washed up and come keep me company. Stuffing the sausage isn't a hard task at all." Ruth was proud of the new skills she was already learning, and was proving to be a hard worker.

"I reckon we need to hunt a bit to add more meat for the sausage," Nat told Tom.

"I'm ready any time you are," Tom said as he washed his hands.

"Let's see what we can do to help," Nat said to Smithy.

They walked into the kitchen, and Nat kissed Marissa's cheek. "What can we help with?"

Maggie handed Smithy a large pan and Nat a long-handled wooden spoon. "Please check the salt. The water should be gone by now. Pour the paste into the pan and set it on the porch rail to set up, please."

"That doesn't sound too difficult," Smithy said.

"Add more water when you finish," Maggie called after them.

"Will do, Maggie," Smithy called back.

After supper, Tom announced they would be getting married in two weeks. "Y'all can stay in Marissa's cabin, and I'll bunk with Smithy until after the ceremony, then Ruth and I'll come back here."

"We will be there with our Sunday best on," Nat promised.

"I don't care what you look like as long as you're there," Tom said.

Marissa laid her hand on Nat's arm. "That means a bath and a haircut for you, my love."

"I definitely need both," Nat agreed.

Tom looked at Smithy. "Are you ready to put in some windows and a stovepipe?"

"I most definitely am. We'll have to boil some pine pitch tomorrow to seal the pipe and the chimney. We need to get you a firepit started anyhow."

"I'll dig it tonight and get the fire set. You can light it and use the pitch in the morning before you head back to town," Nat offered.

"I'll help you," Ruth told Nat.

"We'll be back later," Nat told Marissa and Maggie.

†

Tom and Smithy sealed the chimney and stovepipe the following morning while the rest loaded the wagon with goods. When they finished, Smithy and Ruth climbed onto the wagon while Tom mounted Buck.

"I'm going to ride ahead of you and stack up some rocks to bring back with us later this week," Tom told them. "I'll meet you at the creek."

"Someone is excited," Nat said with a chuckle.

"Me, too," Smithy replied. "We'll see you later this week."

"Safe travels," Marissa told them.

†

"We've got a bed to finish," Nat told them as the wagon pulled away. "I've got the frame done and will drill holes for the rope supports and then carry the frame down to the cabin."

312

"We are just about done with the mattress and pillows," Marissa replied. "We can finish it today."

"I've got two more small carvings to make for the posts, but they won't take long. I'll finish them tonight." Nat started to walk toward the barn. "I'll be back later."

Nat drilled the holes in the bed frame and loaded them onto Quincy's wagon with a spool of rope Smithy had delivered. She led Quincy down to the lake and began assembling the bed. Nat was finishing the last rope support when Maggie and Marissa arrived.

"That came out beautiful," Marissa said as she admired Nat's craftsmanship.

"I'll drill the four holes in the posts to finish the frame." Nat wiped the sweat from her brow.

"I'd like for you to relax on the porch and finish your carving," Marissa said. "When Maggie and I finish the mattress, pillows, and sheets, we will need your help."

"I can do that. I'll check my traplines after I finish carving," Nat said.

"I'll care for Quincy," Maggie said as they walked to the barn.

Nat picked up a small block when she relaxed back in her chair and started to carve. By lunchtime, she had two wolf pups created for the final pieces to the bed.

"Those are nice," Marissa said when she came to get Nat for lunch.

"Thanks, I think they will look great." Nat followed her inside. Warm smoked fish waited at the table. "I don't think I could ever tire of eating these."

"That's such a filling and simple meal to make with chowder," Maggie said. "Gives you the energy to work the rest of the day."

"What else are you cooking that smells so good?" Nat asked.

"I've got a duck roasting in the stove," Marissa replied.

Nat finished her meal and called to Gyp. "We'll be back later." Nat shouldered her rifle and backpack basket before walking into the woods. "I hope we have more beautiful days like today," she told Gyp as a comforting breeze filled the air.

Her traps held two beaver and several marten. Not her best day, but she wouldn't have hours of work to process them. When she returned, she set her catch on the table and got a drink.

Marissa heard Nat whistling as she worked on her pelts and walked outside. "I'm glad you're back," Marissa said. "Maggie has gone to hitch up Quincy for us to take the rest of the bed to the lake."

"It won't take me long to finish here," Nat said. "I'll wash up and help you load the goods."

†

Nat helped Maggie and Marissa carry in the heavy mattress and installed her post carvings before waiting on the porch steps for them to finish. Nat watched geese and ducks swimming on the pond and several moose grazing on the sweet grass near the lake. It reminded her to pay a visit to the other lake she had seen on her way to the bison camp. Maybe tomorrow, she and Hardy would take a ride to explore. Nat was deep in thought when Marissa put her hand on Nat's shoulder.

"We're all done. Do you want to come to take a look?" Marissa said.

Nat stepped into the bedroom. "That turned out beautifully. We make a great team," Nat replied.

"Yes, we do," Maggie said as she tucked the covers under the pillow. "We could probably split a bison hide for a warm covering for Tom and one for Smithy."

"They would make a nice housewarming gift. We shouldn't need covers that heavy for months yet," Marissa replied.

"Now that we've gotten this critical project done, what else do we need to accomplish?" Maggie asked.

"When I rode out to check for the bison, I saw a lake to the east I'd never noticed before. Would you ladies like to ride out with me to check on it?" Nat waited for their reply.

"I think you and Marissa should go. I've had enough traveling for a few days. I can stay and grind up meat for sausage," Maggie suggested.

Nat turned to Marissa. "Are you up for a ride?"

"That would be a nice break," Marissa said.

"We can ride in the morning and be back in the early afternoon. Then we can all check the cove," Nat replied.

†

Nat sat in her favorite chair on the porch while Maggie and Marissa worked on supper. The relaxing sound of the waves and the warm sunshine bathing her body lulled her to sleep.

When Maggie came to check on her and found her sleeping so peacefully, she hated to wake her. She gently caressed Nat's arms. "Time to eat, sleepyhead," Maggie whispered.

Nat smiled up at Maggie. "I guess I got too comfortable."

"There's nothing wrong with a cat nap now and then," Maggie replied. "Let's eat."

†

"Supper was delicious," Nat told them as she pushed her plate away.

"There is one last piece of pie left. Should I get it for you?" Marissa asked.

"Does anyone want to split it with me?" Nat asked. Two head shakes were her answer. "Bring it on then. I can never turn down your pie."

"We need to see if there have been any apple deliveries when we got to town. That was the last of my jars," Marissa told them.

"I will do everything within my power to see that you have all the apples we can use this year," Nat said.

"Unless he has some canned ones, we are out of luck until the fall when the apple harvest begins," Marissa replied.

"You can bet, I'll fill a wagonload when they do," Nat replied. "We better order more jars."

"There should be some berries ripe in the next month or two," Marissa replied.

"Thank goodness for berries." Nat smiled.

†

The following morning, Nat and Marissa rode to the lake. Nat was surprised at how big it was and the abundance of animals in the area. "I think we should start coming here to hunt," she told Marissa. "Keep our animals for when we need them in lean times."

"What do you think about having a cow for milk and maybe have a hog or two? We could help Tom and Ruth build a large barn to house them in. Fresh milk would be nice to have."

"Will one be enough?" Nat asked.

"Maybe two," Marissa said. "We could make cheese and butter with what we don't drink."

"I'll get Smithy to check on purchasing some animals," Nat said.

As they were riding home, Nat turned to Marissa. "Is there anything else you would like to make our home better?"

"Maybe a couple of kids from Tom and Ruth," Marissa chuckled. "Otherwise, I think we are well off."

"We do have a good life here, don't we?" Nat asked.

"It's the best forever home I could dream of," Marissa replied. "A loving partner and family, all the food we can eat, and you can't beat the view from our front porch."

"Forever home. I like that." Nat smiled.

EPILOGUE

Despite Nat's fussiness, Marissa dressed her in her best pair of breeches and a new dress shirt for the wedding. The ceremony was small, and both Tom and Ruth were beautiful as they pronounced their love for one another. Nat, Marissa, and Maggie stayed in town for a few days to give them privacy in their new home.

Smithy's cabin went up smoothly, and within the first month after the wedding, all three families had found their forever homes. Maggie surprised them one morning when they were sharing breakfast. "Would you two be disappointed if I moved into Smithy's spare room?"

"What?" Nat asked. "Are you two in love?"

"No, nothing like that. We are good friends, and we thought it would be nice if I gave him some company and you two could have a home together," Maggie explained.

"You will always be welcome in our home," Nat said. "If you want to live with Smithy, you don't need our permission or approval."

"I have enjoyed living with you two for all this time, but I think Smithy needs some looking after," Maggie said. "Living here is much different than living in town, where he can walk to the hotel for a hot meal or the store when he needs to buy something."

"I get it completely," Nat said and threw up her hands. She hugged Maggie tight. "You won't be but a short walk away."

"That's right, and we'll be working together every day." Maggie smiled. "Thank you."

The three families settled into a welcome routine. Tom, Nat and Smithy continued the building and logging projects while Maggie, Ruth, and Marissa tended the gardens and they all pitched in to harvest the seafood and run trap lines.

Tom and Ruth made the routine deliveries to town and when the bison were delivered, Tom proudly brought home a repeater rifle. "Now we can all hunt well together," he told Nat as she looked over the rifle.

Nat had shown them the lake and the plentiful game. They began hunting there often, to bring in moose, deer, and elk for the smokehouses. Maggie and Ruth tended the livestock and they learned to make cheese and butter from the milk from the cows. The sausage, jerky, and smoked salmon remained a favorite at the general store, so they worked hard to add these items to every seafood delivery or log delivery made to the mill.

Life was good in the wild. Tom and Smithy learned many new skills and took over the traplines, while Nat focused on preparing the pelts for sale.

Two months after the wedding, Maggie, Marissa, and Nat were cutting meat for sausage when Tom came flying from the lake in a panic.

"Slow down and catch your breath," Nat said. "What's the problem?"

"It's Ruth. She has been ill the last several mornings, and she can't keep anything I cook her down."

Tom was gasping for breath when Nat motioned him to sit down. She looked at Maggie and Marissa, who both nodded and then back to Tom.

"Are you ready to be a father?" Nat asked. "It sounds like Ruth might be pregnant."

Tom's face turned ashen, and he would have fallen over if Nat hadn't caught him. "Get some cold water, Maggie," Nat said.

Maggie rushed to draw a bucket of water and splashed Tom's face until he sputtered and his eyes flew open.

"A baby?" he cried out.

"That is sure what it sounds like," Marissa said. "Maggie and I will go check on Ruth. You stay here until you get your wits about you."

Tom nodded and tried to slow his breathing. Maggie and Marissa returned soon from talking with Ruth.

"She's several weeks late on her cycle," Marissa said. "I'm pretty sure she's going to have a baby, but I think you need to have Doc check her out."

"You are planning to take a load of logs to the mill tomorrow, right?" Nat asked.

"Yes, I am. I will take Ruth to see Doc then."

"Maybe spend the night at Marissa's cabin and come home the next day? I bet she'll want to celebrate and make plans with her mother," Nat said.

Smithy walked into the yard and saw the women clustered around Tom. "What's all the commotion? Is everything all right?"

"We think Ruth is pregnant," Maggie said.

"Well, I'll be. Congratulations, Tom." Smithy slapped him on the back.

"He's going to take her to town for Doc to check her out with a load of logs," Nat said.

"He can go today if you help me load the wagon," Smithy said. "I'm not sure Tom can stay focused," Smithy teased.

"Sure, I can," Tom growled back playfully. "I'm going to be a father," he beamed.

"See what I mean?" Smithy broke out laughing.

"Come on, let's get the wagon filled. Will you help Ruth get ready?" Nat asked Marissa.

"Of course," Marissa smiled. "Let me toast a few pieces of bread to help settle her stomach, and I'll be right there."

Later that evening, Nat sat with Marissa on the front steps watching the sun disappear into the ocean. She slipped an arm around Marissa's shoulder. "It's happening," Nat stated.

"What?" Marissa asked.

"The last thing you wanted to make our forever home perfect. A child for Tom and Ruth," Nat replied and kissed her sweetly.

"It already is when I'm with you," Marissa answered, and laid her head on Nat's shoulder.

ABOUT THE AUTHOR

Ali Spooner lives in beautiful northwest Florida with several fur babies. Ali's writing began as a hobby, and with the assistance of the Affinity Rainbow Publishing team has advanced her love of storytelling to a new level.

Ali's characters are primarily everyday people, from cowgirls to psychics. Ali also has created a few supernatural characters in her paranormal series. Several of her twenty-plus books have been Amazon-rated number one choices and always include a happily ever after. Ali's hobbies include photography, reading, travel, college sports, and spending time with family and friends.

OTHER AFFINITY BOOKS

<u>Disconnected by Annette Mori</u>
Vanna has always felt like something was off with her parents, leaving her feeling oddly disconnected. She decides to move across the country and establish a new and independent life after college. On the way to her new position in Flagstaff, Arizona, Vanna meets out and proud Trey, who loves to flirt.

Trey has never forgotten the beautiful young woman she met briefly and is determined to ensure their paths cross again.

Thousands of miles from home, Vanna finds out more about herself, but not her feeling of being disconnected from her parents. Will Vanna ever form the connection she desperately seeks? Does Trey's determination work out?

<u>Darcy Comes Home by Jen Silver</u>
After twenty-five years Darcy and Angie meet again and from the faintly flickering embers of their forbidden

teenage love, a flame erupts. Family complications arise including a reluctant engagement, secret surrogacy, and a persistent ex-wife.

Villagers in Professor Darcy Belsfield's childhood home of Sycamore Haven remember her being sent away to a Christian conversion camp in Canada when her father discovered her making love to her school friend, Angie.

Angie has never married but she does have a past and some unenthusiastic plans for the future. Will the differences in their lives doom the chance of Darcy and Angie discovering if they can build a future together?

Hat Trick by Ali Spooner and K.L. Gallagher

Alexandra "Alex" Hawthorne is on the fast track to the top of one of the most formidable, white-collar, criminal defense law firms in New York. She can ill afford any distractions, especially those with dark-brown eyes, who can rock a power suit while coaching professional hockey players. Not now. Not when Alex is so close to making senior partner. Not after all she has sacrificed.

After a devastating end to her playing career, Janelle Leblanc channeled her passion into coaching and reached the pinnacle of success as the first female head coach in NHL history. Despite her accomplishments, she hears whispers that she was hired as nothing more than a publicity stunt. Janelle's focus needs to remain on the ice if she is to prove them wrong, not on a certain curly haired attorney with the most arresting emerald-green eyes she has ever seen.

Once the spark is lit, their chemistry is impossible to ignore. Can Janelle break down Alex's walls to give them a real chance? Or will Alex's past heartache be too much for them to overcome?

<u>The Lone Star Collection II by Various Authors</u>
Saddle up for a wild ride! *The Lone Star Collection II* has something for everyone! If you enjoy romance, Kris Bryant and Dena Blake have penned hot contemporary stories in *Heat* and *Horseplay*, while *Pins and Needles*, by Julie Cannon, is a historical adventure. Annette Mori also contributes to the romance fare with a beautiful, enduring love story in *Rainstorm*. If you want sizzling erotica check out *50 by 50*, from Renee Mackenzie. What would a collection be without fantasy, paranormal and swashbuckling adventures? *Lured to the Rocks*, a unique work of fantasy by Barbara Ann Wright. In *The Devil's Backbone*, Lacey L. Schmidt spins a thriller about overcoming evil and personal loss. MJ Williamz explores dark passion in *Take Me All the Way*. Del Robertson offers *Return to Me* a classic pirate story, and Yvette Murray tosses in the *Ghostly Galleons*.

<u>Footprints by Ali Spooner</u>
Sandy, the youngest sibling of Gator Girlz, Inc., has worshipped her older sister Cam all her life and wanted nothing more than to be just like her hero. *Footprints* provides readers with Sandy's story of growing up in the Bayous of Louisiana. When the devastating floods of 2016

impact the Baton Rouge area, Cam and Sandy join the Cajun Navy to help rescue families trapped in the rampant floodwaters. The story also revisits Sandy's victory over Bubba Gump and how Sandy's injuries started her down the path to find the love of her life. Food, adventures, and great family relationships fill the pages of *Footprints*.

Love at Leighton Lake by Samantha Hicks

Tallulah 'Tally' Roberts decides that a few weeks staying in a cabin at Leighton Lake will help mend her shattered pelvis and broken heart.

Caitlyn Matthews works at the lake resort her mother owns, loving nothing better than spending her morning swimming in the lake. That is until she meets Tally. Their attraction is instant, but both are wary of these new feelings with their history of previous relationships.

As they get to know each other, secrets from Caitlyn's past come to light. Caitlyn fears her mother has been lying to her and together they search for the truth.

Love at Leighton Lake is packed full of love, drama, and a cow called Houdini who likes to roam the cabins, much to Caitlyn's delight.

The Others by Annette Mori

As a seer and brilliant scientist, Em convinces her wife, Lise, to prepare for the inevitable conclusion, after the chaos caused by foreign countries attacking the United States. Leaving behind a wake of destruction and a new world order, forcing them to navigate a frightening reality. After ten months in their cozy bomb shelter, they emerge to a world where the vegetation is surprisingly unaffected. Should they band together with other survivors, or try to make it on their own? There are others in this unknown world. On the first day outside of their shelter, they meet members of an alternate society. Are they friend or foe? Change is inevitable. But will they change in ways Em and Lise can live with, or will this altered world change them into something unrecognizable?

Affinity
Rainbow Publications

eBooks, Print, Free eBooks

Visit our website for more publications available online.

www.affinityrainbowpublications.com

Published by Affinity Rainbow Publications
A Division of Affinity eBook Press NZ LTD
Canterbury, New Zealand

Registered Company 2517228